ENDORSEMENTS

THE DELTA TANGO TRILOGY is an in-depth journey of one man as he threads his way through personal problems and the challenge of his harrowing career as a U. S. Border Patrol Agent. His life of trials and sorrows rivals any fiction story today.

–Clive Cussler, *New York Times* bestselling
author of the Dirk Pitt series

ESSENTIAL AND GRIPPING. *Delta Tango Trilogy* is a heartbreakingly honest tale of the lives that intersect and are forever changed along our bleak and dangerous southern border. This is an important set of novels, not to be missed or forgotten.

–Margaret Coel, *New York Times* bestselling
author of *Winter's Child.*

T0152431

DELTA TANGO TRILOGY

The DELTA TANGO TRILOGY by Christopher LaGrone follows Layne Sheppard from the day he applies to join the U.S. Border Patrol through the rigors of the Federal Law Enforcement Training Center (known as the Border Patrol Academy) and his alternating exhilaration, anxiety, and drudgery as a field trainee, to the often harrowing moments of shift work on the U.S.-Mexico border. Along the way he deals with his own insecurities, a serious drinking problem, the internal politics of Douglas Station in extreme southeast Arizona (where he's assigned) and, for him, the unimaginable: Falling in love with a beautiful girl who was brought over the border as an infant—one of those illegals known as a Dreamer. Through Layne's experiences, life in the U.S. Border Patrol comes alive in ways few Americans can even imagine.

In Book One—**Fleeing the Past**—Layne strives to prove, to himself and others, that his failures of the past are in the past. As he seeks self-respect and self-confidence, he endures the boot camp-like ordeal of the Border Patrol Academy in sweltering New Mexico—punishing long-distance runs and debilitating hand-to-hand combat. During precious free time he meets Felina Camarena Rivera. Both keep personal secrets and pursue plans for escaping them—plans they also keep to themselves, even as their attraction for each other deepens.

In Book Two—**Felina's Spell**—Layne struggles to overcome the politics of the BP's Douglas Station and advance from trainee to regular agent status—to succeed. As he rides with seasoned veterans, Layne gets a first-hand look at the challenges border agents face on a daily and nightly basis and learns realities that agents either accept begrudgingly or surrender to. Felina's clever plan to become Layne's wife seems headed for success, despite Layne's serious drinking problem, when Felina's brother is charged with DUI and deported.

In Book Three—**Moments of Truth**—Layne realizes the inevitable loneliness and fear of patrolling the border without a partner, and pressure from management mounts. While experiencing many "agent adventures," he faces several moments of truth, both personal and professional, among them dealing with secrets Felina has held. She, too, must come to grips with tough choices; can she rely on Layne? They undertake an audacious gamble, and their futures, individually and together, hang in the balance.

THE DELTA TANGO TRILOGY
BOOK ONE

Fleeing the Past

THE DELTA TANGO TRILOGY

BOOK ONE

FLEEING THE Past

A Layne Sheppard Novel

CHRISTOPHER LaGRONE

NEW YORK

LONDON • NASHVILLE • MELBOURNE • VANCOUVER

Fleeing the Past

The Delta Tango Trilogy - Book One / A Layne Sheppard Novel

Published in New York, New York, by Morgan James Publishing. Morgan James is a trademark of Morgan James, LLC. www.MorganJamesPublishing.com

ISBN 9781631950773 paperback
ISBN 9781631950780 eBook
Library of Congress Control Number: 2020933921

Cover and Interior Design by:
Chris Treccani
www.3dogcreative.net

Morgan James is a proud partner of Habitat for Humanity Peninsula and Greater Williamsburg. Partners in building since 2006.

Get involved today! Visit
MorganJamesPublishing.com/giving-back

To a dream realized
and a legacy preserved

IN MEMORIAM

The unexpected phone call from Nancy came in mid-December 2018. "Denny, I have terrible news," she said. "Chris died."

And that's how the completion of The Delta Tango Trilogy began.

I had gotten to know Nancy as the person in charge of author events at the Barnes & Noble bookstore on Colorado Boulevard in Denver. Over several years she hosted me each time I had a new book, and we collaborated on several Colorado Authors' League events.

One day, I think it was in 2016, she asked if I would be willing to look at a manuscript written by a young guy who wanted very much to be an author; he needed a professional critique of what he had written.

Sure, I said. I enjoy working with aspiring writers.

Chris LaGrone (the brother of Nancy's sister-in-law, I later learned) was then in his late thirties. He had been an agent in the U.S. Border Patrol for a time and had written a novel based on his experiences.

I read it and was impressed with the quality of his writing and the content of his story. But I told him, "No publisher will ever publish this, Chris, because it's too linear. It's just your character's experiences getting into and going through the Border Patrol Academy, being a field trainee, and then becoming an actual agent." I thought it provided insights the public didn't have, but to make a compelling book it needed more.

"Novels," I told him, "have subplots—twists and turns that make the overall story more complex, and thus, more interesting."

I gave him an example: "You're writing about someone whose job is to catch illegal aliens trying to sneak into the United States. Why not have him fall in love with an illegal? That would complicate matters!" I suggested that he read Helen Thorpe's wonderful book *Just Like Us* to learn what a so-called "Dreamer" faces living in America without legal status.

I also told Chris his main character, Layne Sheppard, needed to have a personal issue to overcome—a demon to conquer. I left it to him to decide what that would be.

Chris proved to be the most coachable writer I've ever worked with. He came back to me some time later with a rewritten manuscript that contained love, conflict, and a demon for the main character. Again, I read it. And again, I was impressed. But again, I saw a problem.

"No publisher will publish this, Chris," I told him. "Two hundred fifty thousand words is too long."

But I offered a suggestion: "We could turn this into a trilogy," I said. "This would break nicely into three books."

Chris liked that idea and saw immediately how to divide his story into three parts. Thus began almost two years of rewriting and editing. Chris would send me chapters as he finished drafts. I'd edit them and send them back to him for revisions. He'd return them to me, and I'd add the finished versions to a growing manuscript file.

We had finished Book One this way and were halfway through the same process for Book Two when Chris informed me that he was going to Argentina in August 2018 to improve his already fluent Spanish and learn more about the Hispanic culture. From Argentina he was to travel to Chile and Peru.

Before Chris left Denver, he finished drafts of all of Book Two's chapters, and we discussed a rough outline for Book Three. His absence allowed me time to focus on a book of my own that I was finishing.

In late October I emailed Chris, asking when he would be returning. "We need to hit it once you are back in town," I wrote.

"I'm in South America for another few months," he wrote back. He was looking forward to visiting the Atacama Desert in Chile, where the thirty-three Chilean miners were trapped underground for sixty-nine days before their dramatic rescue in August 2010.

By early December 2018, Chris had made his way to Cusco, Peru (elevation 11,152 feet), via Lima (sea level). He was headed for Machu Picchu, the center of the Inca civilization of the fifteenth century, high in the Andes Mountains.

"Chris suffered from severe asthma his entire childhood," his mother Sherryl told me later. "It continued into his adult life. Changing altitude quickly when he flew from Lima to Cusco, his body was not able to adapt to the thin air quickly enough."

I can't begin to express how stunned I was when I received that startling phone call from Nancy in December 2018. But, somehow I knew right away what I wanted to do.

"This isn't the time," I began. "But when you think the time is right, please tell Chris's mom and sister (Aimee) that, if they'd like to have the trilogy finished as Chris's legacy, I'll volunteer to write Book Three. I have a good idea where Chris was going with it."

By then I had worked with Chris for more than two years. Over countless meetings I had coached him to develop the story as a three-book series. While Book Three wasn't yet in draft form, Chris and I had discussed it at length. I didn't know exactly how he planned to conclude, but he'd put all of the building blocks in place. And I'd edited enough of his writing to have a good feel for how he expressed things; I was confident that I could replicate his style.

I've never been in the Border Patrol, of course, and know virtually nothing about being an agent. Sustaining Chris's intimate knowledge of life in the Patrol would have been impossible for me. Luckily, I had a source who agreed to provide me with insights into Border Patrol policies and procedures and many examples of an agent's adventures. Thus, I knew I'd be able to fill Book Three with the kinds of true-life experiences Chris related so realistically in the first two books.

Just after the start of the new year, Nancy made sure I knew when and where Chris's memorial service would be held, and said she hoped I would attend. I didn't want to miss it, and afterwards I was thankful I hadn't, because, for as well as I had gotten to know Chris, I had no idea how important writing was to him until I listened to speaker after speaker talk about how badly he wanted to become a successful writer. It drove everything Chris did the last several years of his life.

I knew then what to expect, and a week or so after the service I received an email from Sherryl LaGrone that read, in part: "Aimee and I are very much interested in having you finish Chris's work." A week later his mother and I talked by phone, and in March I met her face to face for the first time, before a Colorado Rockies Spring Training game in Scottsdale, AZ.

The book I was finishing when Chris died was my tenth as an author, but all are non-fiction. I had tried writing fiction almost forty years earlier but decided that, as a career newspaper journalist trained in reporting facts accurately, I just wasn't good at making things up. But I'd edited many novels and had been working with Chris for two years. So, I was willing to take another crack at "making things up"—especially since Chris had done most of the hard fictionalizing: creating characters, setting scenes, and establishing the story arc.

My first step was to finish editing Book Two. I decided to end it five chapters earlier than Chris planned, and use those chapters in Book Three. I also had other material from Chris to build on, meaning at least a third of Book Three is his origination.

From there it was just a matter of answering the recurring question every novelist faces, though it was a new one for me: What happens next?

Chris inspired the answers.

I hope I've honored my friend Chris with the way I completed the story he created, and that my attempt to capture his storytelling style reads like the rest of this trilogy.

—Denny Dressman

ACKNOWLEDGMENTS

MY SON CHRISTOPHER was a successful high school and college baseball player, and like most athletes, most of his focus was on his sport. After graduating from college with a degree in marketing and working in various jobs, he discovered that his true passion was not athletics or marketing, but writing. After uncovering his passion, it became his goal to become a published author. Chris began pursuing his dream earnestly while serving as a U.S. Border Patrol agent.

His loving father Mark, my husband, was a high school teacher and Chris's baseball coach at Arvada West High. Mark, too, loved writing but kept it on a personal level. He encouraged Chris to write what became the *Delta Tango Trilogy*. The two of them would talk daily about their love of words, the challenges of working on the southern border, and the importance of pursuing one's dreams. Mark was Chris's rock.

When Mark died of cancer in 2014, the loss was tremendous for Chris, missing his daily visits with his dad. It was then that the LaGrone family's dear friend, Alan Olds, became Chris's confidant and mentor—and initial editor when Chris began writing his first *Delta Tango* manuscript. Retired from a full career as a highly respected and successful high school English teacher in Colorado, Alan guided and instructed Chris, who'd had no formal writing education. Our family is grateful for all the hours Alan spent with Chris, not only on his novel, but also as Chris's devoted and loving friend.

When expressing thanks, the first person who comes to mind is Denny Dressman, whose role is detailed in the *In Memoriam* section. Without Denny, there may never have been a *Delta Tango Trilogy*. For more than two years, he not only edited Chris's work and helped him develop his novel, ultimately into a trilogy; Denny also became a good friend to him during that time. Since Chris's unexpected death, Denny has become a good friend of mine, a mentor who has guided and instructed me throughout the process of bringing the trilogy to publication. I am eternally grateful for Denny Dressman, a true professional who is also kind and compassionate.

Thanks, also, to Nancy Hestera, wife of my son-in-law's brother, who first asked Denny if he would read Chris's original manuscript. And to Terry Whalin of Morgan James Publishing, and everyone in founder David Hancock's Morgan James family who helped produce this book and the entire trilogy.

It is with tremendous pride, as well as a heavy heart, that my daughter Aimee and I see Christopher's dream realized, and his legacy preserved, with publication of the *Delta Tango Trilogy*. We miss both Chris and his father deeply, but we know that they have been reunited in a better place.

—Sherryl LaGrone

Christopher LaGrone

FLEEING
THE
Past

LAYNE SHEPPARD FOUND HIMSELF walking into rooms and struggling to remember the purpose of the trip. It had been too long since the long-term plan he had devised showed promise. The possibility that it might succeed was surreal and was affecting his concentration. He entered the kitchen and opened the refrigerator, pulled a can of beer from its plastic six-pack rings, then put the remaining four cans back and closed the door. He tapped the top of the can with his fingernail and moved to look back toward Fabiola. He stared blankly, daydreaming about the future . . . now that his plan might actually work. The television illuminated the darkness in the living room, and he turned off the kitchen light to enhance the ambiance. He liked the movie-theater feel with her. Looking over the couch at the television, he squinted and gritted his teeth slightly as he cracked the top to the can, trying to make as little noise as possible. Foam filled the rim and he quickly slurped the fragrant bubbles before they overflowed. Fabiola's tiny apartment was cozy in the evening. This was his favorite part of the day, when nothing was required of him.

She didn't react to him opening another beer; it was only his second since they had been home after work. Lying on the couch, she was too focused on the presidential debate to acknowledge what he was doing. Layne observed her staring at the politicians on the television screen while he continued to strategize; she couldn't see him watching her. He knew a conversation was overdue, but he wasn't going to initiate one unless he had no choice—that was, if the dream became reality.

His attention was gradually overtaken by the growing intensity of the standoff between the candidates. They looked prepared and polished. They stood with assertive posture, their hands resting on their podiums. Their suits were striking, tailored to perfection. They were going back and forth about illegal immigration, and they appeared to care sincerely about their differing positions on the issue.

Layne said, "Is it like this in Argentina, where they say they are gonna do all kinds of things and then do the complete opposite when they get elected?" Then he took a sip of his beer.

"Yeah, it's pretty much the same," Fabiola answered without turning to look at him.

He enjoyed hearing her speak, her accent entertaining to listen to. "Do you understand everything they're saying?" Layne asked.

"For the most part. There are some words I don't know." Her eyes were still trained on the politicians behind their podiums; she was captivated. Layne decided to let her watch for a moment before trying again for conversation. But he quickly lost patience. He couldn't listen to any discussion involving illegal immigration without voicing his opinion.

"I wish they would just round up all of the illegals and send them all down there to South America by where you're from," Layne stated with a grin, "so that it takes them longer to find their way all the way back up here again."

Fabiola laughed a little. "That's never going to happen."

"Then they should build a wall from San Diego all the way to the Gulf of Mexico that the wetbacks can't get over, and guard it with turret machine guns," Layne pressed.

"Yeah, right." Fabiola was trying to pay attention.

Layne walked over to sit on the couch and Fabiola curled into a fetal position to make room for him. He grabbed her feet and pulled them over his lap, then retrieved a coaster and sat his beer on the cheap coffee table next to her Yerba Mate bulb. He began pulling her socks off her tiny feet. She protested, but he ignored her and began rubbing them while she resumed her attention to the candidates sparring. He enjoyed their warmth.

The candidates looked like puppets, the puppeteer below the stage squaring each hand off against the other. When it was the Texas senator's turn to respond, he retaliated to a slight from his opponent. The senator looked at his opposition as he began, then faced the audience. "The United States shares a twelve-hundred-mile border with Mexico, and it's no secret that we have an enormous number of illegals coming into this country every day. Let's be honest, the federal government has failed to secure our borders. Migrants are risking illegal entry because there's a magnet attracting them, and that magnet is jobs—plain and simple. I'm being realistic. I don't believe we can prevent illegals from coming into this country by use of force. I think the only way we can stop them is by removing the magnet that attracts them. If I'm elected President, I will see to it that we penalize employers who knowingly hire illegals, with a $5,000 fine and thirty days in jail for the first offense. And a $50,000 fine and a year in jail for the second offense."

The audience clapped vigorously, and the Texas senator waited for the applause to fade before he continued. He faced his opponent again and said, "And you lose all credibility in my book because you hired illegals in your home, and you knew about it for six months before you did anything about it. The fact that you stand here and talk like you're tough on illegal immigration is astounding to me." The governor of Nevada shook his head and looked at his notes, fighting the urge to defend himself until the moderator called upon him. His accuser looked straight at him and added, "And you wouldn't have done anything about it if the press hadn't become aware of it."

The television flashed and lit up the darkness in the room each time the camera angle changed. Layne withheld his comments until the highlights were over. Nevada's chief executive smiled and paused for a second before he responded. "To the best of my knowledge, I don't think I've ever hired an illegal in my life. So, I'm anxious to hear about your findings, because I think you've received bad information. As governor of Nevada, I have taken the initiative of empowering our state police to enforce immigration laws. When you were governor of Texas you were against building a fence. In fact, you put in place an additional magnet by offering $150,000 in college tuition credits to illegals. If anyone is a hypocrite in regards to illegal immigration . . . it's you, sir."

The other half of the audience clapped and cheered.

"It would be nice if they would follow through on fixing this mess," Layne commented, "but as soon as one of them is in office they will do the complete opposite of what they said they would do."

Fabiola didn't respond, so he gripped her big toe with his thumb and forefinger and pulled, resulting in a satisfying hollow pop. Fabiola pulled her foot away.

"*No me hagas mal!*" she said, slightly angry.

Layne laughed and reached for her feet and pulled them back into his control to examine her light blue toenail polish. While she was trying to listen to the debate, he told her, "I said, '*no me hagas mal*' to a Mexican guy at work the other day because you say that. He laughed and told some other Mexicans we work with, and they were mimicking me. They said if you want to tell someone 'don't hurt me' you say '*no hazlo!*'"

Layne goaded her on. "What do people in Argentina think about Mexico?"

"We just think they're uneducated and they listen to stupid music. We never really think about Mexico," she said.

Layne added, "The problem is that they come over here and have anchor babies and multiply, then they become generational welfare recipients. They should let the women in if they're forced to take birth control pills while they're here, and I swear I wouldn't mind seeing them."

"Mexicans don't take birth control; I've never met a Mexican girl in my life who is on birth control," Fabiola said.

"Really?"

"Of course not. They say it's because they're Catholic. It's not Catholic to take birth control, but it's okay to take people's tax money that had nothing to do with them being pregnant?" Fabiola said angrily. "It ticks me off because they make it harder for people like me to get a visa. I waited in line, and Mexicans just run across the border whenever they want to."

"If I make it into the Border Patrol, I'm gonna kick some butt," Layne spouted. "I'm tired of these cheaters coming here and making themselves at home—waving Mexican flags. They left Mexico because they couldn't earn a living there, but they're still proud of it? It makes no sense. And all the lousy construction workers—there's so many of them that they're not even trying to keep a low profile anymore. Every time I get gas, one of them is filling up his truck loaded with landscaping equipment."

He didn't mean to bring up his application to the Border Patrol; it had come out by accident during his rant. Fabiola became quiet. The last time he brought it up things became awkward until it blew over. At first the application didn't matter to her because it seemed like such a long shot. But he had passed the written exam, and his first interview with a background investigator was approaching.

"When is your interview?" Fabiola asked.

"Two weeks from tomorrow," Layne said briefly, regretting that he had brought it up.

Fabiola was quiet for a moment again.

He tried to think of a way to change the subject, but the timing was wrong; it would be too obvious. So he said, "It's not likely that I'm gonna get it, Babe. I never thought I would even get this far. It's so hard to become a federal agent. I've done some bad stuff when I was younger, and I have to get a Secret Security clearance. These background investigators can find out everything there is to know about you."

Fabiola waited to respond again, then said, "Why are you even going through all this then if you don't think you're going to get the job?"

He struggled to think of a misleading reason, but all he could think to say was more truth. "Because my friend Chad from junior college knows this guy in Texas named Matt who made it all the way to the Border Patrol Academy, and he knows what to say to get through the hiring process."

Fabiola listened carefully.

5

Layne continued because she didn't comment. "Chad gave me his number and I've been talking to him on the phone." He had never met Matt in person, but Chad had vouched for him.

"So, you're going to lie to the investigator?" Fabiola asked.

"I'm not really gonna lie. I'm just gonna withhold information, like an attorney."

"As long as you don't involve me in anything."

"Matt said that the background investigator will probably want to interview you, too," Layne said, and cringed, unsure of what her reaction would be.

Fabiola sat up. "What? When?"

Layne became defensive. "I don't know; he just said they might."

"I don't want to talk to any immigration people," Fabiola said, in slight distress.

"He's not immigration. He's a background investigator, like an FBI Agent," Layne explained.

"Layne!"

"You don't have anything to hide, right?"

"Well, I was late filing some things last year, but I'm fine. I just don't want to talk to those people unless I have no choice."

"Don't worry," Layne said to try and calm her, but he sounded feeble after realizing his misstep. She was close to crying, and the situation wouldn't allow for him to pretend he didn't know why. If he were hired, he would have to go to the Border Patrol Academy in New Mexico for four months. If he graduated, he would be living somewhere near the border of Mexico. Her visa restricted her to the state of Colorado. He scrambled within for a way to soft-pedal the developments; it was imperative that he preserve his living arrangement with her. If he was forced to move, he might be stuck with six months to go on a lease when the call came to report to the Academy.

Layne remained silent while he weighed his options, eyes fixed on the television. Out of time, he had no alternative but to appease her. "Do you think you can get your visa changed so that you can come to Arizona with me, in the event that I make it? And be able to work there? I've been meaning to ask you."

Fabiola's eyes smiled but her lips remained pursed. "I guess I could talk to my sponsor and see."

He could tell by the way her posture had changed that she was pleased. He knew what she was thinking: If he was planning to bring her with him to Arizona it probably meant he intended to propose to her—federal employee or not.

The tension blew over and they resumed watching the debate. The governor from Nevada was retaliating to a jab from his accuser about amnesty and the E-Verify system. Layne commented in order to distract her from any questions about their future.

"No good wetbacks," was all he could think of to say to change the subject.

"Why do you call them wetbacks?"

"That's what they used to call illegals in Texas a long time ago, because the border in Texas is the Rio Grande River. So, they would be wet after they swam across."

Fabiola laughed, uncurled her body and stood up to walk to the kitchen. She was wearing soccer shorts and an extra-large t-shirt with the sleeves rolled up. Her legs were tan and smooth; she had removed her eye shadow and mascara when she changed out of her work clothes. Her sandy-blond hair was pulled back into a messy bun with bobby pins so that a few highlighted strands were dangling from the bunch in the back. He had been fascinated by her appearance since the day he met her. Before meeting her, he had thought that Hispanic people from south of the United States were invariably dark with black hair. Everything about her was foreign and exotic. The rhythm in her Argentine accent sounded like Italian to him and seemed to contradict her blue eyes. He often found himself staring when she was looking the other way.

From the couch he could hear the refrigerator door open. He realized it was only Tuesday and the second night this week he had brought home beer. His hangover from the weekend still lingered, prolonged by the beer he had tried to cure it with the night before. The remaining cans of Coors Original in the refrigerator were all that he had available to drink in the apartment. Four beers would be sufficient to take the edge off his discomfort, but six would eliminate the symptoms completely. But if she opened the refrigerator and saw that all the cans were gone it would mean a whole day of dirty looks.

He heard her close the refrigerator and then open a drawer. She still hadn't said anything. Perhaps it was because of the conversation they'd just had. If she only knew the breadth of what he had in the works. The truth was that he had been methodically carrying out his plan for over a year before his friend Kurt introduced them to one another during a summer backyard house party.

Fabiola left the kitchen light on and came back into the living room with a fork and a bowl of something with noodles. She sat down on the couch and leaned against the armrest with her legs bent to her side as she began eating. He pretended to be absorbed in the debate. Under no circumstances could he allow himself to reveal the scope of what he was involved in.

After the attack on the World Trade Center, the President had created a hiring influx by demanding that Homeland Security double the amount of Border Patrol Agents on the southern border. An ever-increasing influx of illegals, and the rumors of large caravans coming through Mexico from other Central American countries, sustained the urgency. The hiring surge was also a response to concerns that terrorist organizations like Al-Qaeda were planning to sneak a weapon of mass destruction across the border, and that the Mexican drug cartels were sending tons of marijuana and other—more lethal—illegal drugs.

The Administration's ambitious quota left DHS with no choice but to make modifications to the screening process in order to hire enough applicants within the allotted time frame. Most significant to the changes was the omission of the daunted polygraph examination, the barrier that dissuaded most people from applying who were otherwise qualified. When Layne learned that the lie detector test had been withdrawn it was his green light to begin work on the blueprint he had laid out. That meant he wouldn't have to answer uncomfortable questions about his past—in particular, his dismissal from two college baseball programs and his shaky foray into minor league ball.

Not even his parents knew the entirety of his mission. He told people that he wanted the personal security of federal employment—a GL-11 Federal Agent earned $80,000 a year—but there were many dimensions to what he was after. He wanted to be taken care of—he knew that federal employees had excellent benefits, and unlike much of the private sector, there was bureaucracy that protected them from being fired. Among the most rewarding spoils would be an irrevocable sense of self-respect, a psychological watermark he would always be able to reference that would keep his mental health stable during doldrums. Deep inside he knew that the true test would be preventing himself from falling victim to his own weaknesses. He had spent the past seven years in search of a way to recapture the self-concept of his youth—the high of being the star player on a state championship team in high school, of being drafted by a major league team, of showing all those kids who made fun of him when he was younger. It was also a way to put his past failures behind him for good, to make his mom and dad, especially his dad, proud after disappointing them so often. The Border Patrol offered a way to attain all that was missing, with one daring endeavor.

After researching the details of the hiring influx he had returned to college for a semester to study in Mexico, primarily to learn Spanish. He foresaw that being a white male with the ability to read, write, and speak Spanish would ensure that he could handle the academic demands of the Academy, which would allow him to allocate the whole of his study time toward classes other than foreign language. The rest of the classes at the Academy wouldn't stand in his way. He had been exposed to firearms at an early age and was an exceptional marksman. Matt had warned him that Physical Training would be torturous, and that it was responsible for the majority of trainees who dropped out. But Layne had been a college athlete, and he was certain that he could handle whatever they threw at him. Long distance running would be difficult, but allowing anything physical to stop him would be a sin. It would be close, but according to his calculations he could survive training and graduate to move on to Field Training at a station on the border.

His eyes remained fixed on the television screen, but his mind was busy envisioning his future: A house, a new truck, and a gorgeous wife preparing dinner for him. The phase of his plan that involved finding a Spanish-speaking girlfriend had fallen into place fortuitously. But the true hurdles still lay ahead—the first one being the interview with the background investigator in two weeks. Matt told him that if he simply omitted certain details about his past, the investigator would have no way of discovering what he needed to hide. Erasing facets of his past from his own consciousness was one more part of the final goal. After passing the written exam, he had resolved to clean up his act so as to fit into the role of the new life he was seeking. He had begun exercising and doing his best to avoid people and places that had been problematic.

Layne glanced at Fabiola. She had never witnessed his behavior when he was at his worst. She forked noodles and looked back at him watching her. She grinned—content, judging by the manner in which she chewed.

The debate broke for a series of commercials and she commented, "I don't want to go to work tomorrow. I have to get one of the units ready to rent, and it's disgusting. Those people aren't getting their deposit back."

"Uh-huh," Layne replied, but he remained withdrawn. His cycle of thoughts moved on to the stage where he imagined what it would be like at the Academy and, if he could make it through, what the border would be like. He vowed to himself that he would become a new person—reborn through military-like discipline. It was his last chance. He was twenty-seven; there was no time left for failure. By any societal standard, he was behind. He had been too embarrassed to even consider appearing at his ten-year high school reunion. He should have had a wife, kids, and a good job by now.

Fabiola set her bowl on the table and looked at him. "You're quiet tonight. What are you thinking about?"

"Nothing, just thinking about who I'm gonna vote for," Layne said. And as he said it, he dreamt about one day being able to tell people the truth. Whatever wrongs he had to commit in order to get there would have to be one last string of white lies to serve as a means to an end and put his life back on track.

2

LAYNE HAD VISITED FABIOLA AT WORK only once before and hadn't noticed her office walls. But on this day a framed print drew him away from his pacing. It must have been there before Fabiola moved into the office, because it wasn't something she would have chosen. The painting depicted a group of demoralized Hispanic migrant workers in straw hats, gazing hopelessly through a barbed wire fence. Layne could just make out the name of the artist in the bottom left corner: Domingo Ulloa. He had never heard of him, but his first thought was that the artist's intention was to gain sympathy from all the bleeding hearts in the United States—those who had been spoiled out of their sense of nationalism.

He scoffed away the painting and looked down at himself to check his appearance; he was wearing slacks and one of his best dress shirts for this critical occasion. He straightened his belt and tried to sit down, but instead gave in to the urge to resume moving as he pressed the dial button and put his cellphone to his ear. Matt answered after three rings.

"I'm sweating bullets," Layne blurted.

"What time is he supposed to be there?" Matt spoke in the thickest Texas accent Layne had ever heard.

"He's supposed to be here at 3:00."

"What time is it now?" Matt asked.

Layne realized that Matt was a time zone ahead as he pulled back the cuff of his shirt to look at his wristwatch. "It's about 2:50."

"Where's he meeting you?" Matt asked.

"He wanted to meet in my girlfriend's office; she's a leasing agent for these apartments. I'm in a leasing office—like a clubhouse." Layne shifted the pattern of his pacing as he tried to remember the primary reason he called.

"Why did he want to do the interview there?"

"I don't know. I was hoping you might know."

"Maybe he just wants to see if you're telling the truth about her job. Usually they will meet you in a library or something."

"It's a pain for her; she's got work to do."

When Layne told Fabiola that Edward, the background investigator, wanted to use her office, she appeared frustrated. She didn't protest, and he let the matter settle. He knew her well enough to be sure that her pouting was held in check by fear.

"Just do what he says," Matt instructed. "He can go anywhere he wants; he'll probably go to your work and talk to your supervisor, too."

Layne felt his pulse surge, and his forehead began to sweat. The conversation finally made clear the gravity of what he was attempting. He swallowed, and said, "Well, we have security at my work. Only employees can go in there because we deal with personal information and credit card numbers and other stuff. I don't think they'll let him in."

"They don't have a choice," Matt said with a dismissive laugh.

Layne began to bite his thumbnail. "Are you sure?"

"Of course, he's a federal agent. He can go wherever he wants, in any state. He doesn't care if he cuts into her schedule or messes with your security at work. This takes priority over everything."

"You went through all this before, right?" Layne said, seeking assurance.

"Yeah, I went through the Academy twice, but I never graduated because I kept hurting my knee in P.T." Matt's tone belied annoyance—he had told Layne the story before.

Layne looked at his wristwatch and looked out the window again. "I owe you one. If I ever meet you in person, I'll buy you a beer."

"No problem," Matt said.

"He should be here any minute. I was just calling to see if there's anything else you can tell me before he gets here." Layne was afraid to let go of Matt's friendly twang.

"You memorized everything you put down on that SF-86, right?"

"Yeah, I remember everything I said. The main thing I'm really worried about is the drugs. Are you sure I should've admitted I smoked weed?"

"Yep, if you say you've never tried anything, they won't believe you and they will start looking even harder for stuff," Matt said.

Layne began to scratch the back of his head while he held the phone to his ear and stared at the floor, searching his racing thoughts for anything else that might help. He had told Matt more about himself than he had ever told anyone. Matt knew the general truth about his past with the exception of a few significant matters—matters too personal and difficult. He didn't know why Layne had been kicked off the University of Missouri baseball team and out of school entirely. He didn't know what happened in Peoria after Layne was drafted by the Cardinals. It was too late to tell him now, and Layne knew that these issues could cost him the security clearance if discovered. But in addition to the fear that Matt would pass judgment, Layne feared that Matt might recommend he save himself the trouble and withdraw his application. He didn't even approve of recreational marijuana use.

"I put down that I smoked it three times at frat parties seven years ago, like you told me to," Layne said.

"That's perfect. Are you sure that's what you put down? You gotta know it down to the year and month."

"Yeah, I'm sure. I quizzed myself a dozen times to make sure I had it down." Layne knew that his mind had a tendency to go blank under pressure.

"Good, make sure you have all that committed to memory; he's gonna try to cross you up with what's on that SF-86."

Layne found himself staring again, this time at the coffee maker, then at some of Fabiola's desk trinkets; there was a miniature flag of Argentina in a coffee cup on her desk. He was trying not to panic.

"I'm also worried about my work history," Layne admitted.

"Why?"

"Well, I've been fired a few times."

"So," Matt said dismissively.

"How could they not care about that?" Layne said, in disbelief.

"Because it's hearsay. They only care about facts. You don't have a police record, right? No DUIs?"

"No, by the grace of God," Layne said, but the memory of his previous good fortune wasn't at all gratifying.

"As long as there's nothing on paper, you're good," Matt said with finality.

"Are you sure?"

"Yeah, if you tell the guy the truth about drugs you've tried, it's ball game, so you have to lie about that. But don't lie about anything you don't have to. If there's a record of anything somewhere, you need to tell him because he'll find it. You won't believe the stuff they dig up."

Based on the latest feel he was getting from Matt, he was leaning toward disclosing everything to the investigator. To risk that the guy would never find out felt more threatening during the final countdown. There were a handful of people from his past that were privy to the information, but Layne speculated that those who knew would want to keep their interaction with a federal investigator as brief as possible.

"Well, if I get past this interview, what comes next?" As he asked, Layne peeked through the blinds again.

"You have to do your Oral Board," Matt answered, then added, "But you can't fail this interview. He's just gathering information; it's not a test."

"I bet that Oral Board is gonna suck. What's it like?" Layne asked.

"They will have Border Patrol Agents there that will grill you about scenarios at the border, and you have to tell them what you would do in the situation. They evaluate you," Matt said.

"Oh, screw me. You live down there; I've always lived up north. I don't know squat about the border," Layne said.

"You'll be alright. Just don't change your answers," Matt warned.

"They're gonna try to rattle your cage. If they get you to backpedal and second-guess yourself, you're done. They don't expect you to know what to do, they just want to see how you perform under stress."

Layne bent a metal blind to look out the window again and did a double take. He saw a man wearing slacks and a dress shirt with no tie coming from the parking lot, watching his feet as he walked slowly. He was carrying a briefcase.

"I think this is him coming now. I better go. I'll call you after I'm done."

Layne closed his flip phone and put it in his pocket. He moved away from the window when he was sure that it could only be Edward, the investigator, arriving along the walkway. He looked around the room and tried to decide what he should look like he was doing when Edward arrived. He elected to wait by the door for a knock and try to look calm. He would wait a few seconds before opening it. If he could pull this whole thing off, he could pick and choose the events in his history he wanted to remember. He would have a clean slate—the new start he had been wandering in search of for years.

When Edward came through the door, Layne made it a point to meet him with his firmest handshake. Edward was a tall, Hispanic-looking man in his early sixties with graying hair and light skin. Layne had approximated his age accurately from his voice over the phone, but the image of the man he had created in his mind was far off—as always.

Layne sat tentatively in Fabiola's desk chair and offered the chair in front of the desk to Edward. Layne wasn't sure how to act . . . or what to do with his hands in these situations.

Edward began opening his briefcase on the desk between them. Layne couldn't withstand the awkward silence any longer. He felt expected to speak and blurted, "Were you a Border Patrol Agent?"

"Yes, I was," Edward answered. "I worked in Calexico for twenty years and I was in the Marine Corps before I entered The Service. I retired a while back and now I do background investigations to stay busy."

"Calexico? Is that near El Centro?" Layne knew where it was but wanted to prolong the subject to delay—even if only for a few minutes—the questions he knew were coming.

"It's farther south. Do you know why they call it Calexico?" Edward asked, grinning.

Layne smiled. He was interested in such things. "No, why?"

"It's one city divided by the Border Fence. On the Mexico side of the border it's called Mexicali, and on the California side it's called Calexico. The letters in the cities are reversed depending on which side of the border you're on."

Layne nodded and smiled. His shoulders relaxed a little bit, as they seemed to be hitting it off. But then he thought maybe Edward was baiting him into letting his guard down to lure him into revealing something about himself he had not intended to. Why did he pick Fabiola's office to have this meeting? What did he know about her?

Edward removed documents from his briefcase and placed them on the desk. "I have a copy here of the SF-86 you submitted on-line. Like I said in our phone conversation, we are going to go over this and fill in anything that's missing."

"Okay," Layne said.

"You've lived in a lot of places," Edward said, his tone sounding somewhat critical.

Layne wondered if that might be a red flag. "Yes, I have, but I had baseball scholarships and transferred twice. I lost a lot of credit hours transferring schools."

This was not the first time he had tried to fit in somewhere and find a new start.

"And since then I haven't been sure of what I wanted to do . . . until now," Layne added.

"I'm not driving to Missouri; I don't give a damn what they say," Edward stated as he clicked his pen. He seemed to be talking to himself. Layne didn't respond and only shifted his posture.

He could hear his internal voice fretting while Edward finished preparing. He tried to appear relaxed, but despite Matt's reassurances, he couldn't muster a glimmer of confidence about exposing his past to scrutiny. His knee bounced. He was embarrassed, and well aware of how far behind he was; he knew he should've been married with a kid on the way by now to appear normal. Edward stopped thumbing through papers and continued.

"I see that you started taking Paxil for depression when you were an athlete at the University of Missouri. What happened there? Are you still taking antidepressants?"

Layne paused to consider his answer. He still used Paxil, but sporadically, only when he felt himself slipping. He had been getting sample boxes of tablets from a relative. They hadn't been on a pharmacy record for years. Matt had advised him to deny using them except for one brief period long ago.

"I went through a hard time when I hurt my arm and lost my scholarship. But I only took it for about a year. There were lots of side effects," Layne claimed.

"What happened to your arm?" Edward asked.

"I tore an elbow ligament playing long-toss."

Edward's face lit up as he read from his paperwork. "You were a major league draft choice?"

Layne anticipated being annoyed, despite the tension.

"Yeah."

"What team?"

"The Cardinals."

Layne thought, *Now he's gonna say, why didn't you go?*

"Why didn't you go?" Edward asked.

"Because I was a draft-and-follow. I was supposed to be drafted again the next year and be offered a signing bonus, but it didn't work out." Layne looked away as he spoke, and scratched his cheek.

He toiled to think of a distraction to lead Edward away from that time period if he persisted; he didn't want him finding out about what happened between him and one of his coaches. Layne interrupted the pause and rushed to deflect any further inquiry. "Do you like baseball?"

"Yeah, I'm a Yankees fan," Edward replied, as he looked up from the questionnaire. He didn't seem to interpret Layne's intent.

"Oh, the Dark Side," Layne said.

"What?" Edward said, confused.

"Oh . . . nothing, it's just something baseball people say. It's a joke." Layne backed off and took a moment to observe Edward while he reacquired his place in his paperwork. He had appeared almost lost when he arrived, and he was repeatedly losing his place within his list of questions. Multitasking between the SF-86 and other documents made him look like he might be approaching senility.

"What is your relationship with Fabiola Estrada? Is she a roommate or a girlfriend? You can just tell me she's a roommate if you want, it's a lot more work if you say she's your girlfriend," Edward said.

Layne tried not to let his eyes show it while he stalled to think. Why would he offer me a lay-up like this? Laziness? Edward knew how to tempt him. To deny a principle relationship would most likely reduce the background investigation by several months. Fabiola being a foreigner was probably a mountain of paperwork. But maybe her status had just now swayed him to set a trap that would eliminate the case completely? Judging by Edward's fatigued body language, Layne was ninety-percent sure he was being sincere.

Edward leaned back and slouched slightly while his writing hand awaited a response. Layne opened his mouth to state that she was merely a temporary roommate, then Matt's southern drawl stopped his lips from moving at the last moment. I warned him not to lie about anything that wasn't a deal breaker. It was too dangerous to gamble with.

"She's my girlfriend right now. She's here on a work visa from Argentina," Layne said reluctantly.

"She is?" Edward seemed surprised by the last part.

Layne was convinced that Edward's behavior was genuine. He was definitely much less adept than Layne had expected—maybe even easy to manipulate.

"She's from the same city as Che Guevara, but she doesn't like to talk about it. I guess it's different down there than the way it is here with the t-shirts and stuff," Layne added.

Edward looked perplexed.

"And she lives in these apartments here?" he asked.

"She lives in that building right over there," Layne answered, pointing toward her building through a large window to his left." She gets a free apartment; it's one of her benefits for being the apartment manager.

Edward glanced at him with an aggravated eye, and sighed. "This is gonna be a pain in the butt. I'm going to have to see her passport and her visa."

Layne reminded himself to keep his guard up while Edward jotted something down. He looked up from his paperwork and glared sharply into Layne's eyes.

"You stated that you tried marijuana three times in college. Have you used any other illicit drugs?"

Layne braced himself and forged his best poker face. He tried to appear matter of fact, but his eyes broke contact with Edward's. He dreaded hearing the word steroids and hoped Edward wouldn't go there. "No, I just tried marijuana three times when I was at fraternity parties in Missouri, but I didn't like it."

"Nothing else, though?" Edward wasn't releasing his stare as he waited for something to write down.

"No, just marijuana. It made me view myself, my life, from an outside perspective. It made me panic," Layne said.

Edward looked suspicious. "Okay, I'll put down that you tried it and didn't like it because you felt bad about it; guilty?"

"Yes, I did feel guilty. If my dad knew, he would be really disappointed." Layne stared at a different picture on the wall for a moment while he pondered the percentage of truth in his statement.

"How many drinks would you say you have in a week?" Edward asked, resuming the stare, but with less intensity.

Layne forced himself to maintain eye contact with him and hoped Edward couldn't tell he was putting forth effort to do so. "I have three or four drinks a week. Unless there's a social situation or something special going on, then I will have two or three more."

"So, seven drinks a week?" Edward asked, his pen waiting.

"Six or seven on average, seven at the most," Layne claimed.

"Any DUIs?" Edward asked, looking at his pad now.

"No."

Edward wrote quietly while Layne crossed his fingers beneath the desk, hoping he would move on to the next subject.

"You said here that you speak Spanish. *Cómo aprendiste Español?*" Edward wanted to know how he learned Spanish.

"*Yo viví en México y asistí a una escuela allí,*" Layne said eloquently. He had practiced this phrase repeatedly while chatting with Mexicans about his life and schooling in their country.

"Where in Mexico?" Edward asked, eyebrows raised.

"La Paz, I was there for almost four months."

"What were you doing in Mexico?" Edward asked.

"I was studying abroad," Layne said.

Edward shook his head. "I'm gonna need to see your passport later on then." He sounded deflated, as if he had pulled the shortest straw of all the investigators. He found his place in his paperwork and continued. "Why did you put Tucson Sector as your first choice of stations to work?"

Layne hadn't anticipated this question. Why does he care? Matt had asked him the same thing, and when Layne told him Arizona, Matt said, "What? That's the worst place on the border."

He felt Edward waiting for an answer while he imagined the desert. "Um, my parents took me to Tucson when I was twelve for Spring Training. I didn't know there were palm trees in Arizona until then. I have wanted to live there ever since."

Edward gave him another bemused look.

Stop elaborating, Layne told himself. *If you can't think of anything to say just be quiet.*

"Have you been to any other countries besides Mexico?" Edward asked as he flipped the yellow paper over to allow himself a blank sheet on his legal pad.

"I've been to Germany, Austria, Switzerland, France, the Netherlands and Czechoslovakia. I mean the Czech Republic," Layne rattled off.

"Why, what were you doing?" Edward asked with his mouth slightly open.

"I was backpacking after I graduated from college," Layne said.

"Backpacking?"

"My parents bought me a Eurail pass and a plane ticket to Munich for a graduation present," Layne explained.

"When was that? How long were you there?" Edward asked.

"Five years ago. I was there a month."

"By yourself?"

"Yeah—well, no. I hung out with an Australian guy from Perth for a week or so in different cities, Paris," Layne said as he transferred his weight to his right buttock.

"Why would you want to do that?" Edward asked, perplexed.

Layne considered the best way to explain that some people found museums like the Louvre interesting, and that it was peculiarly satisfying to witness foreigners within their native cultures going about their daily lives. But he elected to simplify his answer. "I wanted to be fulfilled. It's hard to explain; you just kind of fall in with people you meet." He hoped Edward wouldn't ask about Amsterdam; he had thought about saying Belgium instead, but there was a Dutch stamp on his passport.

Edward leaned slowly back in his chair and sighed. He continued to sift through papers while Layne regretted his nervous mouth. Matt told him they were primarily concerned with a candidate's susceptibility to bribery as well as ties to foreign countries. Layne's time spent abroad had just tripled the amount of research involving the case Edward had been handed. He prayed Edward wouldn't ask him about his work history. When employers saw that he called in sick every other Monday, they knew he wasn't really ill. But Matt had reassured him.

"Besides past employers, there's gonna be people they find that will talk trash about you. They expect that; everyone has enemies. As long as you don't have a police record, you're good. Don't worry about drinking. The Border Patrol lives by the three W's—Whiskey, Women and Wets."

Edward pulled him out of his trance. "Well, I think that's about all I need for now. When do you take the Oral Board Exam?"

Layne stood up after he was sure that Edward was getting up. "I take it in two weeks."

As he walked Edward to the door, he put his hands in his pockets and noticed that he was still trembling. His rear had fallen asleep and tingled with numbness.

"What happens if I don't pass the Oral Board?" Layne asked.

"They will terminate the background investigation," Edward said, as if he expected Layne to know the answer.

Layne tried to chat some more in an attempt to revive the feeling of camaraderie they had begun with. When he sensed that Edward had heard enough, he removed his hands from his pockets and reached out to shake his hand again. Edward fumbled with his briefcase while he closed the door behind himself. Layne took a deep breath. He got a cup of water from Fabiola's water dispenser and returned to the blinds to watch Edward take the path back to the parking lot.

He began to chew the nail on his pointer finger. Getting past this guy was still going to be the longshot he had foreseen. Edward would disregard the people he had listed as references; he would know they were friends and would only speak favorably about him. Matt had warned him of that. Edward would seek out people from his past that he was not in contact with for good reason. He hoped that would not include his former college coaches or anyone in the St. Louis organization.

He allowed the metal blind at eye level to spring back into place as he examined the nail on his finger. It was gnawed to the quick. He involuntarily put the nail of his middle finger between his teeth as he returned to Fabiola's chair to sit and think.

3

LAYNE FOUND A PARKING SPACE CLOSE TO the entrance of the Rocky Mountain Hotel and took a deep breath as he turned off the engine. He checked his tie in the rearview mirror. This was the first time he had ever worn a suit. He hadn't even known where to look to buy one, and had to ask Fabiola for help. She took care of the rest; he had done no more than serve as a mannequin for her.

His hands were already shaking, but he had planned ahead. He reached into his right pants pocket and removed his secret weapon, a blank prescription bottle containing two ten-milligram tablets of Valium. He washed one down with the remainder of his lukewarm coffee, then opened the car door and stepped into the cold morning sun of November in downtown Denver.

He knew instantly that he was in the right place when he entered the lobby. A group of eight young men wearing suits was huddled uncomfortably in cool, thick-cushioned chairs in the lounge. One young man was standing off to the side, wearing a dark blue Air Force dress uniform with a necktie and beret. The lobby was empty except for them. Only two or three were talking, but with hushed voices; the others were quietly observing. They acknowledged him and he sat down in a vacant chair; they resumed talking after he was seated. They were trying to make conversation with one another, but at a volume between a whisper and normal speech.

"What kind of things do they ask you?" one of them said.

"There's no way to know, but I hear it's brutal," another responded.

"Have any of you done your interview with your investigator yet?"

They were talking about what most recently had been concerning Layne, and he couldn't refrain from asking them, "Did you guys put down everything on your SF-86?"

A lanky blond in his mid-twenties who was fueling the conversation, said, "I put down everything I know they will find out about. I was in the Army—you don't even want to know about the stuff we did."

Layne let out a nervous laugh. He knew what he meant; he had heard bizarre stories of deployed soldiers smoking spice and guzzling Robitussin. But to know that others who had applied probably had checkered pasts, as well, didn't quell his worry.

All the other applicants had crew cuts. They looked like they didn't belong in suits, like defendants in court. Layne wondered if he was the only applicant who wasn't active military or a veteran, another concern in addition to the background check and most imminently, the Oral Board Interview.

One of the quiet ones, a solid-looking Hispanic who appeared to be in his late 20s, spoke up. "You guys should be careful what you say. I hear the agents doing the exams bug the lobby."

Everyone became silent for a few heartbeats, then the conversation shifted awkwardly to a topic of no consequence, as eyes wandered.

"How long did it take you to get here?" one of them asked another.

"It was a nightmare, about eight hours on I-70. Me and the wife stayed in a motel last night."

"Where did you drive from?"

"Kansas City."

Layne was surprised; he had assumed they were all from the Denver metro area. The realization that applicants had traveled from other states brought home all at once the critical nature of what lay only moments ahead.

He wiped the sweat from his forehead with the back of his hand and noticed the dampness in the armpits of his Oxford cloth shirt. He looked at his wristwatch—it was five minutes past 8 a.m., bedlam was imminent.

His eyes scanned the ceiling and potted plants for surveillance equipment. Then, before he realized a change, the focus of his thought shifted to the fruity sweetness of his gum. His scalp relaxed and seemed to expand. It had been roughly twenty minutes since he had taken the Valium. The drug began to overwhelm his nervous system like hot fudge over ice cream. He sank into the cushions of the seat, enjoying the temperature of the fabric while he welcomed a general sense of well-being heedless of his circumstances.

At 8:10 a.m. the conference room door near the back of the lobby opened. A stocky Hispanic agent in an all-green dress uniform, duty belt, gun and glistening brass buttons was charging their way, like a bull. He confronted the group with arms slightly bowed and demanded, "Who is going first?"

There was a moment of intimidated silence. Layne reasoned that he should get it over with while the drug was approaching its peak. Without hesitation he stood and blurted, "I'll go first."

The others stared with relief and instant respect for Layne as Bull led him toward the conference room. Layne couldn't refrain from taking in the agent's striking green uniform as they walked side by side. His short sleeves had been ironed and starched to crisp perfection, leaving a prominent fold like a piece of paper through the center of the green fabric. The Federal shield on his left breast flashed as Layne moved past it. It was gold and narrower than the police badges he had taken the time to notice. It was the first time Layne had ever seen an agent in person; for him it was almost like seeing a movie star.

The conference room was empty except for two tables. Two of three chairs at one table were occupied by agents in uniform. The table opposite, about fifteen feet away, had one chair for the examinee. Bull showed Layne to his seat, then sat down between the other two agents to complete the panel. The agent to Bull's right was an overweight Hispanic woman who appeared unenthusiastic—involuntarily detailed to this assignment. The agent to the left was a frail, older Hispanic man who looked like a chain-smoker. His awkward body language made him appear uncomfortable with his duty.

Layne was offended that he would be interrogated by Hispanics about immigration; he considered that perhaps the two agents were unenthusiastic because they were accustomed to apathy while on the border. He tried to clear his mind of negativity as Bull situated himself. Matt had described the Oral Board as another filtration system, a 15-minute melee to thin the herd. "They're gonna to try to rattle your cage," Layne remembered Matt saying.

The female agent spoke first, "What is your name?"

"Layne Sheppard."

She confirmed his name on the file in front of her and said, "My name is Agent Baena. This is Agent Valez, and he is Agent Lopez. Each of us will present you with a real scenario that happened in the field, and you will respond with what you do in the situation as if you're actually there right now."

Layne nodded, "I understand."

She continued, "Agent Valez will start."

Bull read from a sheet of paper. "You are near the Border Fence with another agent and the two of you apprehend a group of approximately twenty suspected illegal aliens. One of the aliens picks up a rock and reaches back to throw it at you. Your partner shoots and wounds him before he can hit you with it, and the rest of the bodies scatter. What do you do?"

Layne thought for only a few seconds before responding. "I would give medical attention to the wounded alien."

Bull: "What kind of medical attention? "

Layne: "I would give him CPR."

Bull: "You would or you do?"

Layne: "I give him CPR."

Bull: "What else?"

Layne: "I call an ambulance."

Bull: "An ambulance in the middle of the desert?"

He felt a jolt of adrenaline that was quickly vanquished by the Valium, which allowed him to think clearly. To make it through this without help would be impossible, anxiety would cause his mind to become blank and stationary, like a blinking cursor.

Layne: "I try to stop the bleeding."

Bull: "How do you call an ambulance, with what?"

Layne: "With my radio."

Bull: "Your radio is out of range, so now what?"

Layne: (Pause)"I call for help with my cellphone."

Bull: "Are you playing games with me, man? That's really what you would do?"

Layne: (Pause)"Yes. I call for an ambulance with my cellphone."

Bull shielded his eyes with his hand and shook his head for a moment, then said, "You're really gonna let twenty bodies go north for one stupid Tonk?"

Bull was almost yelling now.

Layne: "Yes, sir. We can catch the others later; he's still a human being."

Bull nodded slightly. The agents seemed to be satisfied with his answer; indeed, it was a test.

The slender agent, Lopez, picked up his piece of paper from the table and read a second scenario as Layne saw stars. He had two more agents to get through. He reminded himself of what Matt had told him, "Don't reverse yourself."

The grilling followed a similar pattern, but with less force, while Bull sat with arms crossed to allow the others to interrogate. He seemed to disapprove of Agent Lopez's passive demeanor. Layne felt weightless and numb until Lopez let up and deferred to Agent Baena. He held his breath with fear of not being able to come up with any response and being forced to say, "I don't know," while time crawled and the agents waited.

"Involving the scenario with the wounded alien, there's an investigation surrounding the incident and you are to meet with an investigator to explain what happened. The agent who shot the alien approaches you and asks that you alter your story because he's concerned that he will be fired for not following procedure. How do you handle the situation?"

Layne hit a wall. He didn't want them to think he was a snitch; loyalty was all he had left over from before. He knew what he was supposed to say, but he felt hollow saying it.

Layne: "I tell the investigator exactly what happened as I saw it."

Baena: "As you saw it, or the truth?"

Layne: "I tell the truth."

Baena: "Okay."

Thank God, Layne thought.

Bull shook his head with pronounced disapproval. "Wait a minute, some guy throws a rock at you and an agent shoots him, and you rat him out just like that? I want to be your partner, buddy."

Layne: "Well, I would talk to the agent first and tell him what I was going to say."

Bull: "So you could get your twisted story straight with him?"

Layne: "No, to tell him that I am telling the truth to the investigator. I tell the truth."

Bull: "Why do you even need to go talk to the agent?"

Layne: "To let him know that I am not going behind his back."

Bull: "I don't think so. I think the only reason you talk to the agent is so you can get your story straight."

Layne: "No sir, I just wouldn't want him to think I was throwing him under the bus."

Bull: "So you would change the story?"

Layne: "No, I would tell the truth."

Bull: "Are you sure?"

Layne: "Yes, sir, I tell the truth."

There was a moment of silence; the agents exchanged glances and Agent Baena said, "We need you to have a seat in the lobby while we make a decision. Agent Valez will come get you when we are ready. But don't talk with the other applicants about anything that was said in this room. We'll know if you do."

Layne left the room in a daze and floated slowly back to the lounge. He felt the hard tile floor through the lack of cushion in the soles of his dress shoes as he walked. The other applicants received him with great anticipation.

As he sat down the lanky blond said, "You look white, dude."

"I feel lightheaded," Layne said.

"What did they say?"

"They told me not to say anything or they would know."

No one responded, and Layne stared at one spot on the wall in a comfortable state of shock. After several minutes the silence was interrupted when Bull opened the door to the conference room and motioned for Layne to return. He sat back down at the table, expecting bad news. It had been so long since he had experienced success that he felt a sense of fulfillment by simply putting forth a good effort. He told himself that he had done the best he could while he waited for the rejection.

"We decided to pass you. Congratulations. Your investigator will be in contact with you. Don't talk to the others on your way out," Bull said.

"Thank you," Layne said in disbelief.

* * * *

FABIOLA SAT UP STRAIGHT IN HER desk chair as Edward put his badge away into his back pocket and sat in the chair facing her desk. She had straightened up her office as best she could in preparation for his arrival. Her hands were grasping one another underneath the drawer of her desk, below Edward's view. Edward had been placing business cards on the doors of all of her neighbors in the apartment complex and all over Layne's parents' neighborhood. The cards bore the Homeland Security logo in the corner and requested that the recipient "contact Agent Edward Herrera regarding a matter of National Security." Many of her neighbors in the apartments were unlawful and wouldn't answer the door when he knocked, nor would they call the number on the business card.

Fabiola tried not to appear uneasy while Edward thumbed the combination to unlock his briefcase. He couldn't help glancing at her more than once while he opened his briefcase. She had long sandy blonde hair and a European face, completely opposite of what he had expected. She wore an azure shirtwaist dress, and pearl stud earrings. She was interesting to look at—although she looked Caucasian, she exuded a foreign appearance that would be hard for him to describe.

Once Edward situated himself, he focused on Fabiola's blue eyes. "You understand that Layne is applying for a security clearance in order to be accepted into the Border Patrol Academy?"

"Yes, I understand," Fabiola said; her hands gripped one another tighter as she answered.

"I've had trouble getting in contact with the people who live in your vicinity," Edward said with slight frustration.

"I'm sorry about that. But you have to understand, the people who live here probably think you're a police officer, and they're afraid to talk to you," Fabiola explained, her voice sounded unnerved despite her efforts to appear relaxed.

"How long have you known Layne?" Edward said to her, his eyes trained patiently on his paperwork now.

"I have known him for about a year," Fabiola said.

Her accent was pleasing to hear and it charmed Edward; he grinned when she spoke.

"How did you meet him?" Edward asked.

"His friend Kurt introduced me to him. I worked at Purgatory Ski resort with Kurt before my company transferred me here. They own these apartments," Fabiola said, trying to smile.

Edward was becoming increasingly intrigued by the combination of her appearance and her accent as they interacted. "Did you go to college in Argentina?" he asked politely.

"Yes, I went to the National University of Rosario." Fabiola was holding her breath a little after each response.

"What did you study?"

"Medicine, then I changed to Business after the second year."

"Why didn't you continue to study medicine?"

"My dad is a doctor and I felt obligated to study medicine. But after a few years of it, I decided it wasn't for me." Fabiola looked at her hands while she answered.

"I see, and you have an H1-B visa here in the U.S.?" Edward redirected, realizing that he had brought up a sore subject.

"Yes, I do," Fabiola said. She tried to remember what she had rehearsed, but her mind had gone blank.

Edward searched for his next question within his paperwork while Fabiola's palms began to sweat against one another. She was feeling the same way she had when she dealt with U.S. Customs Agents in Argentina while applying for the visa. She shuddered to remember; the Customs Agents were notoriously malevolent and ruthless, and the white female agents especially mean. They spoke fluent Spanish but chose to speak English to the Argentinian visa applicants, to further torment them.

"How long did it take you to get the visa?" Edward asked.

"My company put me into a lottery to get it. It took two years for them to choose my name," Fabiola said.

Edward was silent again, appearing lost while trying to find his place. Fabiola wondered if she appeared nervous to him. Her documents were up to date, but she couldn't overcome the fear of interaction with a U.S. Federal Agent, no matter how politely Edward behaved. He wasn't a Customs Agent; nevertheless, he was not to be toyed with. His attitude was almost leisurely, but perhaps he was a wolf in sheep's clothing. Edward smiled with slight embarrassment as he fumbled through papers and she saw flashbacks of the U.S. Embassy in Rosario where the interview for her visa was conducted. American tourists who had lost their passport and all of their money laid helpless on the sidewalk while the embassy personnel ignored them as they drove past on their way in and out of the gated parking lot. Their apathy toward humanity in general was disturbing, and she cringed while remembering.

"Do you like it here?" Edward asked bashfully.

"Yes, I like Colorado. I miss home, though."

"What do you and Layne do in your spare time?" Edward became aware of the overly friendly impression he was making. He corrected it and his cordial demeanor diminished a little bit.

"We visit my friends in Aurora. I met a girl from Argentina when I got here," Fabiola said with a smile.

"How did you meet her?" Edward asked curiously.

Fabiola couldn't determine if he was being benevolently inquisitive or if he was trying to delude her.

"I was in line to pay at Target and I heard her talking to the cashier. I recognized her accent when she spoke English. Then I found her in the parking lot after I paid," Fabiola said. She enjoyed remembering the first time she met Marcela despite the circumstances under which she was remembering.

"Wow, what a lucky coincidence; I've never met anyone from Argentina," Edward said, his mouth hung open slightly.

"Yes, it was," Fabiola giggled.

"What else do you and Layne do in your spare time?"

"We go to the mountains sometimes; we went to Estes Park a few weeks ago. We go to the movies a lot—Layne loves movies. We only go to the movies that he wants to see though," Fabiola said, laughing a little.

"I bet you watch the World Cup; Argentina is usually pretty good." Edward said.

"I watch every game I can; I wear my Argentina jersey every time they play."

Edward glanced at the miniature blue and white flag hoisted in a coffee cup on her desk. "Does Layne like to watch soccer with you?"

Fabiola's smile straightened. "No, he doesn't like soccer; he doesn't really watch sports at all unless it's the Baseball Series or the Super Bowl."

"Do you visit his parents very often?" Edward's pen awaited an answer, a hint to what questions were relevant.

"No, not really. I have only been to see his parents twice, once on Thanksgiving last year," Fabiola said. She looked unsure about the meaning of her answer.

"Does he help pay bills?"

"There are really no bills to pay. I don't have to pay rent; it's one of the benefits of my job. But he usually pays for me when we go out to eat or to movies, and he always holds the door open for me."

The truth was that Layne never helped her clean. He never offered to help pay utilities, and he only bought food for himself, unless she asked him to buy ingredients that she needed to cook dinner. He didn't pretend to like the *milanesas* she frequently cooked either.

"Have you ever known him to drink excessively, or use drugs?" Edward asked, twiddling his pen.

Her toes curled in her simple pumps. "Well, never drugs, but I've seen him drink a lot. But there were other people drinking a lot, too, at the time."

"Does he change when he drinks?" Edward asked.

"Not really. I don't know. I mean, I think everybody changes when they drink," Fabiola said.

"Have you ever known him to become violent?" Edward asked, his eyebrows raised.

"To me?" Fabiola asked.

"To anyone."

"No. He hates my dog; he says she gets on his nerves when she barks. But I've never seen him become violent."

"What kind of dog is it?" Edward asked.

"She's a miniature Yorkshire Terrier."

"Oh," Edward said, the look on his face showing that he sympathized with Layne to a certain extent. Fabiola looked at her hands for a moment.

"Have you ever seen him mad?" Edward said.

"Yes, I've seen him mad, but I was never afraid that he would hit me."

Edward considered how to ask the next question for a moment while Fabiola sat silent.

"Do you speak Spanish with Layne?" he asked.

"Yes, he gets mad when I speak English to him. Well, I don't mean mad, he gets frustrated when he asks me in Spanish and I answer him in English," Fabiola said.

"Really?" Edward looked intrigued.

"Yeah, well, he speaks in a Mexican dialect."

"You don't like Mexicans?" Edward looked accusatory.

"No, it's not that. It's that I'm just not used to it, I guess."

"When he goes to work in the morning, does he leave on time, or I mean, do you think he usually gets to work on time?" Edward was resuming his notes on a legal pad.

"Yeah, as far as I know. He leaves before me because he has to drive to work, but I've only seen him be late one time and he called his boss and told her he would be late. But that's about it."

"Do you think he gets along with his co-workers? Does he say anything bad about them?" Edward leaned on his right armrest.

"No, not really, he doesn't like to talk about work. He has complained about hours and pay before but never specifically mentioned anyone," Fabiola said.

"What about his character? Would you say that he has good character?" Edward asked.

"He's honest as far as I know," Fabiola answered. "I have never seen him steal or anything. One time, he found a wallet and he used the guy's driver's license to find him, and he gave it back to him with the money still in it."

"Really?" Edward looked surprised.

"Yeah. He's really superstitious about karma."

Edward licked his thumb slowly and backtracked through his

paperwork to jot down another note. Fabiola's gaze fixated on her tiny flag while she thought over some of her answers. She had seen Layne drink a lot only a few times, once when he was drinking Jack Daniels with Kurt in Lodo. Or a time with Robert and Marcela at dinner when he passed out in the car on the way home. But he came home drunk and tried to pretend that he wasn't; he thought she didn't know.

Edward straightened his paperwork and began gathering his things. "Well, that's about all I've got. How long are you planning to stay here?" He stood up with his briefcase under his arm, the question obviously benign.

"For now, I don't know. I'm going to see how it goes. As long as my company can renew my visa, I think I will stay." Fabiola felt relief as she walked him to the door. They shook hands, then she closed the door behind him.

4

LAYNE TYPED HIS LOGIN AND PASSWORD into the Government website for the hundredth time, and read the same information:

Entrance Exam - Complete

Oral Board Exam - Complete

Drug Test - Complete

Background Investigation - Incomplete

Hope was dying a little more with each day that passed. It felt like an eternity since he had taken the initial written exam at the Broomfield Public Library—too much time had elapsed without word from Edward. And it had now been months since the Oral Board Exam. He was certain that Edward had uncovered something disqualifying in his aberrant history, so much so that Layne was expecting a rejection letter instead of a bad news phone call. The notification felt overdue.

The thought tormented him that an investigator like Edward was accustomed to researching choir boys and occasionally unearthing a closeted story about teenaged shoplifting. Even trivial matters could be eliminating; there was no way to know. Edward would be disgusted if he caught wind of one aspect of the truth that Layne was attempting to erase from his memory. It would require a miracle for everything to remain hidden from him.

Fabiola was starting to behave as if what he had told her was true. She was realizing that he probably hadn't exaggerated about his slim chance of being cleared for national security.

The fantasy about seeing "Complete" next to "Background Investiga-tion" was growing faint. But parades still materialized in his mind when he tried, like the celebrations in New York City for the Yankees after a World Series victory, ticker tape, streaming ribbons and marching bands—the trophy being a woman of striking beauty and class, and Layne being the catch on her arm. All of his problems would be solved if he could just make it to the Academy. He needed a ticket to anywhere. He could abandon the wreckage of his life in one, brilliant chess move across multiple squares. He would be a success story, and his gleaming new status would eclipse the rough patch, both to himself and to anyone who discussed him. All of the people he envied—who had respectable jobs and shiny presentable cars that chauffeured gorgeous, proud wives—were living in a perpetual victory party. He imagined champagne and caviar if he could achieve their status.

The dream shimmered in contrast to reality. He dreamed that he would once again experience a feeling that he belonged. He would reach the goal of respecting himself.

Virtually the only thing he owned now that was not disposable was his car and guns. He was too old to live like this anymore. It was painful to come to terms with the realization that seven years had disappeared below his feet. His only hope was to leave now, or live and die this way.

Fabiola was the thread he was hanging from, and the days continued to pass by in a worrisome monotony. He was reaching a point that he preferred to be put out of his misery with confirmation that he was not fit for duty to the torture of not knowing. There was no contingency plan. Working for pennies in a cubicle was unsustainable. Living with the sense of self-worth that accompanied it was, too.

Fabiola had raised an eyebrow when he passed the Oral Board, but her repressed curiosity had faded concurrently with his as time passed. He could sense and see her growing increasingly unfulfilled with his halfhearted affection for her. He concluded that after another week of non-activity, it would be in his best interests to begin accepting her and treating her accordingly.

There were things about her he would miss if the dream came true. He enjoyed her nearness; she made him feel less alone. The lilt and inflection in her South American tongue was an intimation of Latin Romance. She made him imagine what love would be like.

He went through whole days without thinking about the application and the security clearance. More listless weeks, then months, passed without any contact from Edward. On his worst days he felt the Academy becoming another fantasy that would fade into the normality of regular life and discontent. He was holding hands with Fabiola now when they walked in public; she smiled, satisfied just knowing that he was putting forth effort.

By happenstance, the green background of a website he had surfed across reminded him of his nearly forgotten attempt at true life, and on a whim, he loaded the Government website. He strained to remember his login—his password was always the same—and when he pressed "Enter" he stared in disbelief for several seconds at the word "Complete" next to Background Investigation. He stared frozen with shock for several seconds, unable to comprehend what he was seeing.

He wondered how long it had been complete. Perhaps he hadn't responded in time and the Minnesota Hiring Center interpreted his failure to respond as a lack of motivation—that he was no longer interested in the job. Or maybe the completion was of little consequence. Did it mean that the security clearance was in place, or did it mean that the background report had been received and that a decision was pending? There was no urge to celebrate. He called Edward for an explanation, and the investigator assured him, "Everything looks good. You should be at the Academy in a month or so."

There was still no excitement or joy; he was functioning in a state of shock. His mind was quickly confronted with anxious deliberation about how to proceed with tying loose ends. He decided to tell Fabiola that Edward wouldn't call him back in the event that Edward was mistaken. Edward couldn't tell him how long it would take before he was at the Academy, he would need her until then.

The next morning, he became overwhelmed with a sensation, an unprecedented feeling that something was about to change. The urge to leave had been revived, triumphantly, and was consuming him the way a migratory bird knows when it is time to leave for its other home. Visions of his future were appearing everywhere he looked. He would evolve like a misfit high school boy, who leaves for Marine Boot Camp a lost soul and returns home to visit, born again, transformed into a man.

He was told to wait for a call that Edward assured him was imminent. Out of superstition he chose to keep the news a secret from everyone, including his parents, until there was no doubt that it was real. He struggled to go about his daily routine. He couldn't concentrate and could barely function at work, but he couldn't quit until he received confirmation. If his coworkers only knew what he was about to embark on—he tingled when he anticipated their stunned reaction.

At night when he managed to fall asleep, his mind projected its conception of how the Academy would be. He floated vertically through a tesseract, surrounded by trainees in green uniforms moving busily at fast-forward speed on multiple floors above and below him. When he awoke, reality was so surreal that he had to confirm to himself that the website and phone call to Edward had actually happened and was not fictitious among the strange new dreams.

It was difficult to behave normally around Fabiola, and she observed him with suspicion for two weeks until the call came.

He was at work when his cell phone vibrated with a number coming from a strange area code. He disregarded the rule against cell phones during work and answered as he walked swiftly toward the bathroom as confused eyes followed him.

"This is Agent Eagan from Tucson Sector Headquarters. I'm calling to offer you a position as Border Patrol Agent in the Tucson Sector."

"I accept," Layne said.

Agent Eagan was silent for a moment then said, "You want to consider what I'm telling you. We have a position open in Douglas, Arizona, right now. But if you wait a month or two, there will be a position open at Tucson Station."

Layne feared that an unresolvable complication might develop if he chose to hold out. He couldn't risk it. "I can't wait any longer," he said. He was out of breath.

"I know you're anxious, but you want to consider the location," Eagan said.

"Douglas is fine; I've got to get on with this," Layne said, swallowing with apprehension.

"Are you sure?" Agent Eagan asked with sincere concern.

Layne could hear himself breathing more rapidly. "Yes, I accept the position."

Agent Eagan paused again, then continued. "Okay, do you have a pen ready? You need to be at the Holiday Inn on Palo Verde in Tucson on May 19—that's two weeks from today. You will be in Class 590."

Layne felt his heart trying to grasp that he had made it in. "What should I bring with me?"

"We'll send you an orientation packet. When you get there, they will take you to tour your station, then you'll take a bus from Tucson to the Academy in Artesia, New Mexico. Just make sure to bring some good running shoes, and you'll need about $700 to pay for your hotel room. You won't start getting paid until your first day at the Academy."

Layne couldn't wait to resign, and when he walked into his supervisor's office and quit, she reacted with a look of disbelief. He left before she could say anything.

He wanted to tell his parents right away; he imagined their excitement. But first, he had to call Matt. "I couldn't have done it without your help," he told the man he knew only as a voice on the phone. "It went just the way you said it would—even the part about trying to rattle my cage during the Oral Board. Thank you."

After Matt's predictable "I-told-you-so" response, Layne called and told his parents he was coming over to tell them something important. Once there, he told them to sit down in the living room before he would tell them. By the smiles in their awaiting eyes he could tell that they knew what was coming. He tried not to smile as he told them: "I did it. I leave for the Academy in two weeks. I accepted a position as Border Patrol Agent in Douglas, Arizona."

They were speechless as they rose from their seats. His mother covered her mouth with one hand. Her eyes welled up. She approached him slowly, without a word, arms extended to hug him. His dad turned red and erupted. He clapped his hands together and began high-fiving Layne repeatedly while his mother was still hugging him. *No more mistakes*, Layne thought. The watershed was prominent as he surveyed it from over his mom's shoulder. It caused him to swallow hard.

* * * *

THE BEER TOOK THE EDGE OFF, but sitting on the couch alone watching the door was like sitting in a surgery waiting room. He had been putting this off for a week now, each day losing his nerve when he saw her— deliberating, then electing to tell her when the mood was right the next day. He was driving his mom's car. He had sold his old car earlier in the day but hadn't mentioned it to Fabiola. Giving it up was like putting his dog to sleep, a sense of love loss. It was burning the boats.

She was late, and in the meantime, he had drunk eight beers, having originally intended to have two or three. By force of habit he removed the remaining cans from the twelve-pack and folded the box and stuffed it deep down in the kitchen trash underneath the rest of the garbage. She would think he had only bought a six-pack and drank two. When the door opened, Fabiola gave him a dismissive glance, and walked into the kitchen to put her purse and keys on the countertop.

There was intense silence.

Like tearing off a Band-Aid, he forced himself to say to her, "I got the call."

She emerged from the kitchen. "For the job?"

"Yeah, they offered me a position at Douglas Station," Layne said, trying to face her.

"Where is that?"

"It's in the far southeast corner of the state of Arizona." Layne tried to find a comfortable position for his hands.

"When do you leave?"

"Thursday."

"That's in three days. When did you get the call?"

He couldn't make eye contact with her. "I got the call a week ago," he admitted.

"Why didn't you tell me the same day?"

Layne glanced at the surprise on her face then looked away. "Because I was afraid of what you would say."

"But you told me that Edward wouldn't call you back, and you didn't think you would pass the background check."

"That's what I thought. I really didn't think I'd get the Security Clearance." Layne was surprised by how uncomfortable he felt telling Fabiola the truth.

She came halfway into the living room and, as her stability teetered, asked: "Did you really think that, or did you just tell me that?"

He stood up, but she kept her distance from him.

"I didn't think I would get the job. I never thought I'd pass the background investigation," Layne answered.

"Really?" Fabiola said angrily.

"Yes," Layne said.

The silent intervals between them were growing, and Fabiola's voice broke when she spoke again.

"I stopped looking into the visa application because you told me you decided you were gonna stay here." She was trying not to cry. "You never really planned on taking me with you, did you?"

"I didn't think I'd get it," Layne pleaded. The remorse was even greater than he had anticipated. He told himself to get it over with as he looked at the floor. The mission's objective was far more important.

"Do you realize that Edward asked me if you change when you drink, and I told him no?"

Layne didn't reply.

"Do you know how much you put me through? He asked me questions about my visa because of you." She was crying now.

"I'm sorry Fabi," Layne said, finding it difficult to look at her.

"Get out of here," she said sharply. She stepped toward him, her jaw set, one hand raised as if to strike him. "Get out of here now."

She began pushing him toward the door as he tried to apologize. He didn't resist and didn't turn around or stop walking as the door slammed behind him.

* * * *

LAYNE'S PARENTS COULD ONLY ESCORT HIM as far as the security gate at the airport. The female voice announcing departures sounded like the voice of God, her words transmitting the sound of finality. He pretended he didn't notice his mother tearing up in the parking lot. His dad could avoid breaking down under any circumstances; for them, the parting was a standoff of sorts. When there was no more time to delay, his mother hugged him like she would never see him again, her tears breaching the levee. His dad hung on tight and fought hard to withstand the scene. He hugged Layne in a manly way and said what he always said, "I'll see you soon, Big Horse."

Layne threw his suit and carry-on bag over his shoulder and tried to smile. *"Promise yourself that you will be fearless,"* he said to himself as he turned to head toward the gate.

5

LAYNE CHANGED HIS CLOTHES IN THE hotel room and began to admire himself in the mirror. He was getting excellent use out of this suit. But the reflection of himself from the side prompted memories of Fabiola. He remembered her brushing his shoulders with her hand, and meticulously examining the garment's fit from head to toe when he had tried it on. She had directed him where to find one on his budget, and she had combed the racks to select the right color. He put his duffle bag on the bed. He attempted to shake off the memory as he removed his shaving kit and the clothes he would need for the next two days.

Remorse was a useless emotion, but he was powerless to extinguish it. He would have to wait for the prodding to slowly wear off. It was peculiar what his mind chose to focus on, memories woven with guilt from long ago, always being supplemented by new regretful memories he couldn't cease creating. He wished he could be selective with his recollections. They got in the way of what he was doing and caused his mind to wander away from productivity. He could recite song lyrics or Spanish vocabulary spontaneously but became confused by simple verbal instructions. Only distress and anxiety focused his mind on the present.

He looked at his watch. The mailer said that he was supposed to be in the lobby at 10 a.m. He thought it best to be at least a half-hour early. Perhaps immersion into the unknown would expel Fabiola from his conscience.

The elevator settling on the bottom floor disarranged the emptiness of his stomach. It was impossible to eat in this nervous condition. The elevator bell dinged and the doors opened to the drop zone of the ground floor lobby. He was met with the smell of patterned carpet and the murmur of conversations. This hotel was much larger than the Rocky Mountain Hotel where he made it through the Oral Board interview by the skin of his teeth. The lobby here was a wide-open arrangement of multiple banquet rooms and auditoriums and a dance floor-sized lounge with multiple sets of tables and chairs. Scattered among the snowbirds and families on vacation, he immediately noticed young men in suits—some sitting alone, others standing or wandering about the lobby—who resembled those at the Oral Board Interview. He did not see familiar faces. He wondered what had happened to the other applicants at the Oral Board, most of whom seemed so much more qualified than he.

Feeling self-conscious and not knowing what to do, he forced himself to move away from the elevator. It was like holding a cafeteria tray, trying to decide whom to sit alongside at the lunch table on the first day at a new school.

As he wandered aimlessly, hoping no one noticed that he was adrift, he reminded himself to proceed with caution. Experience had taught him that he could expect to gain new enemies each and every time he was immersed into a different work atmosphere—it was inevitable that there would be people who were apt to try to eliminate those whom they perceived as competition. Maybe this time would be different. He truly wished he could feel brotherly with each of his cohorts. But he could bet that he would be swimming with sharks in due time. It was only a matter of how long it would take to identify those he would end up hating; they were usually the ones who initially flew a false flag of amiability.

A group of three he was studying seemed like obvious Border Patrol new hires. One of them was holding court, a shorter, slightly overweight Southerner, judging from a voice that could be heard from a considerable distance. Layne approached them with as much confidence as he could muster and said, "Are you guys here for Border Patrol?"

The Southerner responded, "No, we are here for the A.A.R.P. Convention."

The other two snickered, and Layne responded with a scowl.

The Southerner quickly extended his palm and said, "I'm just kidding. I'm Chad Runyon. We're here to EOD." Layne immediately wondered what EOD meant, but he forced himself to not ask. He didn't want to seem naïve and figured he would find out eventually.

Runyon was the only one not wearing his jacket, just a shirt and tie. The other two introduced themselves. Layne looked them over briefly as they shook hands. Carlos Dos Santos was an atypical example of someone who was genuinely good-natured. He was a pudgy Mexican and seemed slightly self-conscious about his appearance, but exuded a stoic quality and poise derived from a life of fending for himself. He looked to be within a year or two of Layne's age, and he said he was from Tucson. Ryan Schneider looked to be about five years younger and said he was from Minnesota; his enunciation of the letter "O" confirmed his origin. He was tall and blond with chiseled facial features and hair painstakingly molded with defining paste. He looked like he wanted people to recognize that he was adamant about health and fitness.

The attention shifted back to Runyon, who resumed where he had left off. "So, anyway, I figure this job will be a nice resume piece for my application to the F.B.I. They don't take anybody without prior law enforcement experience. The time I spent in the intelligence community chasing terrorists in Afghanistan doesn't count for much with them, I guess."

Schneider asked, "What did you do in the military?"

"I was in Army Intelligence. I was at Fort Huachuca in Sierra Vista for a couple of years; I'm familiar with this area."

"Did you ever shoot at any Taliban guys?" Schneider asked.

"What do you think? I don't even know how many I hit. You can't even see what you're shooting at half the time. There's never a guy out in the open just shooting at you. They're either running or behind cover." Runyon grinned; he was in his element with an audience.

Layne said, "So, where are you from?"

"Kentucky, but I've lived in Tennessee and around the Beltway," Runyon replied proudly.

Layne made a few attempts to participate in the conversation, but Runyon interrupted him midway through every sentence. So, he gave up and joined the others to look at the pictures from Afghanistan that Runyon produced from his wallet. They were shots of Runyon next to a Humvee, wearing desert camouflage and Oakley sunglasses, with a rifle slung in front of him. The photos partially corroborated his story, but in retaliation for Runyon's A.A.R.P. comment, Layne decided to cross-examine him about the details of his deployment. But he abandoned the idea when they sensed activity near the center of the lounge.

The trainees who hovered in the lobby revealed themselves by moving in toward an agent who appeared near the coffee tables. Layne's group of four followed, and he was surprised to realize that about half of his classmates were Hispanic. His perception of the Agency changed suddenly, and his enthusiasm waned. He wondered why Mexicans would want to enforce laws against their own people. How could the government trust these people? It didn't make sense. He expected that Carlos and the examiners in Denver would be a rarity.

His attention returned to the conductor. The Caucasian agent was wearing a different uniform than the agents in Denver—a head-to-toe array of green that resembled military fatigues. The badge on the left breast was a sewn patch in place of a metal one, and he wore cargo pants with a long-sleeve uniform top and a green baseball cap displaying the Border Patrol logo.

"Why would you wear long sleeves in Arizona this time of year?" Layne said under his breath to his group as everyone closed in.

"Because they are always going through mesquite thorns," Runyon replied.

From a close proximity Layne appreciated that the uniform was designed for utility. He was secretly embarrassed to find himself star-struck again in the imposing presence of the agent. The agent carried a radio on his belt and a microphone clipped to the passant on his shoulder. On his duty belt were a collapsible steel baton, a pistol, two ammunition magazine cases and handcuffs, in addition to other imposing instruments that Layne was intimidated to understand.

The agent waited patiently and confidently for the trainees to gather around. Once the circle settled, he gave a series of instructions, all in a compelling but conversational tone.

"All of you that are here to EOD, I need you to form a single file line next to the entrance to that auditorium over there. Get yourselves organized alphabetically and grab a polo shirt from the table. Those two ladies over there will take roll. Tomorrow you will need to be down here at oh-seven hundred. Those of you who are going to Tucson Station, I will be here tomorrow to take you. For the rest of you, an agent from your station will be here to pick you up, so DO NOT be late. You will need to wear that polo shirt with dress pants."

The muttering resumed and Layne moved hesitantly toward the auditorium with the others. He selected an extra-large polo shirt from the table and put the garment to his nose and inhaled a whiff of the pristine, navy blue fabric. He followed the others and made a mental note to use the term "EOD" when referring to what he was doing here to sound more competent. Conveniently, Runyon had deciphered the acronym during the one-sided discussion earlier, explaining that it meant "Entry On Duty" in military jargon. Amongst the mild commotion, Layne identified those with last names starting with "S" and fell into line in correct order. The atmosphere remained free of tension, but no one spoke once in line. The two government women in plain clothes began to take roll with a clipboard, dismissing the trainees to enter the auditorium one by one after their presence was noted.

Layne intentionally chose a seat next to two strangers amongst the large congregation. He was still steaming over Runyon's condescending remark. *Runyon says that stuff when I'm most vulnerable; I should've had a comeback ready*, he thought. *I need to remember to keep my guard up.* He continued to stew as he took in the auditorium, which was reminiscent of the large lecture classes he remembered from college, when he couldn't pay attention for more than a few minutes. A second agent arrived and took the podium to address the twenty trainees who were preparing to enter the Academy as part of the 590th class since the Border Patrol's inception in 1924.

The Human Resources women circulated in the aisles, carrying stacks of paper separated vertically and horizontally in their arms, counting the number of trainees in each row with their eyes. The next several hours droned through the gathering of Social Security numbers, signatures and vital information. Toward the end of the paperwork, a higher-ranking agent arrived at the podium wearing the dress uniform, and the trainees were told to stand, raise their right hands, and swear an oath of allegiance—the U.S. Uniformed Services Oath of Office as required by federal law. Layne read from a card distributed during intake:

"I, Layne Sheppard, do solemnly swear that I will support and defend the Constitution of the United States against all enemies, foreign and domestic; that I will bear true faith and allegiance to the same; that I take this obligation freely, without any mental reservation or purpose of evasion; and that I will well and faithfully discharge the duties of the office on which I am about to enter. So help me, God."

He recognized some of the oath from television—*enemies foreign and domestic* lingered prominently in his mind.

Next they were informed that a union representative would like to speak to them, and that everyone had the right to excuse themselves if they wished. Layne looked around, searching for guidance. Everyone was staying put. A man in plain clothes quickly closed in to pass out contracts to each aisle then took over the podium while the agents and women from HR left the auditorium. The trainees remained quiet and attentive in their seats while the union representative rested his hands on the lectern and waited for the movement to cease.

"My name is Brian Esterline. I've been an agent for ten years."

Layne wondered why he was not wearing a uniform.

"I loved this job when I first started. But five years ago last Tuesday, something happened that changed my life. I was involved in a vehicle stop in Nogales and it turned into an altercation which escalated, and I ended up shooting the driver."

The eyes of all the trainees became fixated on the speaker now.

"He died in the hospital the next day. I was beside myself. I started self-medicating with prescription drugs and alcohol to the point that I could no longer perform my duty. I had to enter a rehabilitation facility for thirty days to seek help."

Layne was drawn in, the speaker looked and sounded sincere. To disclose himself in front of an audience was admirable. His pain appeared heartfelt.

"I didn't have the sick days or the vacation time to cover it, and the union went to bat for me against management. They hired a lawyer for me while the investigation over the shooting was going on. There is no way I could've dealt with all of that with everything I was going through. I can look every one of you in the eye and tell you that the union saved my life, my marriage, and my job. Without union representation you're on your own; Heaven forbid something like that happens to you. There's a hotline number in the information that was passed out to you in case you're having problems and need to talk to someone."

Some of the trainees discretely began to shuffle through their pile of paperwork to find the number.

"That number is only for agents. I don't want you to hesitate to dial that number if you're struggling. There's no shame in it. That's what it's there for. No matter how tough you might think you are, you're gonna run into emotional problems in this job. Some days you'll be angry, and other days you might feel pity for the aliens you're forced to deal with. It's natural. Just remember: You're doing what you're told. You don't make the rules. The higher-ups who make the rules don't have to be face to face with these people."

Agent Esterline paused to let the trainees process the information, "Now, I'm gonna come to each row and collect the contracts. It's up to you, but I want you to think about my story while you're making your decision."

The trainees looked at their fellow strangers with indecision as the union representative moved swiftly into the aisle, applying silent pressure to the first row to accept or reject the contract.

Layne continued to dither while he looked down the row; everyone else seemed to be signing. But his mind was still constructing the scenes the agent had described, too much so to effectively weigh the pros and cons of the obligation. Membership required a twelve-month contract, $25 would be deducted from his paycheck twice each month when pay was directly deposited into his bank account.

Agent Esterline was already standing at his row, waiting to collect the document. Layne signed and dated it and passed it to the trainee on his right while he visualized his interpretation of the chaotic shooting scene. But far more disturbing was the depiction of Agent Esterline laying on a couch drinking from a bottle of scotch with a prescription pill bottle and beer cans on a coffee table.

6

LAYNE'S WRISTWATCH READ 6:45 a.m. as the elevator door opened. Many of the trainees were already in the lobby, assembling themselves into groups correlating to five of the stations in the Tucson Sector: Tucson, Nogales, Wilcox, Naco and Douglas.

Runyon and Carlos were going to Douglas with him, and he rejoined them as the remainder of the class continued to arrive in preparation for the station tours. Layne looked over to realize that Schneider was in the group that would be touring Tucson Station. He felt a twinge of envy.

Standing nearby among the group was a short, frail trainee who introduced himself as Greg. He was chatting with a petite blonde female that Layne had seen in the auditorium during EOD. He'd overheard someone call her Melanie. The two of them separated themselves from the group, but Layne realized they would be going to Douglas as well. *Mexicans AND women*, Layne thought. He sensed that the other white trainees were thinking the same thing.

The atmosphere remained loose, and Layne told himself to enjoy it while it lasted. While they waited for the agent from their station to arrive, Runyon inquired loudly: "Where are we going tonight after the tour?"

No one volunteered a suggestion, so he continued. "We should go out. Get some dinner. Go downtown."

"Do we have anything to do tomorrow?" Carlos asked.

"There's nothing on the itinerary. And we don't leave for Artesia until early on Sunday," Runyon assured everyone.

"The bill for the hotel room is gonna wipe me out. I don't have the money to go to dinner. Let's just go to a bar," Carlos suggested.

The girl in their group looked the other way, unsure if she was included in the invitation.

"You're from Tucson. What bar is good these days?" Runyon asked Carlos.

"The Memphis Queen," Carlos said assuredly.

"You going, Sheppard?" Runyon asked.

Layne thought about it momentarily; he probably shouldn't, but he felt he had earned one last night out. He rationalized that his pledge to transform himself didn't technically need to start until he arrived at the Academy. Starting Sunday, he would be all business. He compromised with himself and decided he would have a few, enough to catch a good buzz but not get wasted. Runyon was waiting for a yes.

"Hell yeah," Layne said.

He stared in deep thought for a few seconds at the logo on Runyon's navy polo shirt. The words *Tucson Sector* with a saguaro cactus were embroidered into an attractive circular emblem on the left breast. It gave Layne an idea of how the shirt looked on himself. He brushed the creases and pinched a piece of lint off the only pair of khaki slacks he'd brought. He was confident that he was dressed appropriately; Runyon was wearing a similar pair of brown cap-toe shoes. Runyon had stumbled onto the one way he could relieve the scorn caused by his comment the day before; the resentment was almost completely forgiven within seconds of the invitation.

At seven sharp, the chitchat faded to silence as agents from each station arrived almost simultaneously. Agent Ortiz from Douglas Station approached them from the entrance with absolute confidence and a cocky, battle-hardened swagger. He was in his late thirties and was two inches taller than Layne, handsome like Che Guevara, and fit from field activity evident from the tan lines created by the temples of his sunglasses. He arrived to stand in front of the group and said nothing; he immediately began counting heads with his pointer finger. When he was satisfied that the number matched his paperwork, he said, "Follow me." The group trailed him outside to a running white van with government license plates parked next to the curb. The trainees climbed in and sat facing one another. To Layne's surprise, Schneider was the last one in. *Welcome to Douglas, after all*, Layne thought. Schneider slid the door closed and Ortiz sped off before they could find their seat belts.

No one in the van spoke. Within a few minutes they were eastbound on Interstate 10 and Layne tried to avoid staring at the blonde female trainee sitting directly across from him. They hadn't made eye contact yet, but he had glanced enough to form an opinion about her looks. She had shoulder length blonde hair and was approximately five foot four with unremarkable breasts. She was somewhat attractive, even with the minimal makeup she wore. He reasoned that she would grow increasingly more attractive the longer they were at the Academy. He glanced at the pinstripes of her slacks and her feminine shoes. The smallest polo shirt they had was too big for her, the sleeves resting below her elbows. He guessed that she was twenty-three, maybe twenty-four years old. He didn't know her name and wasn't going to ask.

The silence of the ride gave him time to assess his experience as it progressed. The personnel was disappointing; people back home would be let down if they could observe him. His preconception of the way things would be was already far off; he expected that, but not in this way. He observed the others while they looked out the windows. By the looks on their faces he suspected that he was the only one in the van that was fleeing the past. The others simply appeared driven by ambition and opportunity.

As the tension slackened with distance from Tucson, Runyon and Carlos began to whisper. When Ortiz didn't scold them, Runyon began to speak aloud. "I heard the cartels are fighting with the Mexican government again. The enforcers for the cartels are bad hombres. Have you ever heard of Los Zetas?" he asked.

No one answered and Runyon continued. "A few years ago, some Mexican singer was badmouthing them at a concert, and they swiss-cheesed his limousine after the show. They're supposed to be a secret organization and they don't want anybody talking about them in public.

"I heard about that," Carlos said, "I heard the guy sang a song about them and they got really torqued."

"Yeah, they used AK-47s. That's what I would use, too," Runyon said.

"You think AKs are better than M4s?" Schneider asked.

"They're more reliable and the 7.62x39 is a better round than the 5.56. I've seen AKs buried in sand and you can just shake them off and they'll still shoot. M4s are really touchy." Runyon smiled to himself as he realized he was in the limelight again. "AKs are easier to field strip, too. You can take them apart and put them back together in the dark. You burn through a thirty-round mag fast with an M4. AKs shoot a bigger, heavier bullet. They've got more stopping power and a slower cyclic rate."

Runyon simulated holding a rifle by making two pistols with his thumbs and pointer fingers, aiming them in unison while he continued on about guns. Layne noticed Ortiz smirking in the rearview mirror, and the others began to drift from Runyon's monologue and began looking out the windows again. Layne joined them, staring with his chin on his palm as the van gained altitude, ascending gradually east on the Interstate.

The population of saguaro cactus thinned quickly until they completely gave way to desert sage and mesquite. He wondered if the others noticed these changes. There were modest brown desert mountains on every horizon, and the earth became yellow with dehydrated desert grass. Always in his periphery, he anticipated what the night would be like downtown. *I can't wait until tonight,* he thought. *It will be like a last supper; it will be fun just to go out and take it easy after all this.*

Ortiz still hadn't said a word to the trainees; he was concentrating on the road as if he were driving a school bus full of children on a field trip. Several times he communicated with an anonymous person via cell phone, laughing about things his passengers couldn't understand.

They abandoned Interstate 10 and turned south on Highway 90 just west of the remote truck stop corner of Benson, creeping ever closer to the border. As they approached Sierra Vista, still almost fifty miles from Douglas, Ortiz turned on the Douglas Border Patrol Station radio frequency. The console to his right awoke abruptly with short bursts of signal transmissions between agents, the numbers and codes arriving in a new foreign language. The communication simultaneously sounded calm and routine, yet hazardous. Ortiz paid no attention to the radio as he slowed and guided the van through the main street of Sierra Vista. The trainees listened without comment.

Ortiz looked back at the trainees through the rearview mirror, wearing swept sunglasses. "You need to look around and get an idea for a place to live. Most of the agents live here. It's a forty-five-minute drive one way to the station. You're not gonna want to live in Douglas, trust me. And Bisbee is for hippies and dopers; they're anti-government and anti-law enforcement there. You're only going to have a three-day weekend for Labor Day to get everything lined-up before you graduate, so you want to start thinking about it."

Ortiz glanced at his side-view mirror and continued. "I know you guys are nervous about the Academy, but just get there and go through the motions—you know, yes sir, no sir . . . whatever."

The drive through Sierra Vista was brief, revealing the recruits' limited housing options, and their enthusiasm continued to decline the deeper they sank into Cochise County. Sierra Vista only existed because of Fort Huachuca Army Base. Activity away from the base was limited to the main strip of Fry Boulevard, east of the military installation. The strip consisted of fast food, franchise restaurants, Walmart, and gun shops. As he gazed at the settlement streaming by, Layne tried to picture himself living there. But it was hard to imagine. Sierra Vista was an island within a desert wilderness, and what civilized comforts it possessed quickly dissipated as Fry Boulevard became Highway 90 again.

They came to a fork in the road and merged onto Highway 80, the last new highway before the border. They entered a river valley and crossed a bridge, passing a sign marking the San Pedro River, where cottonwood and live oak trees swarmed to water along the bank. Layne felt he had slipped back in time; the terrain emanated a theme of juice harps, serapes and lawlessness. Tombstone was nearby to the northeast.

A steep, swerving climb brought them to a brick-walled mountain tunnel. When the end of the tunnel bore light, he found himself in another time warp, surrounded by sun-kissed desert mountains populated by jojoba, yucca, agave and palm trees. His eyes widened as he looked to the left and saw, nestled deep down within a valley, a breathtaking nineteenth century town made of painted metal and rust, like a toy town in a train set. The cypress-speckled mining town was Bisbee, and he gazed for minutes in awe as the others chatted, unaware of his captivation.

The Victorian buildings of Bisbee were behind him in an instant, but their images were pressed in his memory. Ahead were stale wooden mine shaft entrances, copper tailings, and stained gravel cascading along the downhill view of Highway 80, unveiling a vast desert and ancient sunbaked mountains devoid of vegetation far in the distance. The highway was outstretched, reaching for what looked like 100 miles into Sonora and the Mexican frontier. Something extrasensory alerted him that the border was nearby; it was a feeling of surrounding danger. The tattered telephone poles looked weary this far south, like they were carrying grief to a distant outpost.

Mexican clarinets and accordions blared as Ortiz turned the radio knob, finally settling on an American radio station. One by one, the trainees began to speculate about a black linear structure that had appeared with cunning in the distance to their right. It was running almost parallel with them, growing larger, until it was unmistakably the Border Fence. It was the first time Layne had ever seen it, and it didn't look like what he had been imagining.

They approached a vehicle on the southern shoulder of the road and heads elevated with curiosity. As they passed, the trainees shuffled to the right side of the van to look out the window at two four-wheel drive Border Patrol vehicles. Two agents making an arrest didn't acknowledge the van as it swept by. One of the agents was searching an alien, and the second agent was addressing another who was on his knees looking up toward his captors. The alien being searched had his palms on the hood of a vehicle and turned his head to make eye contact with Layne until the van was out of his view. The aura of the men stunned him; their emaciated bodies were obscene with soot, as if they had narrowly escaped the collapse of a coal mine. Their clothes looked commandeered. The scene caught him off guard, like involuntarily stumbling upon an execution—their condition more consistent with animals than humans.

The scene was growing more psychologically disturbing the farther they rolled away from it. Until this moment he had failed to grasp the essence of what he was becoming involved in. How dire must their situation have been to choose to place all of their possessions into a backpack and walk to a different country? He tried to rid the scene from his focus, but the man's expression had laid a foundation in his consciousness. The scope of his desperation could be read in his eyes.

The whispering ceased and he assumed the others shared his sense of shock. He glanced to see the reflection of Ortiz grinning in the rearview mirror, his eyes concealed by those sunglasses.

Layne continued to stare through the window at nothing as the van slowed. The station was just south of Highway 80, and the Border Fence could be seen plainly from the driveway into the compound. Douglas was still five more miles to the east at the Port of Entry, where Agua Prieta sat just south in the Mexican state of Sonora.

Ortiz parked among a fleet of green-and-white vehicles and the trainees hesitated to disembark. Ortiz didn't wait for them, and the group moved quickly to catch up to him as he moved through the parking lot to head into the station. A man wearing head-to-toe camouflage was leaning against the wall near the entrance of the building, smoking a cigarette. He smiled and said hello to the group. The trainees returned the hello with meek voices.

"Who is that?" Layne whispered to Runyon.

"BORTAC. They are like the Special Forces. Hostage rescue-type operations," Runyon said. He appreciated Runyon's knowledge this time as Ortiz flung the door open and entered without looking back. The station was over-air conditioned and smelled like new upholstery. The trainees became quiet, as if they were in a museum, as they shuffled over the United States Border Patrol Logo inlaid on the hallway floor. On the hallway walls were pictures from years past of agents in the field looking through binoculars and riding four-wheelers in a jovial state of mind.

"I've been told they have competitions, between the horse and ATV patrols, to see who can capture the most dope in a month," Runyon said. "Some of the plaques on the walls recognize the teams that brought in the most: This horse patrol, 38,000 pounds of marijuana, that ATV patrol 39,000—in a month! I know what 30,000 pounds of hay looks like. That's a lot of weed."

Layne just stared, wide-eyed.

Ortiz pointed them to the door to the locker room where the bathrooms were, an acknowledgement of the two-hour drive from Tucson. Once inside, separated from Ortiz, Layne peeked at the locker room behind the bathroom concrete; it was immaculate, like a well-kept fitness center. Suddenly, Ortiz entered the bathroom and yelled, "Hurry up! We need to get this over with. And don't pee on the seats!" His voice was amplified by the bathroom tile and caused Layne to jump with surprise. Alarmed, he and the others scurried back into the hallway where Ortiz was impatiently waiting for them with arms slightly bowed.

The trainees sheepishly followed Agent Ortiz through the corridor and avoided looking at him. He seemed to have all of a sudden developed a bitterness about his attachment to the group. They became silent again as he brought them to the camera room, a small dark space where its inhabitants were made visible by light from a wall of small television screens. Three agents in plain clothes sat motionless at each station, guiding cameras with joysticks. Only their eyes moved, their stares shifting from screen to screen. Standing alongside them were two Hispanic women wearing National Guard camouflage fatigues and combat boots. Their job was to move about the room, collecting and exchanging information. Both women had their black hair secured in tight buns. They wore firm expressions as they scanned the screens from over the agents' shoulders. None of the personnel paid any attention to the trainees.

Layne did his best to understand without asking questions. The cameras seemed to supply an infrared survey of a section of the Border Fence that was guided by the controller in robotic movements. The cameras were on top of towers in town somewhere, judging by the vehicle traffic on some of the screens. Radio communications were centralized from the camera room and dispatched by a woman Ortiz called a LECA, or a Law Enforcement Communications Assistant. When agents operating the cameras detected activity along the Border Fence, they called out the movement over a hand-held radio, and the National Guard women relayed information from the agents to the LECA woman. After less than a minute, Ortiz pulled the trainees from the camera room without allowance for questions.

The next stop gave Layne a jolt, as if he had happened upon a room full of naked people. Ortiz introduced the room as the "Fishbowl," a semicircular control console that monitored the processing floor where aliens were detained and fingerprinted. The area was overseen by a supervisor who tracked activity through a semicircular window, occasionally communicating with the agents below via radio.

There were cells filled with unshaven prisoners who resembled the two aliens they had seen on the shoulder of the highway, but there also were cells containing women and children. The worn-out prisoners sat on concrete benches—expressionless, surrounded by an aura of filth. Their dark blue hooded sweatshirts and dirty jeans looked like they smelled putrid, even through the glass. The agents wore latex gloves with their pistols removed from their holsters. The aliens were separated from the agents by plexiglass, and Layne made an effort not to make eye contact with any of them. The aliens who weren't sitting on benches were sleeping on the smooth concrete floors, covered in charcoal colored blankets—

captured and caged.

Layne tried to appear nonchalant about the scene, trying to keep his eyes trained on the agents. The plexiglass that separated them from the processing floor suppressed the majority of sound except for shouts. He observed an agent returning a young man to a cell after being fingerprinted, and could see the prisoner's mouth moving, saying something to the agent. Over the radio, the agent asked the door operator in the Fishbowl to open the cell door and waited patiently for the lock on the door to buzz open. The agent calmly pulled the door open then thrust the prisoner face first into the cell with an explosive two-handed push. The man's arms flailed as he tripped and crashed into several men sitting on benches, and the entire population of male prisoners in adjacent cells broke out in protest, pounding the plexiglass and yelling. The agents who were busy fingerprinting at their computer stations ignored the disturbance and continued pressing fingertips onto glass scanners, concentrating on their computer screens.

Ortiz interrupted the silent staring: "If anyone wants to change their mind, it's nothing to be embarrassed about. Just let me know before I drop you back at the hotel and no one will know. You'll be gone, and on your way back home before you know it. This ain't for everyone."

No one moved or spoke, their eyes averted from each other. Ortiz grinned slightly at the Fishbowl supervisor, who leaned back in his chair gripping his hand-held radio. After a long pause Ortiz said, "Okay, follow me."

He led them next to the Muster Room, where they were told to take a seat. The space reminded Layne of a large high school classroom with tables and chairs facing two dry erase boards. An aisle divided the room, which was used for briefing the agents at the start of each shift, before they went into the field. For this occasion, the room served as the site of an introductory address from PAIC Kramer, the Patrol Agent In Charge, the commanding agent of the station. He was wearing a field uniform, and when he took the podium, his manner suggested that he was about to deliver a canned speech. In his early fifties, bald with a blond Highway Patrol mustache, the trainees knew immediately that he was in charge as his title suggested.

After a brief introduction from Ortiz, the PAIC commenced with his message. "I want all of you who are married or have companions to have your other half come visit Sierra Vista before you go all the way through the Academy. We've had a big problem with wives showing up after graduation and the trainee suddenly quitting because the wife can't handle living in Cochise County. I don't want any more of that chaos. It's avoidable, and it's a big waste of my time."

The trainees began adjusting themselves in their seats, sitting more stiffly upright.

"You all have a tough road ahead of you. I don't envy you at this point. The Academy is rough.

"How many of you speak Spanish?" PAIC Kramer asked.

Layne raised his hand to his ear along with Carlos.

"Good, the rest of you are gonna need to put your heart and soul into studying Spanish to have a chance. I'm going to tell you the truth. Only about half of you are gonna be sitting here in October. Make sure you're one of those people."

As the PAIC's speech was coming to an end, an agent peeked in from the doorway and the PAIC waved him in. The agent positioned himself next to the PAIC like an obedient pet. The trainee looked uncomfortable in his uniform, the green fabric of his pants and shirt more heavily ironed than the PAIC's.

Kramer put his hand on the young man's shoulder and addressed him. "Agent McNeily here just passed his ten-month exam. What do you think so far?" he said, looking at McNeily in a fatherly manner.

McNeily looked nervous and unsettled, as though he had just learned something new and important that he was still processing and trying to retain. He adjusted his duty belt and said, "I'm learning a lot, sir."

PAIC Kramer laughed and said to the group, "He's doing good."

Kramer waited for McNeily to add something, but he said nothing, staring at his feet. Finally, the PAIC said with a smile, "You got someplace you've got to be?"

"Yes, sir."

"Well, go on, then."

McNeily kept his eyes at his feet as he followed the aisle to the door. As he watched McNeily walk all the way to the door, Layne felt the most intense longing he had ever experienced toward another human being. He yearned to be in McNeily's boots the way the Donner Party yearned for California. He was at the end of the road Layne hadn't yet begun to travel; it was unimaginable. But his mind quickly regressed to something gratifying that was within reach at that moment.

Layne anticipated the felicity of what the night had in store after Ortiz dropped them off at the hotel. He couldn't let this night go to waste; it was a once in a lifetime occasion. This would be a last hurrah. He told himself he could bend his rules, considering the circumstances. It was difficult to imagine staying in the hotel while the others were out having fun in an unexplored city. But once at the Academy, he promised himself, he would walk the line from there on out as he had planned.

LAYNE MOVED AT DOUBLE SPEED IN HIS hotel room, his heart beating faster than normal. Time had crawled during the ride back from Douglas in anticipation of nightfall, and he hurried to make up for any lost time. He showered quickly and put on his favorite set of summer clothes: His best sandals and shorts, his favorite bowling shirt, and even his favorite boxer shorts. When the elevator bell dinged on the bottom floor, he was conscious of how opposite he felt from twelve hours earlier.

Runyon and Schneider met him by the coffee tables. Carlos arrived shortly after with two trainees from Tucson Station whose names Layne forgot shortly after they were introduced. He considered poking fun at Runyon's choice of clothes—a Browning Firearms polo shirt tucked in with shorts and sandals, and a Leatherman tool attached to his belt on the hip. But Layne refrained from commenting; he was beginning to take a liking to Runyon despite his pompous behavior. His initiative when planning recreational activities went a long way with Layne, like when someone was funny.

When they exited the hotel Layne's skin was still steamy from his shower; it felt heavenly when it met the warmth of the desert evening. Since Carlos had his car, the group piled in and sped out of the parking lot, headed for downtown Tucson. The timing was perfect, the trajectory of his exhilaration concurrent with the pace at which the sun was going down. The invading darkness lit the fuse the way it had countless times before. When he was a kid on the Fourth of July, he couldn't refrain from lighting bottle rockets and Black Cats before the darkness had a chance to set in. He simply couldn't wait, and it was inconceivable to stop once the first firecracker exploded.

Tonight, he visualized Roman candles and tried to recall how he would feel around midnight when the freight train was at full tilt. It was impossible to rouse the sensation of how it would feel to be at his peak—his brain couldn't recreate the euphoria unless he was dreaming. So sublime were these rare occasions when his fellows were aiming for the same gratification, that he wished the feeling would go on indefinitely. The stars were aligned; it felt like the Fourth of July again.

Six passengers were crammed into a backseat designed for two, and Layne spoke while his head was pressed sideways against the roof. They didn't mind sitting on each other as they laughed and went back and forth about their station tours. The mood was a wide smile on the first night in Las Vegas, as divine as possible.

Once downtown, Carlos parked at a meter and the group helped each other out of the car. They walked swiftly down the college bar strip. Layne felt like skipping in the stillness of the Arizona climate, savoring the new smell of the streets and the grilled meat from the Asaderos along the sidewalks lined with palm trees. The warm night weather felt like bathwater. The full moon in a lukewarm sky and eager smiles parallel with his own made the bliss complete.

They merged into human traffic along Fourth Avenue, passing college students and hippies as they hurried to reach the best bars on the college strip. Tucson felt like the Wild West. Strangers becoming fast friends was inexplicably fulfilling again. From a block away, Layne was caught by a hanging guitar riff and shaker rattle that he recognized as a Rolling Stones jam. It was overflowing from below the The Memphis Queen marquis. They came to a stop at the back of a long line. Only a bouncer on a stool by the door stood in their way, monitoring the bar's maximum capacity with a tally counter. Layne's impatience throbbed as he peered through the window at the people already inside.

Only risks associated with the adventure of travel could create this new taste in his mouth. But striving for the pinnacle of highlife was a one-way street. The thought caused a sense of imminent danger within him. He had known for some time that it was futile to try and use foresight as a deterrent, especially at a time like this. What happened before was a symptom of frustration, under different circumstances 800 miles away, he thought. He suppressed the concern and stood on his toes to get a better look inside. Regrets over failing to seize the day when he was young were the memories that never truly stopped stinging.

Runyon was dominating conversation with talk of bourbon whiskey. "They better have Basel Hayden here or I'm gonna get ugly."

"What the devil is Basel Hayden?" Schneider said.

"You Yankees out west don't know squat about whiskey. All you guys know is Jack Daniels," Runyon said loftily.

"Don't listen to Lynyrd Skynyrd, Schneider. You don't drink whiskey when you're on the border. I'm starting with Tequila, probably Hornitos," Layne said. His mouth watered anticipating the tang of salt and lime.

"Patrón Silver," said Carlos.

"Even better," Layne affirmed.

"It don't matter if I'm in Margaritaville, I'm not drinking tequila," Runyon said, then changed the subject. "We should've invited Melanie to come with us. I feel sorry for her; it would be hard to be the only chick in the class."

"Are you trying to bang her already?" Layne asked.

Everyone laughed.

"No, I was talking to her at the station; she's pretty cool," Runyon said.

"She's pretty hot, too; I'd knock her back out," Carlos said.

"I'm not messing around with any women that we're gonna be working with," Runyon said. "In the Army I saw a lot of guys get into trouble messing with the women that were around."

"What kind of trouble? A burning sensation?" Layne asked.

Everyone burst out in laughter.

Runyon smiled and kept himself from laughing. "No, Sheppard.

Women get ticked at you for some reason. All they have to do is say you commented about their looks or something and you'll be transferred to the North Pole. Or worse. No proof required."

The bouncer nodded and signaled that their group could go inside. Layne inserted his driver's license back into the clear plastic window of his wallet and entered his mind's carnival of glitter, mahogany, done-up girls, and beer taps. He could feel his heart beating to the saxophones and the snap of the drums, amplified through sharp speakers. The ecstasy heightened as he made his way through the mass of people to get a drink at the bar, where he realized that others he recognized from orientation were already there, already drinks ahead of him. Introductions weren't necessary; the trainees knew each other by sight. They kissed tequila shot glasses together, high-fived, and back-slapped each other. *I've got to make this one count,* he thought. *It's a perfect storm.*

Layne scooted sideways between bodies until he made it to the bar. With a stroke of luck, he caught the bartender's eye and she put her ear toward him. He handed her his debit card to open a tab and ordered two Mexican draught beers and two shots of tequila, handing one of each to Carlos. He could feel his smile broadening with satisfaction and his stomach begin to glow with growing warmth as the lime stung the hinges of his jaw.

He leaned on the bar and did a doubletake to observe a group of teenage Rockabilly girls; his eyes studied their thick eyeliner and arm tattoos. Their raven black hair was secured with red handkerchiefs. Girls with the confidence to flaunt a unique style made his blood run hot. He could impress girls with status now, he thought. They might see now that he was special. He would say that he was already an agent; a trainee wasn't impressive enough, although they most likely wouldn't know the difference. He would have to engineer a tactful course of initiating a conversation with one of them, a feat worthy of admiration. Not now, he thought. He wouldn't be able to restrain his blushing cheeks. Maybe later when the inhibition was gone.

He and Carlos set about a scenic tour around the vast room, heading for the pool tables. A loud trainee with a prominent New York accent was beginning to draw attention to the clan.

"Damon Balducci, from Rochester, New York," Layne heard him say several times to whomever he was meeting. He uncompromisingly insisted on breaking, which meant his opponent racking the balls, ignoring the tally. Layne studied him momentarily. He was slightly taller than Layne, but slender with an oblong face, blond hair and blond eyebrows, and a receding hairline, creating considerable power alleys.

Layne and Carlos settled into their own game at the neighboring table, Layne scattering the first rack with a satisfying sledgehammer break that turned heads. He had never felt more like Paul Newman as he surveyed the table and chalked the cue's path through his fingers. He felt the liquor seeping into his bloodstream. He was seeing angles like Tron, executing effortless razor thin cuts with English as the ball rolled with touch into position for the subsequent shot. He communicated with Carlos through eye contact regarding their concern over Damon while they chalked their cues. Damon was growing distinguishably louder by the minute. He chalked his cue and grumbled, "Step up, son," to antagonize passing fraternity boys, who glanced at him and moved on. He pointed at them and simulated an execution with the pool cue, then stood erect to sheathe it like a sword. Layne's eyes swiveled to see the bouncers begin to take notice.

A Caucasian, somewhat muscular trainee Layne didn't recognize, with a high and tight military haircut, was attempting to corral the rowdiness. He passed by Carlos and Layne and said, "No more Tequila," then moved on to pass the word to the next circle of trainees. Layne and Carlos looked at each other, puzzled. Damon addressed the unusual messenger as "Tackleberry," ignoring his warning that Damon could be sent home for his behavior.

The night before, a story aired on a local Tucson news station that three Border Patrol trainees had been caught in El Paso, smuggling 700 pounds of marijuana across the border. The trio had joined a Mexican cartel drug-smuggling operation before infiltrating the Border Patrol. In addition to narcotics smuggling, the news story revealed that the trainees were also involved in kidnapping. The media were aware that the recent problems with trainees were due to the slackening of requirements during the hiring process. A Border Patrol representative stated that they were taking measures to remedy the problem but didn't go into specifics about how. Throughout the day word had spread about the news story, and it had become a topic of discussion amongst the class.

Layne had completely forgotten about the news story until now. His paranoia began to throb as he considered the scandal while attempting to understand Tackleberry's behavior. "You don't think they would have an agent mix in with us to spy on us do you?" he yelled to Carlos above the din.

Carlos took notice. "I sure as hell hope not!"

Layne leaned in closer to yell in Carlos' ear. "You know, a mole, a regular agent posing as a trainee to get an idea who the heavy drinkers are, to maybe pass the information along to the people at the Academy and start weeding people out?"

"Hell, why else would that guy care if we get too wasted?" Carlos said.

The noise made it difficult to hear. Carlos thought for a few seconds then added, "I've heard that they've sent people home for screwing up before they even got to go to the Academy. And now with what happened in El Paso, DHS is probably keeping an eye on us, to see what we talk about."

Runyon sensed the earnestness of the conversation from across the room and approached to join. Layne said to Carlos, without acknowledging Runyon, "They bugged the lobby at my Oral Board interview and I almost let loose to some guys about my SF-86."

Runyon injected, "How would you know if they bugged the room? Did you see anything on the walls?"

"No, but they told me they would know if I gave any questions away to the guys who were waiting."

"Damn, they probably did then," Runyon said.

All eyes were on Tackleberry now, taking half-full beer glasses out of the hands of trainees that were swaying. The room watched him pep-talking drunk trainees, who looked at him as suspiciously as Layne and Carlos had. Layne tried to remember if he had done two shots at once in front of Tackleberry, or if he had admitted to anything in front of him that he had left out of the background investigation.

After a half-hour Tackleberry succeeded in herding the group out the door. But the trainees merely traveled in a swarm across the street to another bar. As the night drew on, Layne ordered his shots and drank them out of view of the others, including Carlos and Runyon. The euphoria from the first few drinks had faded. He had reached a plateau, approaching a decline. But he pressed on drinking, trying to recapture the initial high, all the while knowing the effort would be fruitless.

He woke up on top of the bedspread and realized that he had fallen asleep with his clothes still on. It took him a few seconds to orient himself; he had somehow made it back to his hotel room. He rubbed his eyes and looked at his feet; his shoes were still on. The belt loops of his jeans were mysteriously broken. Flashbacks came to him of waking up in a strange place and looking at family pictures on the wall for clues to determine where was. He panicked as his memory began to fill in, remembering where he was and why he was here. The magnitude of it was almost breathtaking immediately after he opened his eyes in the morning. He sat on the edge of the bed, then stood up and looked out the third-floor window. He told himself that he was okay. Most everyone else had been out doing the same thing the night before, and he had all day to recover. Everything was going according to plan. He licked his cracked lips with toxic moisture from his tongue as his abdomen began to emit the pain of having been poisoned.

For reasons he couldn't understand, the fact that the next morning would be agony was always irrelevant while in the moment. It had once again seemed like a reasonable price to pay, but now he wished he had stayed in and ordered a Pay-Per-View movie instead.

He searched his shaving kit for Alka-Seltzer, trying to remember how he had made it back to his room. As he turned on the shower, he winced to think of what he might have done in front of Tackleberry. What had gone on at the second bar had faded into night. Broken recollections resurfaced, foxy bartender cleavage amidst pulsating music and lights flashing. He remembered fast food drive-through speaker phones and being desperate for bed. He had likely kept his wits about him up until some point, he was sure. But beyond where the recording had shut off, he had no idea. It was distressing, like having had a seizure.

He dropped in the elevator again, immersed in the torture he would have to bear for the day. He would go to almost any lengths to ease the dry fever on his forehead. He sent a text to Carlos and Runyon while he sat slouched in a lounge chair, envying trainees moving about the lobby who appeared as though they had gone to bed early the night before.

Carlos and Runyon came out of the elevator and strolled to the lounge, noticeably less enthusiastic than the day before. They were visibly tired with bloodshot eyes, walking slowly as if their bodies were sore from exercise. They picked up Layne and made their way to the hotel restaurant in a hurry to put something in their stomachs. As they stood waiting to be seated, they kept the pain they were feeling to themselves. A waitress led them to a circular booth where Carlos sat down and scooted in slow motion to the center. Layne and Runyon sat on the ends while she placed the menus in front of them.

Layne guzzled his water until the cluster of ice slid to a stop on his lips. He fiddled pensively with his napkin and silverware while he decided what would be easiest to eat. When his orange juice arrived, he drank half of it in one gulp but was unable to enjoy the flavor, as if his taste buds had been chemically altered. Carlos and Runyon chatted with low energy while they added cream and sugar to their cups of coffee.

Layne deliberated over whether or not to mention his lingering concern about Tackleberry. He feared they might share something they had learned about the situation that Layne wasn't aware of—something that compounded his worry. Or worse, point out something Layne had done that he didn't remember. He was seven years past the age when such antics were laughable. It had become seriously disturbing to be told he had done something that he didn't approve of, now, when he had regained his logic the morning after. If they brought something up, he would pretend it was funny. The contrast in his judgment only twelve hours earlier was something he hoped he would grow out of. The issue of being able to maintain his current state of mind was what he had come here to curtail. But he was succeeding now. He reasoned that the possibility of a bright future would buoy his mood from now on.

"How do you guys feel this morning?" Layne finally said after the waitress took their orders.

"Not bad at all. A couple of Advil and I feel fine," Runyon answered. "The secret is to drink two glasses of water with two Advil before you go to bed. Then two more Advil when you wake up." Despite his talk, Runyon didn't look as though his remedy had worked entirely.

"I feel pretty rough. I got the bubble guts," Carlos said. "Advil doesn't work for me."

"Me neither," Layne said. They each sipped their coffee and re-situated themselves. "You don't think Tackleberry is really an agent in disguise, do you?" Layne ventured.

"No, he's just a brown-noser trying to impress someone by taking on a leadership role," Runyon said. "Someone told me they saw him at their Oral Boards in Ohio."

"So, he was just trying to be a teacher's pet or something?" Layne speculated. He wished he had heard this tidbit in conjunction with the news about the trainees in El Paso earlier the previous night.

"I saw him pull that agent from Tucson Station aside and ask him if he had any tips for the Academy," Runyon continued. "Are you kidding me? What a fag."

"So he's already kissing up? You couldn't pay me to do that," Layne said. He thought silently; he could already feel people jockeying for position. He could fall in with a group when they shared a common goal. But once cliques started developing, he always ended up losing his seat to someone when the musical chairs stopped.

"Did you hear that, like three people, left last night?" Carlos said as he cut his pancakes with a fork.

"What do you mean?" Runyon said.

"After we got back from our tours a guy from Wilcox and two guys from Naco just packed and left for home," Carlos said.

"That's crazy, after that background check and the Oral Boards and everything," Layne said.

"No kidding; that was a pain in the butt," Carlos said. "My background check took eight months. They must have got spooked during their station tour."

Layne wasn't concerned with the departed. His brain had already moved on from Tackleberry and selected a new subject for torment. He was afraid to even ask the others what they anticipated the reception at the Academy being like. He had overheard trainees discussing stories about arrival to the Academy as being the equivalent to the first day of Marine Corps Boot Camp. Their descriptions were consistent with what Matt had told him; he was even afraid to delve too far into the topic with his mentor. He saw instructors in Smokey hats with fists clenched, screaming, nose to nose with terrified faces. He forced himself to address the fear.

"Are you guys nervous for tomorrow?" Layne asked.

"A little," Carlos admitted.

"I'm not nervous; I've been through this kind of silly stuff before in the Army," Runyon offered brazenly. "It's just mind games; Border Patrol is quasi-military. They want it to be like the military when it's convenient for them, but then they don't drill when it's raining."

"What are you guys gonna do today?" Layne asked.

"Lay by the pool and recover, so I'm ready for tomorrow," Carlos said.

"I'm taking a cab to Diamond Back in about an hour," Runyon said. He had been jabbering about it all night; it was hard to forget his rants. It was a gun shop that catered to law enforcement.

Layne declined to accompany him, and Carlos leaned his head back and spread his arms along the booth behind him. He closed his eyes for a moment and yawned. "I'm gonna lay by the pool."

Back in his room, Layne sank into the nadir of his accustomed Sunday afternoon blues. There was no remedying it; he had to be ready for tomorrow. He packed his things and lay on the bed, watching the clock as the relative safety that time represented ran out. The day was passing even more quickly than the night before. Dusk came, and from his balcony he watched with bare feet as the sun set behind the palm trees and desert hills in the distance. Before he was ready, it was time to try to go to bed. He tossed and turned and eventually gave up to stare at the ceiling.

8

IT WAS DIFFICULT TO FATHOM THAT this day had finally come. At curbside, in line silently with the others in blue polo shirts and slacks, Layne waited to load his bags into the cargo bay of the idling charter bus.

There was plenty of room on the bus, and he secured a window seat, gesturing for Carlos, who had boarded after, to sit next to him. The other Hispanics in the class were already beginning to stick together, claiming their own section of the bus. They wouldn't maintain eye contact with any of the Caucasian trainees, and they spoke in low voices to one another in Spanish. They made it obvious that they had already developed their own faction within the class. Carlos was remaining neutral, but Layne could read the awkward conflict in his eyes; the other Hispanics were beginning to ignore him in retaliation.

The same agent who gathered them initially in the lobby on Friday morning climbed aboard, and after a final headcount, he said, "May the Good Lord ride with you all the way; Godspeed." The trainees responded in unison, "Thank you, sir." Then he stepped off and the driver pushed the lever to close the door behind him. The air brakes released their unmistakable pressure and the bus engine began to exert effort as the driver pulled onto Valencia Road, en route to I-10 East.

Melanie and Balducci, the loudmouth from The Memphis Queen, were laughing and joking along with other trainees. Layne and Carlos were amongst the quiet ones; angst wouldn't allow Layne the strength to maintain a conversation. The bulk of his worry redirected itself to the future, both near and far. The seven-hour bus ride to Artesia, in southeast New Mexico, would be a countdown of dreadful apprehension that had begun the moment he opened his weary, bleary eyes that morning. "On the Academy website," Carlos said, "they say the curriculum there is one of the most challenging in all of federal law enforcement." *Just what I need to hear,* Layne thought.

The cactus and treeless brown mountains of southern Arizona were disappearing behind him forebodingly while Layne reflected on his life. He could recall nothing about the previous seven years that could stimulate a flicker of nostalgia. It seemed like an endless series of binges, one hangover after another and one dead-end job after another. His mind wandered farther back in time, and he smiled at parts of his childhood. If he closed his eyes for a moment, he could return to them. But the displacement only relieved him for a few seconds at a time.

The butterflies in his stomach prodded him to frequently shift positions in his seat. The New Mexico Badlands were streaming by like a dream, somehow empty of the enchantment he remembered as a child. A rocky slope called a *bajada* in the distance and pastel layers of sedimentary rock briefly distracted him from the anxiety; his eyes clung to them until they were gone. The terrain continued to morph until they reached the bobbing pump jacks, sometimes called nodding donkeys, of lonely flatland oilfields. It felt like West Texas and meant they were close.

He found himself longing to be back at the hotel, simply for its distance from the Academy. He was incapable of preparing himself mentally, even as the bus reached Alamogordo, marking the final hundred-mile plank into the abyss that he imagined Artesia would be. The conversations trailed off and trainees sitting forward of him began to hug the headrests of the seats in front of them in an attempt to relieve their cramping stomachs. Some tried to continue telling amusing stories, but the responding laughter was forced and bridled by unspoken fear. Only two hours to go.

Layne stared out the window with chin on his palm while his mind played a continuous loop film, his imagination's presage of the Academy reception, that he couldn't cut off. The premonition involved a drill instructor yelling in his face, while he was powerless to make it stop. He was in fear of not knowing what to do while under intense pressure. But the true fear was much more complex and much more deep-seated than the reception. Ever present was the concern about what would remain of his self-concept if he couldn't make it through the rigorous training. Such a catastrophic failure would be difficult to spin to himself. He realized that subconsciously he had set out to prove something to repair his ego. If he was still on his feet after the smoke cleared in four months, he would know that he was not a loser.

The bus crossed the city limits of Artesia late in the afternoon. The town was smaller than he had imagined. The streets were empty, and the town looked as though it had been abandoned some time ago. Main Street still resembled its 1950's appearance, short a soda fountain on the corner of a block. He imagined how different the Academy would look in contrast.

The compound was just outside of town. The bus downshifted and the passengers inside rocked forward and backward in sync with the gear friction, as if they were passing through the base's magnetic field. F.L.E.T.C., the Federal Law Enforcement Training Center, looked like a military base, and Layne swallowed hard as his eyes widened. Barbed-wire fences lined an endless perimeter, stretching farther than he could see. Just before the entrance, a stone sign on a grass lawn labeled the compound, and he was surprised that he had never heard the acronym of the institution where he was about to spend the next four months. He had heard people refer to it only as "the Academy." He had purposely done no research; there had been no reason to scare himself prematurely. He would deal with it all at once.

The driver put forth effort to turn the wheel to steer them off the public road and onto a private driveway that led to a gatehouse. The bus squeaked to a halt just short of a gate and the trainees stared, frozen with fright at the blockade. The clattering idle of the engine was predominant while the driver gestured to the guardians of the entrance. Armed campus police in dark blue uniforms stepped out of the booth, one speaking upward to the driver while the other performed a cursory inspection of the bus.

The guard who was speaking with the driver nodded in agreement with him, and both guards casually returned to their station. The gate ascended slowly and buckled when it reached its vertical position. Layne tried to ask Carlos a question, but all of the moisture vanished from his mouth and he couldn't finish the sentence. Carlos continued to stare at the gate in anticipation. He seemed not to notice that Layne was trying to speak to him. Layne, too, focused on the gate without blinking. Everyone knew intuitively that its opening signified the beginning of their ordeal. At once, Layne realized that there was one benefit to being accustomed to the hardship he had known: It made new hardship not nearly as daunting.

The bus came to a halt inside the compound and the trainees sat motionless, eyes still fixated on the door of the bus as the driver pulled the lever to open it. An instructor in dress uniform and Smokey hat climbed the steps and announced firmly, but at a reasonable volume, "I need you all to get your bags out from under the bus and put them on the lawn next to the sidewalk here. Form a single file line facing that building over there and wait for further instructions."

Layne suspected it was a trick and anticipated a barrage of screaming for any minor mistake he wouldn't know he was making. He merged into the aisle as the trainees rose quickly from their seats. No one spoke as they hurried in half steps to exit the bus. Once their feet found the sidewalk, trainees searched frantically in the cargo bay for their baggage, while the instructor oversaw them with arms crossed. When the bags were on the grass, the trainees aligned themselves facing the building, their posture taut.

The instructor pointed to a building one hundred yards away, "You've got thirty seconds to form a single file line on the sidewalk next to that building. Take your bags with you and put them on the lawn."

The trainees grabbed their bags in a mad scramble and ran as fast as they could. Layne seized his two duffle bags and waddled quickly, more than ran, as his bags restricted his advance. The trainees arrived within seconds of each other and tossed their bags in a pile on the lawn, quickly falling back into line. Everyone looked straight ahead and didn't dare speak. The instructor took his time catching up with them, swinging his stopwatch in a circle by its lanyard while walking slowly. Two more instructors with Smokey hats, arms straight to their sides, arrived and confronted the trainees.

The lead instructor faced the first trainee in line and gripped his stopwatch. "You have fifteen seconds to arrange the line alphabetically with letter A facing me. Go." Everyone scrambled and found their places quickly. At fourteen seconds, minor adjustments made, they were filed. One of the instructors handed the lead a clipboard, and he read aloud: "Allen and Blair, you two are in 212. You've got five minutes to find your dorm room and be back here in line. Now, get moving."

Without rotating his head, Layne looked for the dorm building in his peripheral vision. It was at least a hundred yards away at their two o'clock position. Allen and Blair rushed to retrieve their bags and ran toward the building with maximum effort. The next pair was on their way before Allen and Blair returned. No punishment was specified for failing to return within the given time. When their names were called, each new pair rushed to locate their bags from the pile and waddled toward the two-story dormitory building. The lead instructor periodically glanced at his stopwatch; he appeared enervated and ready for his day to end as he glanced at each pair returning at high speed.

When the pair directly in front of Schneider could be seen sprinting back, the instructor called out, "Schneider and Sheppard, 262, go."

Layne dashed toward his bags and ran when he had a firm grip on the handles. Schneider caught up to him quickly, but when they reached the dormitory, they struggled to find the general location of their room. Panic-stricken, they looked to one another for answers. Then they tried for guidance from the previous pair of trainees, but they were accelerating back to the formation without a second to spare. Layne and Schneider agreed that their room must be on the second floor, judging by the number. So, they climbed the closest stairwell, feeling the strain in their shoulders as they forced their bags to keep up with them. The second floor had a walkway balcony; the dorm complex resembled the front of a motel. The building was L-shaped, and the rooms faced a swimming pool.

They scanned room numbers on the doors while they jogged, and with luck, 262 was within thirty feet of the stairwell.

Schneider opened the door and Layne followed him in. The tiny room had been crammed with two sets of bunk beds. Someone was lying on the bottom bed of the bunks they were facing, reading a magazine. He looked up, and musing at the condition of his new roommates, said, "You guys having fun?"

They didn't respond to him but dropped their bags. Layne glanced at his watch as he closed the door behind them, "We've only got, like, forty-five seconds!"

Breathing heavily, they chop-stepped down the stairs and the moment their feet hit the ground, began to sprint. Once they were back in formation, Layne discretely looked at his watch while breathing heavily. They had made it with ten seconds to spare.

After all of the Arizona section of Class 590 was situated, they marched to an administrative building for individual intake. The three instructors monitored their march from the flanks. Layne attempted to sync his feet with Schneider's, but was forced to stutter step periodically to match the timing and hoped the instructors didn't notice. The sun was going down. He yawned with his mouth closed and followed with extreme caution, careful not to bring attention to himself.

Following several more hours of paperwork the trainees were dismissed, and they headed back to their new dorm rooms in broken groups. It was June and already warm at night here in this new world. A giant orange moon observed them as they walked with heavy feet in relative darkness until they reached the lackluster lights of the dorm complex.

The trainees wandered from room to room to join huddles of conversation with veteran trainees who were already acclimated to the Academy.

"We better go talk to our new roommates," Schneider said to Layne. When they arrived, the roommate who had been reading a magazine on the bottom bunk was just coming out of the bathroom. Layne and Schneider introduced themselves.

"I'm Ricky," the stranger said. "What do you guys think so far?"

"Not as bad as I thought it would be," Layne said, overcome with relief and smiling.

"That's because you guys got here at the end of the day and the instructors were too tired to mess with you," Ricky said. "You guys lucked out. When I got here, it was just after lunchtime and they chewed our butts out the whole time."

"I heard we are still waiting for our California, Texas, and New Mexico people," Schneider said.

"Just California and Texas," Ricky said. "The instructors have to stay up until those buses get here. You guys don't have any people from New Mexico. It's the state that has the least amount of activity, so they don't need as many new agents."

"How do you know all of this stuff?" Layne inquired.

"Everybody knows everything here. So, don't tell anybody anything that you don't want the whole Academy to know." Ricky held up a uniform top, preparing to iron it. It was the same field uniform as the agents in Tucson wore.

"Where's our other roommate?" Schneider asked.

"He's hanging out in his buddy's room. He's kind of a weirdo—doesn't talk much. I don't think he's gonna make it." Layne and Schneider had to move out of the way so that Ricky could get to the outlet. He plugged in the cord for the iron to heat up, and said, "Let's go outside, there's no room in here. You guys are gonna get sick of these rooms real fast."

The three of them leaned on the balcony railing overlooking the courtyard with its pool and sand volleyball court. Floodlights lit up the dorm complex, and humidity flowed through their beams. Masses of bugs orbited the lights, and crickets chirped in the surrounding darkness.

Schneider excused himself to go meet someone, leaving Layne and Ricky alone. Layne enjoyed the privilege of being able to finally relax amid interesting conversation. "How long have you been here?" he asked.

"A month and two days."

"What's it like?"

"It sucks, man. Everyday you've got to be in formation at 7:00 a.m., and you have to march to all your classes and to the buses."

"Are the classes hard?"

"Law is a killer; the others aren't that bad. Did you go to college?"

"Yeah, Missouri," Layne answered. "You?"

"UT San Antonio."

Ricky looked and walked like an athlete. Layne thought he was probably a football player in high school, but he refrained from bringing up sports, not wanting anyone to know about his past. He was about five foot nine, a light skinned Hispanic who could easily be mistaken as white, especially when he spoke. He was confident but not cocky, like many athletes Layne had known. Layne was enjoying his company.

Ricky went back inside to tend to his ironing board.

"Any hot chicks here?" Layne asked as he followed him back in.

"There's a few, but guys are all over them. My buddy got one of them last weekend. But I don't even try. It's too hard, too many dudes."

"Where are you from?" Layne asked.

"The Valley."

Layne looked confused.

Ricky clarified. "It's in south Texas. I'm gonna be stationed in the same town where I grew up. I've been around Border Patrol my whole life. I can remember when the trucks were lime green. Where you from?"

"Denver," Layne said. The dorm room door, which they had left cracked, creaked open. Damon walked in as if he were walking into his own room, looking for Schneider.

"Damon Balducci, from Rochester, New York," he said to Ricky without invitation.

Layne almost immediately wished Damon would leave, his insolence quickly making Layne bristle as they stood elbow to elbow, looking around for a place to stand comfortably.

"What did you do before this?" Ricky said to Damon.

"I was in the Navy for eight years," he answered with indifference. Layne didn't comment.

"Eight years! What was *that* like?" Ricky said.

"It was alright."

Ricky hung up his uniform and Damon followed them back outside to lean on the railing again. Layne fought the urge to give details about himself as they resumed their view of the courtyard. Matt had warned him, "If the PT Instructors find out you were an athlete, they will mess with you every day. Everyday they'll compare how easy college sports must be compared to PT."

"How old are you?" Ricky said.

"Twenty-seven; you?" Damon replied.

"Twenty-seven," Ricky said.

Some of Layne's insecurities began to wane—everyone was about his age. It would have been embarrassing to be older than everyone else.

"You party here?" Layne asked.

"You got it! There's a bar right over there." Ricky pointed to a building that did look like a bar, less than a hundred yards from the dorms, in the middle of campus. "It's on, every weekend, starting Friday night. I got a twelve-pack in my ice chest waiting for me after class at four o'clock."

"A bar on the base?" Layne was still feeling the sour stomach and general discomfort from the previous Friday night in Tucson. He reminded himself of his vow to himself; he was intent on staying away from the place or he would have no chance of making it through.

"Yeah, it's called Sandy's, and the bartender is blind, believe it or not," Ricky said.

"Blind?" Damon said.

"Yeah, and don't screw with him. Some guy ordered a beer a couple of weeks ago and handed him a five and said it was a twenty. Someone saw it and told an instructor, and he got sent home."

The three of them walked back inside the dorm room. It would be impossible to make this cage feel like home, Layne thought, but then, no place except the house he grew up in had ever really felt like home. Ricky's duty belt was hanging from the post of the bunk, and Damon took Ricky's rubber pistol from the holster without asking and began aiming it at things.

"Careful, man," Ricky said. "Never take that gun out in front of instructors. Some guys were playing laser tag in one of the temps a few months ago and an instructor walked in. Both of them are gone."

At that moment, Ricky's bunkmate came in and squeezed through. He was unmistakably Hispanic, and without acknowledging anyone or introducing himself, he began preparing his things for the next day, using the top bunk as a table. The three of them didn't acknowledge his presence; it seemed to be a courtesy to him.

Damon said, "So all you have to do is pass all the classes to graduate?"

Ricky shook his head with an unsatisfying grin, preparing to enlighten them. "No, there's PT—Physical Training. You've got to go through Stacking and OC and running. My class got screwed; our PT Instructor is a marathon runner. A couple of pussies quit the first day; they almost died. He ran us, like, five miles the first day."

Layne's heart began pounding again.

Damon said, "What is Stacking and OC?"

"They do it to you in PT. Stacking is the worst. You have to fight off four guys at once with your baton for two minutes or you don't pass."

"OC?" Layne asked.

"An Instructor sprays pepper spray in your eyes and you have to handcuff a Red Man while your face is burning."

Damon scoffed. "I went in the tear gas chamber for the Navy; it wasn't that bad."

Ricky disagreed again. "I heard about that. The guys who were in the military say OC is way worse. I still have to do both of them in a couple of months."

Ricky started getting ready for bed, and Damon took it as his cue to leave. Layne looked for a vacant locker closet to put his clothes in, but there were only two lockers for four people. They were both taken—by Ricky and the silent roommate. Schneider hadn't come back yet; they would have to figure out the locker situation when he returned.

He put the majority of his clothes under Schneider's bed, then looked for footing to get up to the top bunk—there was no ladder. Ricky asked him to turn out the lights as he was climbing. The silent roommate still hadn't said anything. He was lying on his top bunk wearing headphones and looking at his cellphone. Layne stared at the ceiling in the quiet of the dark room. There was no use trying to go to sleep this early, but he tried to, out of respect for his new roommates. Schneider would wake them up anyway when he came back. He felt like he was at camp, the way he did during naptime in daycare. The hotel in Tucson now seemed a distant memory.

9

FELINA CAMARENA RIVERA'S TIRED FEET climbed the last step to her second-floor apartment. It was already becoming uncomfortably hot in Tucson, and it was barely May. Her weariness was compounded by the heat. As she reached the landing, she pulled her hair behind her ear and looped her arm through the handles of her purse to select the apartment key from her key ring. As she turned the key in the deadbolt, she tried to ignore the sound of a toddler crying and adults arguing in the apartment next door. She felt herself frowning; she knew she would continue to hear the argument once inside. The walls were so thin—she would likely be able to sense things being thrown during the argument as well. It was embarrassing for her to be seen entering this building, and she was anxious to get inside and lock the door. At least the neighbors hadn't left trash bags outside their door today.

She set her purse and keys on the kitchen counter and looked around the living room of her studio apartment as she leaned her head sideways to remove her earrings. Her couch and furniture hardly went together, which frustrated her every time she came home. Life felt like treading water. The used car she had recently purchased had wiped out her savings, and her budget was so crimped she was eating Ramen noodles most nights.

She enjoyed having her own car, but her prized possession was her soft bed. She was already dreading the next morning, when her alarm clock would force her to exit her soothing sheets. She wished she could somehow remain lucid while asleep, so she could experience the complete tranquility of being immersed in her dreams. But before she knew it, the alarm was going off. She usually set the buzzer to sound a half an hour earlier than necessary so she could hit snooze and enjoy the relief of knowing she could go back to sleep, even if only for fifteen more minutes.

She balanced herself with the countertop to pull off her shoes and sighed as she sat down on the couch and crossed her legs. She retrieved the TV remote from the coffee table; hopefully there was something on that would distract her from the bad news that was less than an hour old. It left her painfully more despondent than normal, so much so that she didn't have the strength to call Marianne. She had told her boss that she had scheduled a doctor's appointment for feminine issues. But instead she had missed the second half of the day to go through with something that she had been apprehensive about for days on end. Now, she wished that she had stayed at work and had never gone through with the appointment. The result was draining what was left of her hope.

She had just met with an immigration attorney, an appointment she had scheduled three weeks prior. She had been living optimistically on an aspiration that, with the assistance of a legal professional, there would be a way out. She had never known life without the burden. She often fantasized about what life would be like if she were like everybody else—if she were a legal resident of the U.S.A. She would look forward to waking up each morning.

She tried to convince herself that she had lost nothing by seeking counsel. But she relived the demoralizing scene at the appointment and began to cry while she searched the TV guide screen for something to distract her thoughts. It was of no use; she couldn't expel the conversation from her mind. She had felt exposed while telling the lawyer the truth, despite the attorney-client privilege he reassured her of. Upon her request, the attorney closed the door to his office.

Felina interpreted the attorney's body language, and immediately felt vulnerable instead of secure. As he returned to his seat behind his desk and asked what he could do for her, his busy demeanor conveyed that his time was valuable. He interlaced his fingers and rested them on his desk and leaned back in his chair to hear what she had to say. She took a deep breath and explained to him that she was born in Guadalajara, Mexico, and that her parents had brought her across the border when she was three years old.

She was too young to remember life in the country of her birth, she said; she recalled only unpleasant, blurry clips of the one-way journey into Arizona through the night during a three-day stint. They had made multiple changes in vehicle transportation along the way; the intense desperation of the voyage was unforgettably terrifying, even for a child so young. The ordeal lingered in her memory, largely due to the acute distress her mother had been under. She remembered being too exhausted to stand, and that her mother had insisted that she remain awake. Despite being only three years old, she knew that something momentous was occurring, and it was disturbing to witness her mother in a defenseless capacity, pressing on in faith.

The attorney's expression grew more pessimistic the more she revealed. He adjusted his tie and shifted positions in his chair, but his indifferent facial expression didn't change. She continued anyway; it was peculiarly relieving to speak aloud about what had troubled her most of her life. Only her family, and her best friend Marianne, knew the truth about her—that she had been living in the United States illegally for almost the entire twenty-one years of her life. The attorney wasn't taken aback as she had expected, being that she spoke English perfectly with an American accent. He seemed to have already known the punch line as she was building up to it.

She expected him to show at least a discernible amount of empathy— he was, after all, Hispanic himself, though born in El Paso, Texas. But he exuded an arrogance of superiority without allegiance to his race that was difficult to look past. She had become envious of Chicanos when she was fourteen and began seeking work with false documents. He made no reaction at all the moment she confessed to a crime by simply being there, and she realized that he probably heard similar stories on a daily basis. He looked down over his chin to check his tie and reclined slightly farther back in his chair. He separated his hands and began tapping the eraser of his pencil on the desk while she made an effort to impact the disinclined look on his face.

She made her case as to why legal status was imperative to her. She was exceptional and didn't belong in the confines that her immigration status limited her to. She had graduated from high school with a 4.0 grade point average and had scored a 27 on the ACT on her first try. Her unwavering passion to attend the University of Arizona had begun her junior year, and she was certain that she would eventually be accepted into medical school. She was naturally intelligent and a relentless learner. Her teachers in high school had, time and again, insisted that she apply for an academic scholarship. She explained to the attorney without breaking down that she had no choice but to mislead her admiring educators. She was ineligible because of her immigration status, and she couldn't seek a Pell Grant without a Green Card. She hadn't even bothered filling out a FAFSA (Free Application for Federal Student Aid); without a legitimate Social Security number, she couldn't receive student loans either.

The attorney raised a feckless eyebrow at her accomplishments but sighed and went on to tell her that it would be futile to apply for status as a Lawfully Admitted Permanent Resident. Even if she could afford his fee, the government would reject the application when they discovered that she had been living in the United States illegally for all this time. Only if she had entered the country legally with an immigrant visa would USCIS (U.S. Citizenship and Immigration Services) consider her, and even on that basis, it could take years for them to process the application. He went on to dissuade her by pointing out that by applying, she would be revealing her illegal status and physical location to government officials, who could dispatch ICE Agents (Immigration and Customs Enforcement) to detain and deport her back to Mexico.

She was upset and embarrassed when he asked her if there was anything else that she would like to discuss with him. She interpreted the question as a hint that her time was up. She was too proud to cry in public. She gathered her purse, thanking him for his time while she suppressed the urge to justify her argument that she had earned the right to higher education.

The United States was the only country she had ever known. She had family in Magdalena, Sonora that she had never met in person, and the rest of her family was in the State of Jalisco. She had grown up talking to her grandparents over the telephone; she knew what they looked like only from photographs. Visiting them had never been feasible. Getting there would have been no problem, but avoiding the Border Patrol upon return would have been too risky. It would have been senseless to attempt to cross the border back into Arizona without an immigration record.

She didn't feel like a criminal. She pointed out that she had never crossed the border illegally on her own accord. The only crime she had willfully committed was the use of a fraudulent Social Security card and driver's license that she had been using since she was sixteen. But it was a crime of necessity in order to drive and work. The driver's license had her picture and name on it, but it hadn't been issued by the state of Arizona. Her family had connections to people who made fake IDs. The counterfeiter had stolen the laminates from a DMV in Yuma. He made a photocopy of a genuine Arizona Driver's License then cut and pasted to rearrange the serial number and replaced the original picture with Felina's picture, name and birthdate. The ID even had the holograms and magnetic strip on the back, but if it were run through a scanner it wouldn't contain any information.

Felina always took added caution to follow traffic laws; she had never been pulled over while driving. But in the event that she were ever stopped by a police officer, she had purchased a fake Mexican driver's license. And if necessary, she could speak English with a Spanish accent to play the part. She had put studious effort into mimicking acquaintances who spoke English with a heavy Spanish accent.

She stared at a vase of flowers on the top of her entertainment center, in deep thought, while the TV guide screen waited for a selection. Pursuit of happiness seemed like an impossible struggle. She uncrossed her legs and attempted to move on. It would take time for the sting of the appointment to subside.

She opened her laptop computer and began looking at the cost per credit hour at Pima Community College; her inner drive compelled her not to give up. The screening process for junior college was more easily bypassed. She would have to apply as an international student because she didn't qualify for in-state tuition. The tuition cost under international status was unrealistic, but she would have to somehow come up with the money to get started on her prerequisite classes. She would go from there, and hopefully God would show her how to sidestep the immigration obstacles to complete the subsequent two years and receive her Bachelor's Degree.

She was too tired to continue; she sighed and closed her laptop. Every aspect of her life was problematic. She stood up to draw the curtains and shed the last of the day's sunlight on her mood and stared momentarily at the fading light moving across the Catalina Mountains. She couldn't refrain from staring at the houses in the foothills again. She wanted to knock on the door of one of those beautiful houses and ask the person who answered how they had done it, how they had achieved such a utopian existence?

At least tomorrow was Friday. After work she was planning to stay at her parent's house on Tucson's south side. She continued to take in the view as she thought about her family. She looked forward to the visits; her brothers Javier and Eduardo would be there, and the family would play cards until late. She would likely sleep on her parents' couch if she was too tired to drive back home. She drove only when necessary. It was second nature for her to constantly check her rearview mirror while she was behind the wheel.

The only aspect of the time she spent with her family that she didn't enjoy was speaking solely Spanish. She was continually improving her English vocabulary. She had grown up speaking Spanish at home and translating for her parents when they needed her to. It was a reminder of her limitations. She had never been outside the boundaries of Arizona; she had never been on an airplane. When she needed to borrow money, she pawned her jewelry. She couldn't get credit cards, which compounded her financial stress.

She made up her mind that she wasn't going to ask her parents how they were doing during this visit tomorrow night. She felt herself becoming fidgety when she thought of her mom paying their bills at the first of each month. At least her dad still wasn't drinking, as far as she knew. And the job cleaning houses her mom had gotten lucky in finding was appearing to stick.

She continued to stare unproductively out the window. She needed to make sure that she wasn't late to work tomorrow—her boss yelling her name for her to come to his office was all that she could take. For him to threaten her about being late again was enough to bring tears and draw attention from her gossiping coworkers. If they ever discovered the truth about her, her boss would surely also know the same day. But she wasn't sure what his reaction would be. She was fairly certain that he knew that many of the company's best cement finishers were illegal. He might not fire her; more likely he would lower her wage, since she had no recourse except to quit. She felt the job was beneath her—it was menial in relation to her intellectual capability—but it was the best she could do. At least that's what she told herself every day. To her, working for a low wage was worse than slavery. At least slaves had their room and board provided for. In a job such as hers, not only was the money inadequate to offer a sense of security about basic needs, but the burden of worrying about her well-being was additional labor that went uncompensated.

It was time to stop thinking about things she couldn't change, and time to change into her pajamas. She couldn't help but prolong the intermission from work, even at the expense of sleep, although she knew she would regret it in the morning. She couldn't anticipate the next morning's groggy regret as motivation to get to bed early, so she reopened her computer and continued to search the Internet for a way around her problem. It was strange, but on weekend nights she went to bed early; the night didn't need to be savored when there was nothing to dread the next morning.

She placed her hand on the bedpost to balance herself while she pulled her socks and jeans off to get undressed. Her right shoulder cracked as she reached behind her back to unsnap her bra. She reminded herself to set her bedside alarm and make sure the volume was turned up, and to charge her cellphone and set the alarm on the phone at 6:05, five minutes after the first alarm went off. For backup, she told herself.

10

MOVEMENT IN THE DARK WOKE LAYNE at 6:00 a.m., and for a few seconds he couldn't determine where he was. As he came to, he realized he had forgotten to set the alarm on his cell phone. But there had been no need. Ricky and the silent roommate were already getting dressed as quietly as possible, and their movement had awakened Schneider as well. Layne could feel him moving in the bed below. While Ricky buttoned his uniform top, he noticed that Layne was awake and said, "Is it okay if I turn on the lights?"

"I'm getting up," Layne said.

He stared at the ceiling, his face close enough to observe the subtle pattern on the tiles. The memory of a dream he was having sometime during the night was still vivid, and he was waiting for it to subside while he lay there. In the dream he just realized that he had gotten a nonsensical tattoo of an eagle, or something that he would never choose, on his arm. It was a dream he had experienced before, and it was followed by one with a familiar theme. He was desperate to complete an impossible task and he uncontrollably made one mistake after another while he moved in tiresome slow motion as time raced. Ricky and his bunkmate were putting on their green rough gear uniforms. Layne admired the regalia of the uniforms as they dressed. He wasn't sure if the creases that were ironed into the sleeves looked better pressed through the middle of the Government patches or around them to the rear. The crease through the middle left a fold in the patch that disrupted the panache of the Customs and Border Protection seal. He examined Ricky's web gear as he fastened his duty belt with a hollow click.

In addition to the rubber pistol, Ricky and the silent roommate had been issued a rubber radio. The model items were perfect replicas and were accurately heavy, like a well-made toy. Layne looked down at the top of Schneider's head, as he sat still on his bed waiting for his two new roommates to finish so there would be room to walk to the bathroom. Schneider turned his head upward to see Layne looking down at him.

"Do you want to shower first or do you want me to?" Schneider asked.

"You go first," Layne said, and then to the others, "Why are you guys up so early? Don't you have until 7:00 to be down there?"

"We always go to the cafeteria to eat breakfast," Ricky said.

Layne rarely ate breakfast. The thought of pancakes and eggs was even more unappealing this strange morning.

"You guys will want to shower and iron your uniforms at night. It makes it easier to get ready in the morning," Ricky advised.

"When do we get our uniforms?" asked Layne, eager to blend in and to see what he looked like in the uniform.

"They will measure you for them today or tomorrow. You should get them on Friday. You'll get your duty belt and rubber gun today. They'll give you your backpack and all your equipment, too. What class are you guys?" Ricky asked.

"590," Schneider said.

"Enjoy the blue and grey uniforms until your greens come in, because all you have to do is wash and put them on. It's a different ball game once you get your greens. You have to iron the pants and shirts every night. If you go to class and your uniform isn't crisp, you'll get a memo. You don't want that." Ricky ran his fingers down the crease in his pants one last time.

On Ricky's backpack Layne noticed a black patch that said Class 572 in embroidered yellow letters. As the silent one adjusted his duty belt, Layne could see his Velcro name tag: Cabrera; his first name started with the letter "J".

"What are we supposed to do when we get down there?" Layne asked.

"Your law instructor will come find you. Don't worry, he'll tell you what to do."

"Why the law instructor?"

"His classroom is like your homeroom, and he coordinates everything for your class."

Layne stepped down from the top bunk carefully; the metal frame of the bunk bed was cold on his bare feet. He could hear birds chirping in the warm humid morning air as Ricky and Cabrera opened and closed the door to leave.

Schneider came out of the bathroom with a towel around his waist, and steam fogged up the mirror above the sink as he opened the bathroom door. "There's no water pressure in the shower. It's like standing under a mister on a Mill Street bar patio."

"Great," Layne responded.

He showered quickly, using a miniature bar of soap and a little bottle of shampoo from the hotel in Tucson. He considered that this was the third day that he was wearing the polo shirt and his khaki pants without washing them.

The trainees from Class 590 found one another in the courtyard as the sun came up. The California and Texas trainees had arrived in the middle of the night, and Layne was revolted to see that sixty percent of them were Hispanic. There were only a few quiet conversations taking place, everyone else waiting silently. Layne whispered to Runyon: "Are you kidding me? Over half of the class is Mexican! No wonder so many wetbacks make it up here."

Runyon frowned in agreement. "I know; it's a total farce. You've got to take into consideration that this is the only way that these Mexicans can make over eighty grand a year without doing construction. It's like being an electrician; it's a job that dirt heads who didn't graduate high school can still get and make a good living. And once you're a career agent you're pretty much untouchable."

Dozens of other classes, in uniform, were already in tight formations in the courtyard, preparing to march to the buses that would take them to class. It would have been a beautiful summer sunrise in a less daunting environment.

Half of Class 590 had been enlisted in the military, and they quickly helped assemble everyone into formation in multiple rows before the instructor arrived.

Instructor Luis Baca arrived at exactly 7:00 a.m., in dress uniform, his Smokey hat tilted slightly forward, secured by a leather strap which clung to the back of his head. His high and tight haircut was fresh, the sides almost shaven to the skin. All of the brass on his uniform gleamed. He was a fit, thirty-eight-year old, handsome Hispanic man with light skin, like a Spaniard. It was evident by the expression on his face that he had been detailed to the Academy against his will. He surveyed the class with annoyance then demanded, "Who has prior military experience? I need two Squad Leaders."

A trainee named Guillermo volunteered, to the relief of the rest of the class of fifty trainees. Guillermo was from the late-arriving Texas group, and he looked to be one of the oldest trainees in the class. The oldest was a thirty-seven-year-old Puerto Rican from New York City who had spent ten years in the Army but wanted no leadership role of any kind. Instructor Baca divided the class into two groups of twenty-five. Guillermo was Squad Leader of Layne's group—Group A. No one volunteered to lead Group B, and Instructor Baca quickly lost patience.

"Everybody with prior military experience raise your hand!" he growled forcefully. He pointed to a white, twenty-eight-year-old Marine Corps veteran who had raised his hand.

"What's your name?" Baca demanded.

"Osborne, sir."

"Osborne, you're Squad Leader for Group B."

Osborne's face looked displeased, like he was chewing something disgusting, even while Baca glared straight at him for several seconds, daring him to object.

"You Squad Leaders, take five minutes to show your squads the drill commands and how to march in formation," Baca ordered.

As Baca observed, Guillermo and Osborne demonstrated parade rest, at-ease, left-face, right-face, and about-face, as well as the proper separation distance between each foot in inches. When the five minutes was up, Baca marched them to class registration, uniform measurement, equipment checkout, and Spanish aptitude testing for placement in classes. As the trainees would be quick to discover, when on campus between 7:00 a.m. and 5:00 p.m., the squads would march to every destination for the next four months.

At 11:00 a.m. Layne's group marched to the PT Building to be issued temporary uniforms, the outfit Ricky advised him to enjoy. Until their regular uniforms were scheduled to arrive in two weeks, they were to wear navy blue cargo pants and grey t-shirts with the Homeland Security Seal on the left breast. They were issued two identical shirts. The same shirt would be worn with gym shorts for PT when the dreaded class was integrated into the schedule in two weeks.

Layne was relieved when noon arrived. Baca instructed the Squad Leaders to march their squads to the cafeteria for lunch. Baca followed them into the building and took off his Smokey, then left to sit with the other instructors at their private tables.

Layne exhaled when Baca was gone. He picked up a warm tray from the spring-loaded stack and stood in line to get to the buffet. The damp tray was blue with the Homeland Security eagle emblem in the middle. He filled his tray with roast beef, mashed potatoes, salad with ranch dressing, a bowl of banana pudding with wafers, and an orange-colored drink from a punch dispenser.

The cafeteria of green was packed and bustling with conversation. After scanning the congregation for long seconds, he spotted the group of blue polo shirts in the far corner. He squeezed into an open space on a bench at a table where Carlos and Runyon were sitting, along with

Damon, who appeared to already be making the others uncomfortable, judging by their body language.

Among five hundred trainees in uniform, tables in the far corner of the cafeteria were reserved for new classes, the exiles who still lacked their green uniforms. Only one rung above Class 590 were two classes wearing the blue cargo pants and the PT shirt sitting at the neighboring tables.

"Damn, this place is packed," Runyon said. "This place is way over capacity." He unraveled his silverware and put his napkin in his lap. The trainees in green placed their hats on the table before eating.

"Not as packed as my room," Damon announced to the entire table. "I got some guy's butt in my face while I'm lacing my boots in the morning."

Runyon added after he finished chewing: "That's why there's all that construction going on over there by those other dorms. They're hurrying to make room for the influx. This place was designed for a couple hundred trainees. There's got to be three times that here right now."

"It's worse than prison. Tackleberry is my bunkmate," Damon complained.

Everyone laughed.

"Even with a pillow over my head he sounds like a weed-whacker, snoring," Damon added.

Layne looked discretely to his right as he picked at his lunch. Tackleberry was only a few places down the bench, pretending not to hear. Still, no one knew his name.

"Where do the instructors live?" Layne asked the group.

"I heard in those temporaries behind the PT Building. Two of them share a temp," Schneider said.

"That's why Baca is such a pain; these mattresses are like sleeping on a park bench," Damon said. His voice was prominent and piercing as usual, and Layne looked around to see if any of the trainees in green reacted to the comment.

"What do you expect? He's supposed to be that way," Runyon said.

"You know everything," Damon said, in response to contradiction. "Were you in Black Water before this?"

"Army Intelligence in Afghanistan; what about you?" Runyon fired back.

"I was in the Navy for eight years," Damon retaliated.

"You mean the Gay-vy," Runyon grinned.

Everyone at the table laughed.

"When we start PT in two weeks and put on the boxing gloves, I'll show you how gay I am in the Octagon," Damon said. Layne couldn't tell if they were joking or not.

"We better get going," said a trainee from 590 at the adjoining table, rising and looking at his watch.

"Who's that?" Layne asked Carlos.

"I heard someone call him Danielson," Carlos said while he grabbed his tray and rose with everyone else at the table.

The group weaved through the tables to head back out to formation, stacking their trays near the kitchen door.

"I think half of our classes are in temporary buildings that are like a mile from here," Layne said, walking with Schneider. "Out where we took the Spanish test."

"What class did you test into?"

"Group two; you?" Layne said.

"Me, too."

They had learned that there were four Spanish groups total. Group One was for Mexicans who grew up speaking Spanish. The term the instructors used for them was "Nativos." But there were so many of them that half of Layne and Schneider's Group Two was also composed of Nativos. Group Two was intended for trainees who had learned Spanish in school, and for those who had been exposed to Spanish but didn't speak the foreign language on a daily basis. Schneider was earning credibility as someone Layne could trust and express himself to. He was sharp, like Runyon, picking up on things that Layne was initially unable to see. But unlike Runyon, Schneider was completely unpretentious.

"How did you learn Spanish?" Layne asked.

"It was my minor in college. You?"

"College," Layne said, "and travel. I lived with a family in Mexico for a while a couple years ago."

"When do we start Firearms?" asked a 590 trainee—another Hispanic, Layne noticed—who had caught up with them. He was walking with Runyon, and the four fell into step and into conversation.

"Same week as PT," Runyon said.

"What kind of pistols are we getting?" inquired Schneider. He knew Runyon would have such information.

"HK P2000, I'm pretty sure. But they store them at the range," Runyon said. "They use a .40 caliber. It's a high compression round, pretty much standard for a police cartridge."

"Do you know if the M4's are full-auto?" Layne asked. He knew that his own familiarity with guns would prove to be an asset, as he had planned. Hopefully, his proficiency in firearms and Spanish would be the linchpins he was depending on them to be.

"They are. They're M4 A-1s," Runyon said.

"Not three-round burst?" Layne suggested.

"No. The Border Patrol never updated them after Vietnam. They still have the old M4s. It's a carbine version of the M-16; it's actually an AR-15, the "M" was just designated by the military. Most people think AR stands for Assault Rifle, but it actually means Armalite, the company that produced Eugene Stoner's design."

"I know what an M4 is," Layne said.

As it often did, his attention shifted to something that prodded him with distress. He announced to no one in particular, "I've got to remember to go back to the dorm and switch the books in my backpack to Law and Applied Authority."

"Me, too," said Schneider. "My backpack already weighs twenty pounds from the morning classes."

"What do you think Baca would do if you didn't have your Law books?" Carlos said.

"Write a memo," Schneider said.

Layne blocked himself from voicing his thoughts. *I don't even want to think about opening my backpack and realizing I forgot my book in front of Baca. I wonder how many memos you get before you're fired?*

By the second night it was obvious that it would be impossible to study in his dorm room. There was one desk, but there was a television on the wall in the corner above it that Ricky and Cabrera watched from their bunks until they fell asleep. The only place to study was an empty classroom or the television lounge behind the pool.

In the television lounge there was sufficient space to have a notebook and textbook open at the same time. But the lounge was as distracting as his tiny cell of a dorm room. When he arrived there to study, Carlos, Runyon, Schneider, and Blair—another trainee who had fallen in with their group—were already sitting at a round table, pens in their hands and heads turned to the big screen TV. Everyone was wearing basketball shorts and flip-flops. Some trainees that Layne didn't know had green lanyards around their necks with the yellow letters, USBP, attached to thumb drives.

Layne found a seat at the round table with his back to the TV. He removed his Nationality Law book and a notebook from his backpack and clicked his pen. At the other two tables, trainees from other classes were studying, several spitting excess saliva from tobacco into Gatorade bottles, others cracking sunflower seeds with their back teeth.

"I can't believe all of the information they expect us to learn," Layne said. He knew as soon as he said it that he was again saying out loud what he was thinking. He scolded himself; displaying the neurotic inner workings of his mind could bring trouble in this environment. Those at his table took notice and nodded in agreement. A muscular trainee with a spit bottle at the far table leaned backwards to see who had said it.

"It's a lot," Blair said.

Blair was from Utah, Layne had discovered. His behavior suggested that he was a Mormon. He hadn't yet cursed and seemed to be avoiding caffeinated drinks. Layne remembered his name after he introduced himself, because he had blue eyes and dark hair, almost black. He was the same size as Layne but looked like a non-athlete; he was duck footed. The others commented, welcoming more distraction from their study.

"Nationality Law for two months, then we have Immigration Law for the last two months?" Schneider said.

"I hear Applied Authority is worse than Law. And we have PT and Operations to worry about, too." Layne hoped he was not the only one who was concerned. "How do they expect us to handle all of this while we're living in a room with three other dudes?"

A trainee sitting on the couch in front of the TV—a senior, judging by his body language—overheard the conversation and turned around to say, "Don't worry too much about Ops. Some guys from a year ago stole all the tests from an instructor and made copies." Several heads near him looked up from their books and smiled in agreement. "Check with your roommates if they're ahead of you, they should have copies. The questions are all pretty close to the real exams, the same just worded differently and in different order."

"That's awesome," Carlos said.

"The Ops 1 and 2 tests are almost exactly the same. It's like fishing with dynamite. You gotta waste time so you don't turn it in too fast," the senior continued with a grin. "But be careful with them. About a month ago the Campus Police raided all of the rooms looking for hard alcohol and found a bunch of the tests. Almost a whole class got fired for having them."

"We can't have hard alcohol in our rooms?" Carlos asked.

"Beer, but not hard alcohol. We used to be able to have hard stuff in our rooms until about three months ago. Some guy ended up in the hospital for alcohol poisoning and they changed the rules."

"Runyon wants to know what their policy is on wine coolers," Layne injected.

Everyone laughed.

"Screw you, Sheppard," Runyon said, laughing a little himself.

"That's sweet they have the tests," Layne said, charged with enthusiasm now. "Fraternities in college do that. They have file cabinets with a tab for each professor and all of his tests. That's how those guys can party every night and still pass their classes." Layne was sailing on the hope now that there was a shortcut through this stage. He would just have to set aside some rules for himself to follow religiously.

"I bet our Applied Authority teacher changes his tests, though. He looks like he's on the ball," Schneider said. "I heard he makes over a hundred grand a year."

"You mean Greenberg?" Blair asked.

"Yeah, he's a civilian permanent instructor. He doesn't have to iron a uniform and polish boots every night before he goes to bed. Guys like that are on tenure. He can't really get fired," Runyon said.

Runyon leaned back, putting his mechanical pencil on the table beside his open book. "All of the permanent instructors are like that. They all live in Roswell and have to drive an hour to work in the morning. I don't blame them. Better than living in Artesia. I heard Walmart can't even find people that can pass a drug test to work there. This town is one big meth lab."

"What's the difference between a permanent instructor like Greenberg and one of the ones who wears a uniform?" Layne wanted to know.

"Greenberg is a civilian contracted by the Government to teach," Runyon said. "He probably has a PhD. I think most every other instructor, the ones that wear a uniform, are detailed here. That's why they look like they're as miserable as we are."

Everyone laughed, entertained by the conversation.

"I think the only permanent Border Patrol instructors are those old guys that teach Ops and Firearms," Runyon continued. "Everyone else has to pay their dues and live in those temps for four months."

"They have to be better than the coffins we have to live in," Layne said.

"Did you guys hear about the Glop?" Schneider asked, putting his pen into his open book as a marker and closing it.

"Do I even want to know?" Layne asked.

Schneider had the attention of everybody at the table. "Dude, the gun range where we have Firearms Class is like ten miles off the base, out in the boondocks. There's a road that goes out there. Supposedly, before you graduate you have to run all the way out there without stopping or you don't pass PT. The PT instructors drive alongside you in golf carts the whole way."

"I heard Ricky talking about that," Layne said. "It sounds like so much bull. I think the senior classes are just messing with us. I can't run that far; Ricky said it's AT LEAST ten miles."

"What's the difference between Reasonable Suspicion and Probable Cause?" interrupted Carlos, who was the only one still focusing on his Applied Authority book.

No one said anything.

Finally, Runyon said, "I don't know."

Everyone laughed.

"I don't understand all of those search and seizure exceptions," Blair admitted.

Layne looked around and realized that he needed to bear down. He realized that he hadn't changed since college; he couldn't keep from daydreaming. He copied down everything the professor wrote on the board, to feel like he was being productive. But he never once went back and referenced what he had written.

"I can't get anything done here," Layne said. "I need to go find an empty classroom or something to study in."

He stood and put his books in his backpack.

"I'll go with you," Blair said.

11

"RIGHT FACE, MARCH!" Guillermo ordered.

The days were settling into a routine and Layne was surprised to find that he enjoyed marching. It reminded him of what it felt like to be part of a team. He marched thoughtlessly, watching Schneider's heels until the squad halted at their bus stop near the cafeteria. The trainees appreciated the punctuality of the bus drivers. Some mornings it was already close to ninety degrees and trainees had to stand rigidly at ease, hesitant to even wipe the sweat off their faces while Instructor Baca stood searching for an opportunity to yell.

When the yellow school bus arrived, Group A boarded, pulling their hat bills over their eyes and gripping the straps to their backpacks as they climbed the steps. Everyone could relax once inside and seated. Layne sat next to a window near the back of the bus and put his backpack in his lap. As the others chatted, he stared out the window. The bus traveled five minutes on a dirt road to a collection of temporary buildings. The driver stopped in front of the second of five buildings on the right side of the road, and Guillermo got out first from his seat by the door. Group A filed out and assembled into formation in front of him. After a minute of standing at attention, Instructor Baca came out of the temporary building, nodded to Guillermo and said bitterly, "Bring 'em in."

The trainees filed in order up the stairs and into the classroom, settling into assigned seats at tables. An index card at each place displaying each trainee's name reminded them of their assigned seats. Baca waited at the podium until everyone was seated. It was evident that he was especially angry for some unknown reason and itching for something critical to aim at the class. "Before we start today I want you all to know that if any of you have a problem with the way I teach my class, if you have any *cohones*, just come up and tell me before you get back on the bus." No one spoke or moved. "After I kick your butt, we'll get you out-processed in a few hours, then you can go back to working at Target or whatever dead-end job for the rest of your life."

Layne looked over at Blair; somebody must have dropped a dime on him. Blair was stunned, his face white. During the fifteen-minute break the day before Blair had told a small huddle that he had been a general manager at a Target store in Provo, Utah before he was hired for the Border Patrol. During the same conversation he complained that he didn't like Baca's teaching style.

Baca scanned the class for several seconds with a challenging look on his face, the room dead still except for the sound of the air conditioning unit running. Then he moved over to the podium and said, "Open your books to 119."

The tension blew over, and Layne toggled back and forth from daydreams to copying down like a court reporter what Baca wrote on the dry erase board. He looked at the clock on the wall every five minutes, longing for Friday night to return. Toward the end of class, after twenty minutes of silence in a dark room illuminated by PowerPoint slides, Baca did a double take at something going on in the back of the class. He looked pressurized as he left the podium, and he walked to the back, left corner of the room. Melanie nudged Damon before Baca reached their table.

Baca read Damon's name sign on his table and said, "Balducci, it's way too early to start ticking me off. Sit up straight and get out your pencil and paper. Write this down, because I'm only gonna say it once."

Damon straightened himself in his seat and rubbed his eye.

Baca grew angrier. "Memo, due before class starts tomorrow. Subject of memo: Why I can't stay awake in Agent Baca's class. You will also want to add what your plans are for staying awake in the future. Don't screw with me again, got it?"

"Yes, sir," Damon said, though the tone of the acknowledgement could have been interpreted as facetious.

Baca pointed at Damon and resumed his rant. "Make sure everything in the header is correct. If you don't know what the chain of command is, ask one of your senior classmen. For you, that means you put a lowercase "t" in parenthesis next to BPA, for Trainee."

Layne looked straight ahead and wrote the acronym BPA on the cover of his notebook with a question mark next to it and pointed to it, nudging Schneider. Schneider clicked his pen and wrote Border Patrol Agent underneath the question as Layne nodded.

Preoccupied with his anger, Baca returned to the podium and tried to continue his lesson. He removed the cap from a dry erase pen, then turned back to the class and stated, "When I went through, you had to earn your badge. Now they just sew it in your uniform the day you arrive."

Damon sat upright in his chair waiting for Baca to move on, trainees all around Damon grinned spitefully when Baca returned to the board to demonstrate the proper heading for a trainee memo.

"One misspelled word or missing punctuation and there will be two more memos," Baca warned.

Once dismissed, the class filed silently out of the temporary building. Blair stayed behind without being told to. It was assumed that he had done so in order to apologize to Baca. The white trainees whispered to one another in formation; the conclusion was that it must have been Squad Leader Guillermo who had reported Blair's comments to Baca.

As the bus departed, Damon berated Instructor Baca from the rear seats, loud enough so that everyone on the bus could hear him if they wanted to. Guillermo's name rang out in the tirade, and there was little doubt that it reached Guillermo at his front-most seat by the door.

Damon ranted, "I can't figure out what that mange is on the back of Guillermo's neck." Melanie's voice was distinguishable among isolated laughter. Damon was referring to pronounced acne scars that Guillermo bore from adolescence. Damon carried on: "Guillermo drag-bunted by me in line at the cafeteria the other day after he got his tray. I had to breathe his egg salad fart until the cloud lifted. I couldn't get away from it; I would've lost my place in line."

The laughter only inspired Damon to continue entertaining. "I was trying to hold my breath but I already received it. It was too late; I was gagging. I only breathed twice in about two minutes. I was afraid I would taste it. The guy's a gremlin, man."

Guillermo pretended not to hear it as the white trainees continued to laugh hysterically.

The wind picked up and blew dust across the road as the trainees looked through the windshield to see where they were going. The bus brought them back to the main campus near the PT building and obstacle course, and what looked like an abandoned railroad car. Two men in their sixties were standing, waiting, both in blue jeans and cowboy boots. They were wearing the same navy blue polo that the trainees had been issued in Tucson, but without the cactus emblem. The men looked like the veteran agents the trainees had heard about.

The trainees dismounted and formed up for Operations Class. After the instructors introduced themselves, the class followed them toward the train car. They settled near a smooth dirt strip the size of a long jump pit.

"I need one volunteer," said the instructor who had identified himself as Agent Marshall. The pair appeared wise, like Texas Rangers who had become old men. It was interesting to be in their presence. The second instructor, Agent Garner, stood aside with arms crossed, as his counterpart asked for a volunteer.

Guillermo raised his hand.

"What's your name, son?"

"Jorge Guillermo, sir."

"Go ahead and walk straight across this area here." Instructor Marshall pointed to a strip of dirt the width of the long jump pit. Guillermo walked across and turned around to face the group.

Marshall uncrossed his arms and approached the dirt. "Sign cutting is ninety percent of what you will be doing as an agent, so what we are learning here in Ops 1 is the most important skill you will learn in the Academy. I don't care what your Law Instructor says. All that nonsense will fly out the window as soon as you cut your first group, and it will all come down to whether or not you can track sign. You're gonna learn hundreds of different kinds of visas and other useless stuff. When you get to your stations you will say to yourselves, 'by golly, that old man knew what he was talking about.' You'll probably go your whole career without seeing one document, except for a Mexican identification card that most likely has a fake name on it. Knowing all those documents is for Customs Agents at the Port, not for us."

"Isn't that racial profiling, sir?" Guillermo said.

"No, it's country profiling," Marshall said with a reactionary, off-guard response.

Several in the class looked at one another in disbelief as the instructor recovered his train of thought. He knelt down to look at the prints that Guillermo's sneakers had left on the dirt.

"After a fresh drag you will be able to tell if a grasshopper walked over this. After twenty years I could cut a group and be able to radio ahead to somebody two miles north and let him know where a group was gonna cross to within a one-hundred-yard section of road."

The trainees exchanged glances again.

"Now the first piece of information that you want to determine is the age of the print. I can tell instantly if sign is good or if it's too old to follow. Besides dragging a road, Mother Nature resets the dirt with wind and natural erosion. Unless the dirt was wet when the print was made it will only last a few days. If you find a print that's over an hour old, it's probably too late, and whoever made the print is in a van on his way to San Antonio."

Instructor Garner took over. "The next piece of information you need to take from sign is the number of people in the group." He removed an umpire brush from his back pocket and brushed smooth Guillermo's prints from the strip of dirt. Then he said, "I'm gonna turn my back on y'all and I want two or more of you to walk across this strip." Garner turned and walked twenty feet away from the trainees, his back to the group. Damon stepped forward, walked across the strip, and eight other trainees followed him, walking back around the edge of the dirt strip.

"Are you ready?" Garner asked.

The group responded in unison, "Yes, sir."

He returned to the strip, and without kneeling looked at the mess of prints on the dirt for three seconds. The stampede of footprints overlapped one another and looked completely meaningless.

"There were nine of you," Garner said.

Layne resisted the urge to clap, the rest of the group exchanged impressed facial expressions.

Marshall continued. "The next piece of information you want to determine from sign is the direction. Most of the time a group will continue in the same direction as they crossed. But when you cut a group, you want to follow it for about fifty yards north of the initial cut before you radio ahead. Usually it's not an alien's first time to cross, and they will maneuver to try and throw you off."

Marshall paused to let the information resonate, and some heads nodded.

"Now, the aliens or their guide will do something that we call brushing-out. After they cross dirt that leaves prominent sign, they will double back and cover their tracks by rubbing them out with a stick or something. The problem is they can't continue to brush-out their tracks the whole time they're moving; it takes too long. And when you get some experience you will be able to spot brush-outs just as easily as footprints; they'll be obvious to you."

Marshall knelt down and with the palm of his hand he brushed out half of the prints and left the other half remaining untouched. "Y'all get the picture?"

"Yes, sir," the trainees responded at once.

"Now, Instructor Garner and I are gonna show you all how we check different kinds of transportation, like trains."

The group followed them to the train car and the instructors climbed in, grunting with the effort, and told the trainees to follow. Once inside, Garner resumed: "It depends on where you're stationed, but some of you will be checking both stationary and moving train cars. What I mean is, you might be riding on a train to its next stop, because you won't have time to check every car while it's stationary."

This was the most practical lesson, so far, Layne thought. He noticed that all the trainees were focused on Garner's explanation.

Garner continued. "It's common sense that you don't walk into any kind of room without cutting the corners first. If you just walk in blind, someone can hit you over the head with something. You'll learn in PT that you never turn your back on an alien. That's rule number one." He glanced over at his partner, who smiled and nodded his head, having heard the coming story before. "I was checking a train in Big Bend one time, when I was about ten years in. There were three aliens aboard and the train was moving, about twenty miles per hour. I turned my back for a second and an alien pushed me out. I was so ticked; I radioed ahead and tried to get the train stopped, but by the time we got it stopped these guys had jumped off."

It was evident that the memory remained vivid from the way Garner clenched his jaw.

"It's probably better that we didn't find that guy," Garner added.

He looked at his watch. "Alright, your bus will be here in five minutes. Squad leader, get your group in formation and ready for the bus."

The sun heated Layne's face as the trainees knelt to climb down out of the car. He was overtaken by a fantasy as they marched back to the bus stop. Garner's story added a cinematic element to his conception of what it would be like to be an agent. He visualized himself as the hero of his own train car scene—those back home would be so overtaken by the glamour that they would be speechless. Women would be shy in his presence. The feeling faded quickly as he looked up at the sun swirling its heat; the fear of PT caused reality to set back in.

12

LAYNE FELT A SENSE OF ACCOMPLISHMENT; one week under his belt and their uniforms had arrived faster than usual. He examined his reflection in the mirror and grinned at the image he projected in the green rough gear. He turned to the side to view how the duty belt and its utilities appeared from another angle. When he looked in his own eyes, he communicated the secret with himself—he had infiltrated; he felt like an impostor. But he shook off the thought and swapped his morning books for those he needed for the afternoon and zipped his backpack, heading to the cafeteria.

The silent roommate, Cabrera, had packed his bags, so there was one less body in the room. It was a secret that the three remaining roommates had sworn to keep to themselves in hopes that administration wouldn't discover the vacancy and fill the spot.

His Spanish class had given him confidence. His facility with language was a valuable asset; he knew after the first class that Spanish would be a rout, requiring minimal effort, even amongst the *Nativos*. In addition, the instructor, Agent Nunez, was a former computer techie who had left the corporate world for a career with the Border Patrol. He was turning out to be a soft touch. Ops 1 was a tap-in putt, which meant there were two classes he could brush aside. But the first day of PT was Monday. He rarely made it through an hour without terrifying visions surfacing about Stacking and OC. But today was Friday, and Friday was a long way from Monday. On Friday night he was capable of saving his worries for another day. Anticipation of weekend revelry always sustained him through the week with thoughts of a temporary escape from routine.

In the cafeteria buffet he filled his tray with more food than he could eat, more mashed potatoes instead of salad, and chocolate milk in addition to his orange flavored drink. He searched the sea of green uniforms and eventually noticed Runyon, then Carlos. He smiled big and they acknowledged him with a grin and a nod.

"What are you so happy about?" Runyon said as Layne straddled the bench to sit.

"It's Friday."

"Are we getting it on tonight?" Carlos asked.

"Is that a rhetorical question?" Layne retorted.

They all laughed.

"You look good in your uniform," Runyon said.

"Do you find me attractive, Runyon?" Layne felt jubilant, his hangover from the weekend before a distant memory.

"Screw you," Runyon said.

As Layne took his silverware out of his napkin, he noticed trainees from Class 542 entering the cafeteria wearing real Motorola radios, the microphones clipped to the epaulets on their shoulders. His mood declined and leveled off. The radios were a sign that the veteran trainees were in the final stages of Ops 2 training, only a week away from graduation. These trainees carried themselves differently, knowing at this point the only obstacles that lay in their way were written tests, hardly a threat for most if they had made it this far. They had survived Stacking and OC; the tribulation and uncertainty was behind them. Half of their class had been fired for failing a class or had resigned just before they had to face Stacking and pepper spray. Layne had been paying attention to the grapevine, and reasons for resigning were always the same: "Family obligations" or the plain admission that the Border Patrol wasn't for them.

"Man, I hope I don't look bad in Stacking when it comes." Layne had spoken his thoughts out loud again.

"I don't care if they hogtie me in front of the whole Academy, as long as I graduate," said Melanie's friend Greg. Layne was surprised to hear him speak up; he seemed to have made himself anonymous on purpose throughout the week. Layne only knew his name because he was also in Spanish Group 2. The others at the table observed him, waiting for him to follow up his comment with an explanation. But Greg looked embarrassed that he had spoken aloud and looked down to continue eating half a grapefruit with a spoon. The first thing Layne had noticed was he wore extraordinarily large boots for his height; his feet looked cumbersome when he walked. He was frail with boyish looks, only about five foot six, and approximately twenty-five years old with sandy blond hair in a buzz cut. His taciturn demeanor seemed to come from a lack of confidence around peers. But it appeared that he had become fast friends with Melanie; they were becoming inseparable, which Layne found strange.

"What are we doing tonight?" asked Runyon, maintaining his status as social coordinator.

"Getting trashed," Carlos said, as he and Layne and most of the table stood up to leave.

They agreed to meet in the courtyard after the last class. And the minute Layne hopped off the bus at 4:15, he gripped his backpack straps and raced back to his room, took off his uniform, grabbed a towel, wrapped it around his waist, and turned on the shower. Refreshed to be in shorts and sandals again, he put on his deodorant in two quick strokes. He sprayed a fine mist of cologne on his neck—there might be local girls and waitresses at The Wildcat, their agreed-upon location for dinner that evening.

Damon had been at the Academy long enough to have made a weekend trip to retrieve his vehicle, a compact pickup truck, and offered to drive. Being that he was one of the few trainees in the class with a vehicle on base, they agreed to overlook any qualms about his behavior in public and decided to tolerate his company in exchange for a ride.

Layne braced himself in a rear corner of the pickup bed, as the wind disheveled his hair.

"One week down!" Runyon yelled to him from the other corner of the truck bed.

"Fifteen to go!" Layne yelled back to him.

Damon parked at a meter, The Wildcat just around the corner. Downtown Artesia looked different than it had six days earlier; it was no longer threatening. The warm summer evening seemed to welcome them to their first Friday night in the Academy. They walked swiftly, the way they had in downtown Tucson the weekend before.

Once inside The Wildcat, a high school-aged Latina hostess showed them to a table and Damon gestured to her buttocks and gave a thumbs-up while her back was turned. Layne realized it probably wasn't a good idea to be seen in public with him, but they had no choice if they wanted to go anywhere outside the base. The restaurant had a pleasing steakhouse ambiance that Layne enjoyed, and was filled with a haze of delicious-smelling beef smoke. Hopefully none of the instructors ate here. The waitress arrived to take their drink order and removed her notepad and pen from her apron.

"Coors Light," Damon said, and she jotted down his order on her pad. Damon smiled deviously and asked, "*¿te gusta mi bigote?*" Damon was growing a highway patrol mustache and was trying to convince the others in his crew to do the same. He had been asking people if they liked it in Spanish since the group assembled in the courtyard. It was the first phrase he had memorized in class. The waitress rolled her eyes, already seasoned enough to have put up with more than her share of trainee nonsense. She looked at the premature blond stubble and said, "You don't have a mustache."

Damon laughed and said, "I just learned that this week."

She laughed a little with a smile as her pen awaited the next drink order.

Layne tried not to be obvious about noticing her low-cut top or the way her dark hair shone in the lighting of the dining area. The trainees were already feeling the effects of being deprived of interaction with women. Layne ordered a Coors Original—The Banquet Beer, a beverage designed for occasions such as this. He decided that it was reasonable to have one with dinner; two was his limit.

When the food and drinks arrived, Layne cut into his ribeye and its juicy flavor was accentuated by a week of cafeteria food. He chewed it more than necessary to extract every bit of taste. He took a sip from his frosty glass of beer as he chewed and looked at the others eating their steaks. They looked even happier than they had at The Memphis Queen in Tucson.

"Can you guys believe what a dipstick Baca is? It took me four hours to write that memo," Damon said.

"You better quit tweaking him. You don't want to go to your station with a stack of negative memos," Runyon said.

"You can't keep a good man down," Damon said as he prepared his baked potato with the usual butter, sour cream, and bacon bits.

Before he realized that he was offering too much information about himself, Layne asked Damon a revealing question between bites of his steak. "When they asked you what drugs you tried on your SF-86, what did you tell the investigator?"

"I told him I never tried any," Damon said while he cut his steak and chewed.

"And that's true?"

Damon laughed. "I've stayed up for a week straight before on crystal meth. After about the sixth day I started hallucinating. I finally crashed and slept for two days."

His dinner companions looked at one another.

The quiet caused Damon to follow up. "Why would you tell them you tried anything? There was no lie detector test." Layne realized Damon was right; he spent too much time worrying about things that were out of his control. What a waste of time it was worrying about all those things for so long. He pulled at the last gulps of his second beer as the four of them coordinated the check.

Back at the Academy, the gate rose and the Campus Police in the booth waved Damon through. Layne lounged against the corner of the truck bed and his head swayed backwards slightly with the relaxation of a beer glow as Damon accelerated onto the base. The night sky was a few ticks away from becoming completely dark. He felt completely alive, surrounded by new people in a new environment on a summer night. It was as if one could tell that it was Friday night simply by the climate and the energy in the atmosphere. Layne looked up at the stars; they were much more vibrant above a small town. Everything felt new and foreign. Damon parked and stretched as he got out as Layne and Runyon straddled the tailgate to dismount.

"Sandy's?" Runyon suggested to the group.

Everyone agreed, but Layne was indecisive as he reminded himself of his personal vow. The mild buzz from the two beers at dinner was fading; he despised the groggy comedown from only a few drinks. The only way to bypass it was to go to sleep. He prepared himself mentally to return to his room and watch a DVD movie and doze off. It would be nice to enjoy the freedom from worry—worry about issues that often developed as a result of the weekly carousel. *I'll be proud of myself and glad on Monday*, he thought. When he committed himself to something his volition was impressive; like how he made it through the hiring process to get here. His mind continued to operate and weigh options even though he had already told himself he had made a decision. He looked at his feet while he walked.

The group could hear commotion coming from the dorms and the courtyard as they approached campus from the parking lot. It sounded like a riot from a distance. When they turned the corner, Layne skipped a stride in near disbelief. The courtyard was illuminated by temporary lights and occupied by hundreds of trainees holding red keg cups while music blasted from six-foot tall speakers. Trainees in shorts and flip flops were mingling, drinking, and playing sand volleyball and horseshoes. He looked to his right to the balcony of his dorm complex, now a convivial debauch, people elbow to elbow, leaning over the railing with beer cans, yelling. It looked like Bourbon Street during Mardi Gras. It was madness. *I can't believe they allow this,* Layne thought.

"Did any of you guys get beer?" Layne said to his companions.

"Me and Runyon went and got supplies last night. We took the bus to Walmart and got two cases," Carlos said.

Layne thought for a moment. If he stayed in his room, he would be the only one on campus to do so, and Ricky and his friends were moving in and out the door. It would be impossible to sleep with this noise. It looked as though the Government expected them to party on weekends, and encouraged it. He was just an Average Joe here.

"Can I have a few? I'll pay you back," Layne said. "I think Ricky has some, too."

"Sure," Carlos said.

Layne climbed the stairs in a flash, weaving through the crowd on the second level to get to his room. He ran into Ricky on the balcony; he looked like he was already halfway drunk. Ricky was happy to see him; his eyes were red and watery, and he yelled and cheered with his arms raised when he saw Layne coming.

"Can I get a beer from you? I'll pay you back tomorrow?" Layne threw his rules to the wind, reasoning that he had a tendency to overthink and exaggerate things. He reasoned that no one could be expected to abstain from a festival of such splendor. To be here at this place in time was a once-in-a-lifetime experience; the only thing to do was enjoy it.

"Ice chest in our room," Ricky answered, motioning his head over his shoulder in the direction of their room.

Layne finished the can of beer on his way to Runyon's ground floor room, and when he entered, Runyon handed him another from his own ice chest. "Hey, hold on Sheppard. You gotta shotgun that beer from Carlos' beer bong, it's the rules."

"You brought a beer bong?" Layne had been afraid to smuggle a can of Copenhagen into the Academy the day they EOD'd.

"Hell yeah," Carlos produced the apparatus from the upper bunk.

Layne got down on one knee and put his thumb over the opening of the tube, while Carlos held the funnel high. Runyon cracked a beer and handed it to Carlos.

"You ready?" Carlos poured the beer into the funnel and the tube filled with beer and air bubbles.

"Burp that hummer," Carlos said.

Layne relieved pressure from the opening and the tube became air free.

"No stopping, muchacho," Runyon said.

Layne put his mouth on the opening and unkinked the hose. The icy beer rushed down his throat, and he began to panic. Both Runyon and Carlos chanted, "Go, go, go." When the tube was empty, Layne dropped it and gritted his teeth, pacing around the room until the sting in his throat subsided.

"Let's go check out Sandy's," Carlos laughed.

The courtyard looked like Spring Break in South Padre Island, with groups of trainees barbecuing in large metal barbecue pits, all with drinks in hand. The three of them wove through the mingling bodies and the heat from the barbecues toward Sandy's. The bar was a beacon of merriment, like the revolving beam from a lighthouse. They could hear the crowd inside roaring from fifty yards away. From a distance it looked like a Mexican cantina south of the border, where gunfighters drank tequila and mezcal.

They were overwhelmed by cheerful noise as Runyon opened the door. Multiple lines, six people deep, waited to order a drink from the blind bartender and his partner. The bartender moved at normal speed, while the woman who helped him streaked back and forth, pouring two beers at once from the taps. Carlos, Runyon, and Layne joined the line to order drinks. The trainees ahead in line were carrying away two beers and holding a shot with their fingers in a triangle shape, concentrating so as not to spill.

"Looks like there's no rules against double-fisting here," Layne yelled to Carlos and Runyon. He was feeling peculiarly mellow despite the chaos. He concluded that he could be a hypochondriac from time to time. Perhaps he had just been surrounded by the wrong people after college; now he had finally found a like-minded group where he fit in.

Some of the trainees passing by with their orders staggered and looked too drunk to communicate clearly. The crowd extended out past the pool tables and out the back doors. Mobs danced with fists in the air on the patio outside, fueled by 70s rock music from large outdoor speakers the height of a man. *I was afraid I was too old for this anymore,* Layne thought as he advanced in line. They were partying with the energy and excitement of high school kids. The scene was taking on a dreamlike euphoria as he watched from his place in line, three people between him and the bar. He wished he could freeze the moment in time and live there permanently. It was perfect, when he was ready to go home he could simply walk to his room and be in bed within minutes. The fear of getting a DUI that usually lingered in the back of his mind was nonexistent here; there was nothing to spoil the experience.

Layne stared in one spot and recalled the countless times he had decided to risk it and try to drive home, praying for empty roads at 3:00 a.m. Inevitably headlights would appear behind him, the focus of his eyes alternating between the speedometer and his rearview mirror. *Please don't be a cop*—the prayer would spin in his mind. When the headlights would close in behind him the rush of adrenaline would almost make him sober. Then, the vehicle wouldn't pass and he would accept the fact that he was caught, only to realize when he reached a stoplight that from a few car lengths away, what appeared to be emergency lights on top of the vehicle were actually ski racks. He would promise himself it was the last time trying to make it, but he would find himself in the same situation again.

His mind wandered again. He knew Blair was watching a movie in his room. To join him now was unthinkable. He couldn't walk away if someone paid him.

Layne concentrated on the pint glasses and shot he was carrying, balancing them in order not to spill a drop. He joined Runyon and

Carlos to stand at a round stool table they had commandeered. Layne was successful in preserving his drinks; he sat them on the table and tossed his shot back.

"Can you believe these teases?" Carlos commented as he surveyed the crowd. The three-percent female population of trainees had spent considerable time preparing for the evening. They were all dolled up, with heavy eye makeup, lipstick, and meticulously woven French twists and bobs. It was difficult not to stare; he could almost smell their perfume and finishing powder from looking at them. The horde of male trainees catered to them and hurried to buy them drinks, surrounding them like a pack of coyotes on Animal Planet.

"You should buy one of them a drink," Layne suggested sarcastically to Runyon as the burn in this throat from the shot subsided.

"Screw that. These chicks are ruthless, teasing us like that," Runyon said, but his eyes were still fixated on one in particular as he complained. Her shoulders were tan beneath the spaghetti straps of her white top. It was torture to look at her.

"I'm just gonna go without for four months, like Ricky was talking about," Carlos concluded.

"If a dude lands one of these chicks, the whole Academy is gonna know every detail," Layne said.

The wisecracks came in rapid fire; quickly, they were bent over with laughter.

Layne felt the pull to get back in line for another round of drinks; his second beer was halfway gone. Staying in his room reading a book seemed ridiculous now. He just needed to not get carried away; just relax, that was all. He couldn't imagine a problematic scenario, except a fight, but the trainees were getting along wonderfully. "I probably shouldn't get too wasted," he said out loud.

"Why not?" Runyon asked.

"I don't know. I planned on just having a few beers," Layne said with remorse.

"It's a little late for that. How many shots have you had?" Runyon said between laughs.

"Two shots of Crown and a Car Bomb. I'm taking it easy," Layne said. They all laughed.

"I got some catching up to do," Carlos said.

"Screw it," Layne reasoned, as much to himself as to the others. "We still got tomorrow night. We can recuperate Sunday."

It's Monday that I dread, he thought, then he blocked out the thought to seize the moment.

13

FELINA PULLED UP AS CLOSE TO THE curb as she could to park. The best spot she could find was two houses down from Marianne's. It was evident that there was a party going on, as an abnormal number of cars were already parked along the street.

Marianne had told her that everyone would start getting there around five, so Felina chose to arrive around 5:30 so as not to be uncomfortably the first one there. She froze momentarily with her thumb and forefinger on the key before she rotated it to turn off the engine. She thought she heard a knocking sound while the engine idled without the sounds of driving to interfere with her ear. The needle on the heat gage was hovering higher than normal. She turned off the engine and told herself not to worry about it today. She looked at her wristwatch; it was 5:39, just about right.

She looked in the rearview mirror to inspect her makeup, and carefully removed a fallen eyelash from the corner of her eye with her pinky and pointer finger. She got out and straightened her jean shorts before she closed the car door. It was May; it would still be another month before stepping outside would feel like opening an oven door. She had on a bikini bottom under her jean shorts and a bikini top underneath her t-shirt. But she hadn't decided whether or not she would reveal her swimsuit unless most everyone was getting into the pool. It depended on who was in there. There were more cars on the street than she expected, all the way to the cul-de-sac at the end of the street, and cars were parked in Marianne's driveway.

She used to look forward to the barbecue pool parties in Tucson. But recently, things that made her smile were becoming fewer and farther between once her aspirations hit a wall. She felt no sense of belonging anymore. She could hear the music from an ice cream truck somewhere nearby. The memories of her carefree youth brought back bittersweet feelings as she walked up the driveway to the front door. Once on the porch, she realized that everyone was out back, and she headed around the house to enter the backyard through the gate in the picket fence.

Felina felt hesitant and self-conscious as her flip-flops snapped in a slow rhythm over the dirt yard. As she navigated her way through the prickly pears and reached for the latch, she considered turning back; no one knew she was there yet. She could hear the splashes of people plunging into the pool in concert with laughter and ebullient sounds coming over the fence from the male voices.

It was uncomfortable arriving at gatherings of this type, being single. She planned to go straight to Marianne and say hello as people watched her come upon them. She had promised Marianne that she would make an appearance. But it was awkward deciding who to just greet and who to hug. Consistent with her culture, her male relatives always hugged her and kissed her on the cheek. But she thought that, in general, people she knew hugged each other too much.

She knew that she should introduce herself to anyone she didn't know, for possible opportunities to network for better jobs. But she knew that she would end up letting Marianne make the introductions. She wouldn't introduce herself to the guys unless the situation cornered her.

Felina struggled with the latch while simultaneously lifting the wooden gate to open the uncooperative fence just enough to squeeze through. She recognized most of the girls sitting at the patio table under the umbrella. They did a double take at her unnatural stride, and she forced a smile. Some of the girls she had once been somewhat good friends with, until their lives had become consumed with "baby dads" and kids. Some of the guys were in the pool throwing a football while others sat in lawn chairs at the edge of the pool with board shorts dripping and silver beer cans in hand.

The girls were barefoot and gossiping at a poolside table while their boyfriends ignored them. They all wore bikinis—although some of them shouldn't have, in her opinion; she told herself she might have to show hers in order to fit in. She would see how it went. She considered who she should mingle with, and who to just say hi to. She was concerned that sometimes she appeared to be rude, even though she didn't intend to be. Some of the couples she had been introduced to, enough to say hello; she knew most everyone's name.

Marianne came around the pool to meet her halfway, and as expected, gave her an excited greeting and hug. The others waved hello but didn't call her by name. Felina waved hello at everyone as a whole, then they quickly returned to their beers and conversations.

Marianne went out of her way to designate a lawn chair for her, and Felina sat down beside her. The discomfort had been quick. She was glad now that she had come; she held dear Marianne's advice and ability to counsel her when she was feeling low or in distress.

"So, how are things?" Marianne asked, the attention on her face confirming the genuine interest for Felina's well-being.

"Oh, they're okay," Felina said as she pushed the cuticle back on her right pointer finger. She noticed that she was unhappy with her nails too.

"Just okay? What's going on?"

"Oh, I'm just in a rut. Work sucks. I pretty much hate my life right now."

"Oh honey, I'm sorry. You should talk to Trisha over there; she's doing loans for Old Pueblo. She's making bank. I bet she could get you on."

"That would be nice, but doesn't she have a degree?"

"I don't think you need one to work there; we'll see. Are you getting close to being ready for Pima?" Marianne was trying to be encouraging and optimistic.

"No, I can't afford it yet; hopefully next year. I don't even know if it's gonna be worth it though, if I can't get into a university afterwards." Felina sounded disheartened.

Marianne didn't respond immediately, and Felina could tell her friend was trying to think of a topic that she would lighten up to.

Felina decided not to undress into her bikini until she had a beer, her boobs were embarrassingly large, and no swimsuit top succeeded in concealing them. Guys would make an effort not to look at them for too long while their female companions were there. And she could never get a good read in the mirror on how her butt looked with this particular bikini bottom. It was too big as well, but she didn't have the willpower to lay off of her mom's beans and tortillas, especially when she was depressed. It was of no consequence as she looked around; there were no guys there she was interested in drawing into a conversation. There were only one or two single guys that she could tell, but she wasn't interested in them. Most of them had children with other women; she vowed never to spend any of her time taking care of another woman's child.

"I'm so sorry about the immigration attorney," Marianne whispered into her ear. She looked at Felina and exaggerated a frown to show that she was sorry.

"It's okay; I'm over it. I wasn't pinning a lot of hopes to it anyway." Felina tried to sound strong, although the heartbreak still remained.

"I don't like you sitting around your little apartment, sulking all the time. You need to get out and do something," Marianne said in a motherly fashion.

"I know. I just have to figure something out," Felina said. "I'm gonna find a way to do it; I can't stand working for much longer."

"You need a boyfriend to split the rent with," Marianne said.

"No, I don't want to get distracted." The guys around the pool were looking at her. She glanced at them and they returned to sipping their beers, pretending to have been looking behind her.

"How is Ryan doing at the Academy? Do you miss him?" Felina asked, trying to change the subject.

"He's hanging in there; I can't wait until he's done. I'm so lonely with him gone. That's why I need to have friends over, to cheer myself up," Marianne admitted.

"Well, it's not that long, and you're gonna be set once he graduates. And aren't you going to New Mexico in July to visit for Family Day?" Felina's envy was apparent in her tone.

"Yeah, I can't wait," Marianne said. She lit up, reminded of something she had been planning to mention to Felina. Marianne looked around to make sure no one was listening, then lowered her voice: "You know what? I meant to tell you. Ryan has some friends that are BP agents now, and they say there's a lot of agents who are married to girls they met when they caught them crossing the border."

Felina looked skeptical. "No way."

Marianne nodded convincingly. "I swear. I guess it's really common, especially in places like Naco and Ajo. There are no girls in those towns that the agents want anything to do with, just trailer trash. And those poor guys are so lonely; there's nothing down there."

Felina was listening, but she didn't understand what it had to do with her. The women she was speaking of were living in Mexico. She remembered what the attorney told her about having lived here illegally for so long.

"I guess the guys are so happy. Those women are so grateful; they take such good care of those guys," Marianne explained.

"I can't believe the agents would do that. How is that allowed?" Felina asked with skepticism.

"They meet the girls when they are detaining them, then they start going into Mexico to visit them on their days off," Marianne said, letting out a little laugh.

Felina stared at the people in the pool trying to float on a big beach volleyball while she pondered. "But how's that legal?"

Marianne nodded assuredly. "The agents put in for a fiancée visa for them and the girls come to live with them once it's approved. The girls go to the American Consulate and get a Green Card and apply for residency. Once they tie the knot, the women are citizens."

"But the women would have an immigration record if the agents met them when they were in jail," Felina said with confusion.

Marianne shrugged. "I don't know, but they do it. I guess it's kinda common at those little stations. Lots of guys are happily married to them. Not so much here, because the Tucson Station Agents live up here and work in Sasabe."

"But theirs is the opposite situation as mine," Felina said, trying to understand her point.

"I don't know; the agents make good money. I was just thinking you could hook up with one of them and maybe he could pull strings for you or something," Marianne said, realizing that Felina's skepticism was valid.

Felina disguised her aggravation; Marianne's optimism was ill-informed. Besides having studied the immigration process, Felina considered it to be common sense that no one could pull strings to have someone's immigration status changed. Even those who went about it properly had to wait years, even decades before their cases were reviewed. There was a backlog that would be miles long if the applicants were physically waiting in line. Only a high-ranking official in the federal government, like the Secretary of State, could break the rules and grant citizenship to someone, especially a criminal.

Marianne took a big pull from her longneck beer. She could tell that her suggestion only further discouraged Felina. They smiled at each other while they were quietly mulling over new topics for discussion.

Felina put on her sunglasses and took in the scene of a few couples and their attitudes toward one another at the pool. They looked like they were pretending to be happy while in public, but it was evident that they argued continually. The two couples who had brought their small kids looked like their relationships had completely changed once they became parents, like they were handcuffed to one another. The girls looked like the high school puppy dog love had worn off and they despised the child's father now.

The couples that were taking responsibility were tolerating one another for the benefit of their child. But at least they tried. Most guys from Tucson disappeared, and the mother had to track them down for child support. She had sworn not to have kids until she was married and established, ideally if she was out of college and financially secure, hopefully when she was around 27. Likewise, she vowed never to have kids with someone she didn't want to be with permanently. But part of her was envious, even slightly jealous, at the sight of the young mothers.

Felina turned to look at Marianne when she said, "You should totally come to our party over Labor Day, though. Ryan is graduating in the middle of September and he's inviting some of the guys from his class. We're having a barbecue."

"That would be fun," Felina said. She tried to sound enthusiastic out of gratitude toward the invitation. But she was already thinking of an excuse in advance why she couldn't make it.

"Yeah, his classmates from Tucson Sector have to use the three-day weekend to find a place to live," Marianne said.

"Oh, cool," Felina muttered. She knew what Marianne was getting at, but she was not interested. The socioeconomic situation in Tucson made it hard to find guys with a future, who earned a good salary. Living with one of them might solve her financial difficulties temporarily; she might be able to go to Pima to get her prerequisites out of the way. But the arrangement would fall short of fulfilling her objective. She still wouldn't be able to attend the U of A without a Green Card.

Marianne became restless, unable to think of something to say that would cheer her up. "Let me get you something to drink; I'll get you a beer," Marianne said as she stood up.

"Okay," Felina smiled politely. She stared at the pool and wouldn't look at the guys who she could feel staring at her. She wanted nothing to do with them; they would lead to the lifestyle she was trying to avoid.

She could tell that they were waiting for her to take off her shorts and t-shirt. She would leave her clothes on. She elected to finish the beer that Marianne was fetching then say that she had something pressing that she needed to attend to.

LAYNE WOKE UP SUNDAY ON HIS BUNK, wearing only his boxer shorts and socks. Ricky was asleep on his stomach, facing the wall, and he could hear Schneider snoring beneath him. The bone-dry heat circulated pain through his limbs and was filling a reservoir in his stomach. There was an unbearable, nagging pain in his core combined with indigestion that caused him to belch sweet acid and sweat. He climbed down slowly, painfully from the bunk. Ricky turned over but didn't wake up. Layne unzipped his backpack carefully and reached in and pulled out two warm cans of Coors Light, quickly wrapping them in a towel.

In the bathroom, he turned on the shower and flushed the toilet to camouflage the sound of the tops cracking. Streams of water penetrated to his scalp as he finished the first can, the suds tasted completely different warm. He sat it down on the shower floor and picked up the second can, pouring the relief effort in gulps. Despite the taste, the beer spread soothing warmth throughout his body in coalition with the hot water from the shower head. It rounded off the edges of the pain and reduced the feverish toxicity to a tolerable level.

Saturday night had been a stepped-on rerun of the first night, an attempt to recapture the sensation he felt when they first arrived back on campus after dinner at The Wildcat. But only a small number of the trainees had shared his enthusiasm to chase it. The majority seemed to have had enough from the night before. It was already 10:00 a.m.—the Sunday afternoon blues were closing in fast.

By afternoon, the loathing of a looming Monday drained the last sands of happiness from the hourglass, and he felt the day already creeping toward an impending dusk. The morning medicine had long worn off. For now, the entire population on campus was either sleeping off a hangover or sitting on plastic chairs on the balconies, wearing basketball shorts and flip-flops, polishing boots, quietly. He went outside to stand next to Ricky, who was recovering slowly himself on the balcony. They leaned side by side on the railing overlooking the courtyard and the pool.

"I better polish my boots," Layne said, rubbing his stomach.

"Are your pants and shirt ironed?" Ricky asked.

"Not yet."

The thought of ironing his uniform was depressing; the Academy seemed like so much more of a grind than it had on Friday.

"Make sure the crease in the front of the pants and on the sleeves looks like a fold in a piece of paper. Use lots of starch," Ricky advised.

"I'm worried about running in PT," Layne said. Since little league football he had been afraid of being forced to run and not being able to stop when he needed to.

Ricky nodded in agreement. "I know what you mean; I played football in Texas." But the thought didn't seem to hit him as hard as it did Layne.

Before Layne knew it, he was standing in formation, waiting for the bus on Monday morning. He could barely speak a word. He could only answer questions, barely able to manage short sentences while immersed in the malaise. Those around him spoke to others instead when they realized he wasn't in the mood to talk. He told himself he couldn't afford to fall back into this habit. His existence felt aimless. He resolved that it was the last time he got smashed two nights in a row, no matter how enticing it seemed. For now, he would just have to gut it out.

Every activity down to lacing his boots would require extra effort for the next few days, like duties for an astronaut in a space suit. To comprehend that it was Monday morning was like facing the rack. The sickness felt like a strange influenza combined with mild depression and paranoid anxiety. He couldn't show himself evidence otherwise; nothing could make him laugh or even crack a smile. His advantage in Spanish and firearms felt irrelevant now. It was imperative to his survival that, from here on out, he steer clear of Damon and anyone else like him. He would surround himself with people like Blair, without alienating Runyon and Carlos.

The squad leaders, Guillermo and Osborne, faced their squads and chatted to kill time while the class waited for their buses to separate them. Layne took mild comfort in making small talk with Blair, who seemed to sense something was wrong without making it public. For Layne, chatting with Blair had a calming effect.

"What did you do all weekend?" Layne gathered his strength to ask.

"I just watched a few DVDs and studied Law. I got my uniforms ready. All three sets are ironed so I don't have to mess with them until Wednesday." Blair looked primed and enthusiastic—the way Layne wished he could feel.

"I wish I would've hung out with you all weekend," Layne said with sincerity that Blair could read. Layne didn't feel the need to keep his guard up around him, for some reason; something in Blair's disposition urged Layne to speak the truth to him.

"Did you drink too much?" Blair asked.

Layne considered that he might already be earning a reputation as someone who went over the top, even amongst a sea of heavy partiers. Matt had warned him to try to remain anonymous amongst the gossip.

"Yeah, I shouldn't have drunk as much as I did. I don't feel too good today," Layne admitted.

"You're welcome to hang out with me on Friday and Saturday night if you want," Blair offered.

The thought of laying low and preparing for Monday all weekend was immensely appealing at this moment. If only he could make himself feel that way on Friday.

"I might take you up on that," Layne said.

Blair nodded.

"You think everything is alright with Baca?" Layne asked to change the subject.

Blair reacted uncomfortably in remembrance of Baca's Target comment. Despite being the straightest arrow in Class 590, Blair was already all over Baca's radar. "Yeah, I talked to him. You've got to be careful what you do and say around here. Guillermo tells Baca everything he hears."

"I know," Layne said. He was lucky he hadn't said anything negative about anyone, except maybe Damon.

Layne whispered, "Do you think Guillermo tells Baca what the Mexicans do and say, or just us?"

"I don't think so," Blair whispered back. "I think he just tells on the white guys. I wish we had Osborne instead; he's cool."

Blair changed the subject into a normal tone as the bus arrived to take the group to PT. "Are you ready for PT?"

"No, but what choice do we have?"

On Friday PT hadn't seemed like the doom that it did today. With regret he remembered having said "screw it" to himself. "Screw it" was a foolish thing to say, he realized, as ludicrous as saying, "it is what it is." He should've run around the track on his own Saturday and Sunday. He had been hoping that it would be overcast today. The sun made the sky glow blue. It looked like it was just waking up, ready to be relentless. It would be unforgiving when it reached its zenith.

After the short ride, Osborne counted heads for his half of the class as they disembarked, then said, "Hey, Damon, how was Juarez?"

Damon had invited Layne to come with him to Mexico, and from what he had already heard about Damon's Saturday night in Juarez, he was glad he had declined.

"I killed it," Damon gloated, inviting more interest.

Damon seemed as energetic and obnoxious as usual, despite his long weekend.

"What did you guys do?" Osborne asked.

"Just beatin' up guts," Damon bragged.

The white trainees, including Melanie, laughed. Damon had ended up spending Saturday night in Mexico with a trainee named Vallon from Class 548. Vallon was the only trainee he could convince to join him on the road trip. It was nice to have a break from Damon for one night. The class's first paycheck had been electronically deposited on Friday, and Damon let everyone know he was headed 200 miles to the border to spend a good portion of his on prostitutes. Damon had to search far and wide for a travel companion; the trainees at the Academy were forbidden to visit Mexico. Baca had specifically warned Class 590 the previous Friday.

Osborne asked, "Was she hot?"

"One of them was okay, but the other two were bush pigs."

Laughter burst out and Layne began to squirm over the subject matter in the presence of so many likely detractors. To him, the conversation implied that Damon considered the country of origin for half of the class to be utilized solely as a receptacle for depravity. Damon had become accustomed to spending tax dollars on drugs and hookers during his time spent on leave in the Navy. He considered the Academy's location near the border to be an opportunity to treat the weekends like leave at an Asian port.

"How many did you do?" Osborne asked with unimpeded intrigue.

"Two Saturday night and one yesterday. I was gonna do two yesterday, but I was drained."

Damon spoke with a straight face, but some of the white trainees laughed hysterically. Others, including Layne and Blair, refrained amidst the awkwardness. Damon continued with unprintable commentary.

Layne cringed at Damon's shipyard mouth; he wanted to hide. Melanie and the Hispanic girl in Group B, Lupita Gorda, from the Valley, were just as present as everybody else. He surveyed the angry expression on the faces of the trainees from the Valley.

Osborne caught his breath. "How much did you drop?"

"About three hundred bucks. We went to the bars, too, though. I learned more Spanish—*cuanta cuesta la Panocha?* I might be conjugating the verb wrong and I'm still polishing my pronunciation, but it translates to how much does it cost? I should be ready to move up to Group One with all the *Nativos* pretty soon."

The Hispanics weren't laughing. Damon's insolence was appalling to those with common sense. But Osborne kept on. "How many did Vallon do?"

"Two, I think. We were screwed up. Vallon got this one with a cast on her ankle. He said he was resting it on his shoulder when he had her in the buck." At that, Damon had to laugh himself.

"He should've signed the cast after he paid her," Osborne said.

The laughter escalated again. Layne and Blair looked at one another in disbelief.

Osborne tried to become serious, "Did anyone come up with a class motto? Baca is gonna ask us again today. We gotta come up with something like the other classes, like 'Class 590, nowhere to run, nowhere to hide, Class 590 beaming with pride.' Something like that; it doesn't matter if it sucks, we just gotta have something tomorrow. I don't wanna tell Baca we don't have anything."

Damon responded with an off-color suggestion in the spirit of the moment, and it was greeted with scattered laughter.

The Hispanic trainees whispered to one another, wearing angry scowls, then the class spotted Instructor Baca coming and they straightened their formation and all stood at attention. Baca arrived to stand before the class without a word. He looked angry, as usual, but he glared specifically at Damon for a long moment.

* * * *

THE SUN SCORCHED THE GROUND FROM a cloudless sky as Group A marched in formation to the PT building from the bus stop. Two PT instructors were waiting for them outside the double-door entrance of the building. The trainees stood motionless facing the building in two columns, still unsure of what to expect. In close formation the group smelled like sunblock. Their foreheads and arms cooked for five minutes before they all were guided inside, single file, in absolute silence.

The PT building was a wide-open, domed edifice with high ceilings and an ice-cold linoleum floor. One by one the trainees were issued another PT shirt, two pairs of green gym shorts, and three pairs of old style gym socks with two green stripes at the top. Layne peeked ahead to the front of the line, where trainees were also being issued a green plastic canteen and given a piece of athletic tape to print their name and class number with a black marker. Each in turn applied the tape to the canteen and passed the marker.

After everyone had been issued a locker and combination, one of the instructors commanded, "You've got five minutes to be in mat room number six in your PT shirt, your PT shorts and socks and running shoes. Do not forget to bring your canteen and DO NOT wear a watch."

Layne felt queasy as he walked toe to heel on the concrete bench between the lockers to get to his bottom locker, a continuance of the self-inflicted fever that had begun Sunday afternoon. There was no room to get by, and he had to wait until Blair and another trainee were done dressing before he could reach it. He looked at his watch, which barely reminded him to remove it. Agitated, he spun the combination dial with care; time didn't allow for him to overshoot any numbers. While trainees hurried out of the locker room carrying their canteens, he put on his PT uniform in a rush and wished he were in Group B, sitting comfortably in Applied Authority.

He also wished he could turn back the clock on his weekend bender. He would be absolutely sure to be prepared next week, something he had sworn to do before he got here. It was too late for regrets.

Once inside mat room six, he was overwhelmed by the smell of wrestling mats. The two PT instructors stood ten feet apart at the front of the class. They wore the same shirts as the trainees, but with coaching shorts. The first instructor introduced himself as Agent Ramirez. Layne put him at about five-foot-eight and forty years old with what looked like two percent body fat, a distance runner's body, and a shaved head. He looked like a Mexican gang member without tattoos. The other instructor, Agent Pyatt, was six feet tall—Layne's height, but twenty pounds heavier and roughly the same age as Ramirez. He looked like a gym teacher. They assembled the class into three rows, and everyone stood quietly, awaiting further instruction.

Instructor Pyatt's voice echoed off the walls of the room and escaped into the hallway through the open door. "Get into a pushup position!"

Both instructors and trainees quickly knelt down into a pushup position and waited. Layne's arms and chest quickly strained with the effort of supporting his body weight. He could see veins in his hands pulsing.

"Ready? Down," Pyatt said strictly.

Several seconds passed. "Up!"

"Down!"

The class still moved as one. *He will probably have us do ten reps,* Layne hoped.

"Up!"

By fifteen repetitions, Layne could feel the veins in his neck and forehead bulging, and his arms were beginning to burn and shake from muscle failure. The moaning started with leg raises and escalated as the seconds lingered during planks. Instructor Ramirez interrupted the moaning and yelled, "Shut up! Suffer in silence!"

The pair demonstrated each exercise without the slightest hint of strain.

As the class and instructors repositioned themselves back into a long-sustained, push-up hold, Ramirez said in a compassionate tone, "This is not for everyone. If you feel like you can't continue, just let us know and we'll get you out-processed. It doesn't mean you're a bad person. If you want to do so in privacy, come talk to us after class."

Layne's midsection began to sag, succumbing to muscle failure. He glanced when he could from a push-up position at Instructors Pyatt and Ramirez in hopes of skipping a rep when needed, while the tandem continued to call out the count of each push-up. He was already in survival mode. Just when he thought he might be able to slack, when the instructors were focusing on someone in the back row, they switched exercises and began jumping jacks.

"We're going to work in here until the walls sweat," Pyatt declared. And they did.

It was noticeable through peripheral vision that one trainee in the middle row on the other side of the room stood out from the rest, flailing to his own beat. Layne snapped a look and realized it was Blair. When his legs formed a Y shape at the end of the first half of a repetition, his arms were at his hips. And when he jumped, his arms and legs came together into a diving position. Blair looked around desperately to try to sync his rhythm, like a drunken beginner attempting to simulate a line dance by sight.

Agent Ramirez yelled, "Stop!" Everyone halted. Ramirez approached Blair and said, calmly, "What are you doing?"

Blair, drowning in humiliation, responded, "I don't know, sir."

"What's your name?"

"Blair, sir."

"Do a jumping jack, Blair," Ramirez said.

Blair attempted a jumping jack and it still came out wrong despite his effort to correct it. Agent Ramirez let out an accidental laugh, then forced himself to be serious again. He assisted Blair slowly with the timing of the exercise, as everyone watched and tried not to smile. When Instructor Ramirez was confident that Blair could perform as needed, he let him do a series of ten on his own, like a dad pushing his boy on his first bicycle. Then he returned to his position with Instructor Pyatt at the head of the class and the tandem resumed exercises.

Just when Layne thought he could not lift himself off of the mat for one more bodybuilder, the instructors reassembled the group into two columns in the hallway. Ramirez disappeared, and Instructor Pyatt began to lead the column toward an exit.

Twenty-five pairs of running shoes squeaked and echoed off the temple-like ceilings. There was still no cloud cover and the midday June sun reheated the sunburn on his forehead and forced Layne to squint his eyes. They moved in step toward the outer fences of the compound. He had hoped that the timing of the background investigation would have put him here in autumn; instead he was surrounded by the heat of summer dawn. He forced himself to accept that the baking fireball overhead would compound the pain exponentially.

The track was a dirt route that hugged the anti-climb fence of the perimeter. He could barely make out a turn in the chain link and barbed wire far in the distance, at what looked to be a mile away. Another class was finishing its run of the perimeter, carrying model M4s and shotguns made of the same orange rubber as the pretend pistols. Instructor Pyatt led the two columns farther toward the end of the reprieve, and their feet left concrete and began to grind on dirt. Layne followed the trainees in front of him at the mercy of his captors, like a prisoner of war. The trainees took drinks from their canteens, then decided which hand to carry them in.

Instructor Pyatt yelled, "Okay, double-time!"

The group began to move much faster, and Instructor Ramirez swung around next to the two columns in a green John Deere Gator vehicle. He briefly stayed in pace with the middle of the column where Layne was, then he accelerated and performed a whipping U-turn and settled at the rear of the columns. The sound of the Gator's engine drowned out the sound of his own breathing for a moment.

"What's that golf cart for?" Layne said to the trainee next to him between breaths.

"If you fall too far behind, they drive you to the front. That's what that little truck bed in the back is for."

They could hear Instructor Ramirez yell from behind them, "If you feel that you can't carry on, just fall out. You can relax back here, and I'll take you to Building 26 to be out-processed. But there's no stopping."

Layne tried to put the Gator out of his mind, but the horror of being trapped hurt with each step. In ten minutes, he knew he would be unable to muster the strength to glance at a bad car accident on the road next to them if they passed directly by one. "I bet we'll stop at that turn in the fence," he muttered to no one in particular.

The separation between trainees was already beginning to stretch, as those in better shape passed those who hadn't trained for the run at all before arriving. Layne had jogged in Colorado, but not enough. He began flowing with sweat prematurely as the toxins sought escape through his pores. He knew he should've run more before arriving here. The weight of the full canteen he was carrying had begun to wear on him. He looked ahead in agony and great hope at Instructor Pyatt, who was approaching the left turn, but his hope was obliterated as Pyatt took the turn without breaking stride.

Recollections of suffering from forced runs in high school and college resurged with the desperation in his lungs and the cramps in his calves that concentrated themselves in his Achilles tendons. He had already fallen back several more places in formation. Four trainees in front, who had made the turn in stride, proudly trotted like show ponies behind Pyatt in the distance. Layne was in too much pain to muster jealousy or hatred or shame, as a few more from behind passed by him among the heavy breathing.

"If you stop running, you quit!" Ramirez yelled from the Gator.

A piercing side ache stabbed through Layne, and the sweat from his forehead allowed him to see out of only one eye at a time. Just as he thought he could possibly die, two-hundred yards past the turn in the perimeter fence, word was passed down from the front of the columns in short breaths: "We are about halfway there." The trainee in front of him gasped to relay the information.

Damon was two trainees ahead and began chanting, "Hey, hey," in an intentionally low baritone voice so that the pain assumed the rhythm of a chain gang song.

"What an idiot," someone cursed under his breath.

As he watched his feet trade off in front of him in agony, Layne battled thoughts of returning to Denver and homelessness. He glanced up to see those in front of him stumble and pour water on themselves from their canteens to extinguish the grease fires on their heads. He attempted the maneuver, concerned that he was spending precious strength unscrewing the canteen cap while trying to maintain speed. When he managed to remove it, bringing water to his mouth caused his bicep to burn and disrupted the timing between his upper and lower body; he tripped but kept from falling. He poured the water on his sun-heated hair and the cold sizzle caused him to skip a breath. But by the time the water flooded to his neck and shoulders it had already reached body temperature and seemed to evaporate on his back instantly.

Instructor Ramirez sped past them in the Gator and dust entered Layne's lungs, causing him to cough. Ramirez was schlepping someone from the rear of the columns that Layne couldn't identify. The trainee appeared to be mortally wounded, curled up in a fetal position in the bed of the Gator, being brought to execution in the front. Don't look at him, Layne told himself as he looked down at his struggling knees and feet.

When they finally reached the second turn, he was sure it had been several miles since they started, and he began to let go of concentrating on the distance. He slipped into a rhythmic, bouncing daydream about his childhood, elementary school playgrounds, and friends long since gone. He thought that perhaps he was hallucinating. To eliminate the weight he carried, he poured the remainder of the contents of the canteen on his head then began alternating the hand that carried it when each bicep failed. He had suppressed all thoughts of stopping for water when he began to believe he was seeing a sanctum in the distance through refracted heat rays fluttering from the dirt path. As the object became more real, he embodied a stranded plane crash victim waving at a rescue helicopter, as he watched those far in the front circling the object in a walking pace.

Finally arriving at the oasis, he joined the carousel of red-faced survivors orbiting a water fountain and struggling for breath with their hands on their heads. It resembled a short version of a circular shower faucet in a gym locker room. The trainees ahead of him in the rotation took turns in sets of two replenishing their canteens, barely able to wait until the sound of the fill reached its peak at the neck of the canteen before they brought life to their lips. But as he walked and watched, he wasn't convinced that the water would relieve his thirst. Walking decreased the pain from running but seemed to aggravate his gag reflexes. He suppressed the impulse to vomit, his strength of will welling from his relief that it was over. They would probably be made to run back to the PT Building, but it was only a few a few hundred yards away.

When his turn came, he bent over and anxiously waited as the stream of water changed tone toward the threading of the green plastic canteen. When he rejoined the carousel, he poured a mouthful and instantly inhaled half of it. Unable to slow his breathing, he coughed and walked and tried again, feeling the hose water flavored liquid travel down his esophagus and settle in his abdomen. When his breathing calmed, he continued to walk. Then unexpectedly, Pyatt yelled, "Line up!"

In disbelief, Layne followed the others as the trainees re-formed their columns to run back along the perimeter in the opposite direction.

Pyatt yelled, "Let's go back. Ready. Double-time!"

15

THE WORN ASPHALT AND YELLOW LINES of the two-lane highway that led from the base to the gun range seemed to be longer than ten miles. The view down the aisle to the driver and the firm feel of the booth-like seats reminded Layne of a field trip in elementary school. The yellow bus slowed and pulled right onto a dirt road, but the diversion from pavement was brief. The driver engaged the brakes slowly, and the tires skidded on gravel as dust rose from the tires up to the open windows. Through the dust cloud the trainees saw a wooden-roofed firing range facing a quarter-mile long bay enclosed by bulldozed mounds of dirt. Rows of targets divided by distances of hundred-yard intervals waited downrange. The dusty range looked junk-ridden, like a movie set where the Road Warrior would practice firing his weapons at rusted car frames.

Five instructors with pistols on their hips were waiting for the bus to arrive. There was no doubt who was in charge—a tall, slender-yet-solid man with a red uniform polo shirt, green Border Patrol hat, khaki cargo shorts, and black boots. Everyone had already heard about "General Lee." His thick, orange, almost Civil War mustache was prominent beneath the blue, swept lenses of his sunglasses, and a whistle on a lanyard hung from his neck. The skin on his arms and legs beneath his shorts down to his boots was red from lack of cover from the sun. The bill of his hat was lower than that of the trainees and his assistants. Hands on hips, he surveyed the evacuation, as the trainees dismounted from the bus, grasping their backpack straps as they hurried down the steps.

The trainees speedily joined in formation on Squad Leader Guillermo's lead. General Lee's assistants, dressed in matching uniforms and standing to his sides, were all trying to look intimidating. General Lee looked tough for real, like Andrew Jackson or a seasoned Texas Ranger. Arms crossed, he ordered the class to sit in the metal bleachers behind the range. Layne scaled the bleachers and sat in shade.

General Lee moved slowly to the front of the bleachers and his assistants settled themselves at his sides. He slowly scanned the group, left to right and back again, then spoke after a long pause. "I've been in the Service for twenty-five years now. The last five in the field I spent with BORTAC. I've been involved in multiple hostage rescues, and I can't even begin to estimate the hours I've spent in underground tunnels, when I didn't know which side of the border I was on."

Layne liked the twang and drawl of General Lee's West Texas voice. Arms still crossed, he paused briefly while gathering himself to continue his address. His gaze fixed on the ground in front of him. His assistants seemed on guard, which prompted the trainees to be, as well.

General Lee continued: "I got lots of rules—I just can't remember them all right now. One of them is that I want all of you to shoot every day in practice like you're qualifying. And don't slam charge the guns. They can go off if you got a bad primer. Don't be like one of these fatsos at my station in Big Bend—clock-punching government workers doing the bare minimum every day, never getting out of their truck to follow sign the whole shift. And don't ever mention the word BORSTAR around me; ridiculous waste of taxpayer money. Rock climbing to get water to stranded Tonks—makes me want to get on my hands and knees and puke. I always kept an extra bullet in my shirt pocket in the field, so if I was ever stuck somewhere, I could shoot myself in the head before BORSTAR could rescue me."

Layne felt his eyes widening and noticed others in the class straightening up to display their undivided attention.

"I like to hear those stories about ranchers shooting holes in the water stations that the earth muffins set up for aliens." General Lee began to pace back and forth slowly, looking at his feet with his arms still crossed.

He tipped the bill of his hat up and wiped his forehead with his arm. "I'm so all over the place today, I can't even think straight. The wife is driving me crazy; I don't even want to go home. I wanna pitch a tent, under this roof here. If I'm not here one morning, it's most likely because I shot her and I'm in jail. If I don't show up, Agent Huston here will take over and lead drills from the speaker box." General Lee pinched the bridge of his nose. He uncrossed his arms and wandered over to a wooden platform with vertical wooden dowels supporting two dozen gorgeous black pistols hoisted with slides retracted, exposing the chamber and barrel of each.

General Lee still appeared to be thinking about something unrelated to class, but commenced because of time constraints. "The Government landed a deal with Heckler and Koch, so y'all will be using the HK P2000 instead of the Beretta we used to carry. You're lucky; these are right out of the box. It's a hell of a gun. Those Germans are evil toy makers. We use the .40-caliber round with this just like we did with the Beretta. This gun is double-action and has no safety, so you don't have to mess with it when you draw. For now, they all stay here. You'll have one assigned to you when you graduate."

General Lee removed his HK from his holster for a visual aid. "This gun is a lot different than the Beretta. The Beretta was a true semi-automatic. With a semi-automatic, when a round is fired, the action ejects the empty cartridge and loads another round into the chamber, and the hammer stays locked back so that just a touch of pressure on the trigger fires the next round. This gun is double action, but not like a revolver. More like a semi-automatic, but the hammer doesn't stay locked back after each shot. When you pull the trigger, the pressure of your finger cocks the hammer just like a double action revolver, so the trigger-pull on the first shot is heavy. And after the first shot if you don't let off the trigger the hammer will stay back. So, the next shot is light on the trigger like a semi-automatic, but with some resistance against your finger. It's tricky, but you'll get used to it. There's what we call a 'speed bump' in the trigger-pull we'll show you how to find."

Layne could smell the guns as his turn in line came to claim his issued pistol. The steel slide of the pistol above the composite handle felt top heavy in his hand without a magazine in it. It was obvious which trainees had not been exposed to guns by their hesitation to touch one when their turn came. His dad had gotten him his first gun on his twelfth birthday, and he had hunted—birds, rabbits, squirrels, deer—for years. He was confident in his shooting ability, and thankful for his years of experience in this important area.

One of the assistants said, "Leave your rubber guns on that table over there. Once you get your gun you need to holster it and come over here."

The trainees were brought to the half of the range designated for pistols. Targets were posted at various distances up to twenty-five yards from the shooter's position. The trainees assembled on the midway concrete platform, fifteen yards away from their individual targets. Assistants shifted from one trainee to the next, tutoring each on how to grip the pistol properly and how to operate the action. The new grip felt awkward to Layne, but he enjoyed holding the pistol. It felt solid yet light in his hands, and the action was tight, flawless. He examined the etched specifications on the slide. The pistol was so attractive that it was hard not to look at, like a Porsche 911; it felt sinister in his hand.

Without magazines in the pistols the trainees performed basic drills, drawing from the holster and aiming at the targets without shooting. The targets were in the shape of a man from the waist up, and they rotated like a shutter: to open for a few seconds, then closed automatically, to create a window of opportunity to shoot. General Lee continued to survey without speaking while the assistants went over a dry run of the different stages of qualifying.

Huston said aloud, "You will be drawing the pistol from the holster almost every round. Everyone go to the five-yard platform and wait for instructions from General Lee."

General Lee's voice came over the loudspeaker. "The first round will be fired from the hip from five feet away without aiming. When the target opens, draw your pistol and fire one shot from the hip."

Trainees loaded full magazines into the pistols and chambered a round. The pistol became instantly heavy. Then they topped off their magazines, replacing the round that had been chambered. They holstered the loaded pistols, closed the safety latch, and stood ready.

"Everyone ready?" General Lee said over the intercom.

Everyone nodded. Layne felt like a gunfighter.

"When the target opens, I want you all to draw the pistol and fire one round before the target closes."

The target snapped open and Layne reached for his pistol, unlatched the lock, and drew. He aimed by feel and the round kicked the pistol upward in his grip and a hole appeared just inches from the bull's-eye. The target closed and he re-holstered the pistol and closed the latch to secure it.

"Move back to your fifteen-yard platform. From this platform you're going to be aiming with the sights and firing three rounds," General Lee explained through the speaker.

The first trigger-pull to draw the hammer back was heavy, as General Lee had described. The target rotated open and Layne drew the pistol quickly, but simultaneously he felt fearful that he might shoot himself in the foot. With arms locked straight the fluorescent dotted night sights to the rear made the matching dot on the front sight easy to find under the bull's-eye. Through the earmuffs, the rounds thumped his eardrums as empty cartridges somersaulted and pinged on concrete. The pistol discharged with a sharp impact against the web of his hand and re-aimed itself after it disposed of the empty cartridge. The action cycled too quickly for the naked eye to see. From twenty-five yards the trainees fired from a barricade to complete the qualification.

When everyone was finished with the first practice qualification, several empty magazines lay on the platform and dozens of spent shell casings were scattered on concrete like popcorn.

"All clear?" General Lee's voice blared from the speakers.

Everyone nodded.

"Approach your targets."

Layne pushed his ear protection forward to his temples and adjusted his clear plastic glasses while the class moved ahead as a wave to score the targets. General Lee came out of the box and surveyed the targets, arms crossed, as he slowly moved from left to right down the firing line. He stopped just past Schneider's platform then backed up.

"Hold up for a minute. Show me your arm," he said to Schneider.

Schneider pretended to be confused and showed General Lee his right forearm. The swept blue sunglasses masked the expression on his face.

"What happened to your arms?" General Lee asked.

"I don't know sir," Schneider replied.

"There's no hair on your arms, like a woman."

Layne looked toward Melanie, who was going about her business, smiling but not looking. Then he thought of Schneider lying on his bunk reading Men's Health, and tried not to laugh. He was one of the show ponies in PT.

General Lee said aloud. "Everybody stop what you're doing. How many arm shavers do we have here?"

Nobody raised a hand.

"Another one of my rules is that I can't have any shaved arms in my class. Bodybuilder or not, it's too gay to be associated with me," General Lee said. The class resumed changing magazines, and General Lee continued to wander slowly to his right. "Unacceptable," he said aloud.

As one of the assistants recounted the bullet holes within the five-ring of Layne's target and tallied them with a marker, Layne sensed silent approval from over his shoulder when General Lee passed by him and stopped briefly. "Well done. You're an expert on your first Qual."

Those who had missed hitting paper with half of their rounds glanced in Layne's direction, curious about why he wasn't being offered any corrective instruction. It's so easy, he thought. He pretended not to notice the faction of Hispanics staring with begrudging looks.

"YOU GOING TO RUIDOSO WITH US, SHEPPARD?" Damon said from across the classroom. Baca was outside, in the middle of the private briefing with the Squad Leaders that he conducted before each class period. The rest of the class was reviewing for the Nationality Law test, pretending not to be interested in the conversation that Damon was making public.

"Who all is going?" Layne asked. He could feel the heat coming to the surface in his cheeks and forehead, embarrassed that everyone was listening.

"Fleming is going. It's just us so far," Damon said.

"Alright," Layne said self-consciously. He was becoming tired of Sandy's and the barbecue in the courtyard.

"Fleming is going so he can play Texas Hold-Em," Damon said. "He thinks he's Matt Damon." The Hispanics were pretending not to be interested but were listening for something to pass on to Guillermo.

"How can he play, he's only twenty?" Layne said as he glanced at Fleming, then cringed and wanted to walk it back.

"He's got a fake ID," Damon said.

Fleming looked up from his study materials at Damon, shaking his head in disbelief that he would announce such a thing.

Layne looked away from Damon to hopefully put an end to the publication of their plans. He rubbed his throbbing shins while he continued to cram. He was worried that he had developed shin splints, a common affliction at the Academy. Concern over the symptoms in his tendons was as serious as worrying about symptoms of the plague. Five days absent from PT meant going home and checking the mailbox twice a day for a year. To imagine repeating a single week was sickening; to imagine repeating a month was unthinkable.

Baca, Guillermo and Osborne came back in and the class became quiet again. Baca handed out the test. As Layne read the first multiple-choice question he considered the possibility that he had been studying the wrong material; he couldn't even narrow the answers down to two possibilities.

The second part of the test was a series of questions involving paragraphs weighed down with dates and information that he initially disregarded as storytelling until he worked toward a solution like an algebra problem. He went back and realized that every word in the paragraph contributed to the answer. When he thought that an answer was obvious, he reread the question. Natalia, who was born in Moscow in 1958, had been arrested for shoplifting in 1979, which he had assumed would disqualify her from gaining citizenship. But he looked on the chart and saw that only a felony would disqualify her. Shoplifting was a misdemeanor, but he had to consider whether or not she had been a "LAPR" (Lawfully Admitted Permanent Resident) for long enough for the crime to even matter. He needed to calculate how old she was and how long she had been in the United States, and how old she was when she was arrested for the misdemeanor.

By the time he was finished converting the paragraph about Natalia into a profile of her on scratch paper, those around him were turning pages. Once he came to a conclusion about her status, he reread the question again to be sure he was satisfied with his answer. Then he noticed that Natalia had been ARRESTED for shoplifting. The text didn't mention that she was convicted. Knowing helplessly that he was wasting more time, he reread the paragraph again and reversed his answer. Then he erased his previous choice more efficiently from the answer sheet, afraid that the computer that read the answers might make note of a bubble that had been filled in mistakenly.

"Five minutes left," Baca announced to the class.

Frantically, Layne began filling in the bubbles to questions that he had never gotten a chance to read. Baca began counting down with pleasure, "Five, four, three, two, one." Layne continued filling in bubbles as quickly as possible, considering which letter he had previously chosen the least amount of times.

"Pencils down," Baca ordered.

Layne tried to put the test out of his mind; he would worry about it Monday when the scores were posted. It was Friday.

There was still twenty minutes remaining in the class period as Baca collected the tests and answer sheets. With the time remaining, he decided to get started teaching the next section in the book. As he wrote on the Dry Erase board the door to the temporary opened and bright light peaked into the classroom. The trainees turned to look and see who the visitor was. An agent from administration in dress uniform and Smokey stood in the doorway, propping the door open with his back. Baca turned from the board with marker in hand and stood waiting for an explanation for the visit without greeting the agent.

When the agent realized that Baca wasn't going to welcome him and ask how he could help him, the agent said, "Can I speak with you in private?"

"I guess," Baca said, in an aggravated tone.

The agent let the door close behind him as he stood to wait outside on the wooden porch. Baca put the cap back on the marker and threw it at his desk. He put on his Smokey as he walked toward the door. "Why not? It's not like I've got anything else to do," he muttered as he stormed toward the door. The trainees waited until the door shut behind him before they began to whisper to each other with curiosity as to the purpose of the interruption.

After several minutes, Baca opened the door and leaned in through the doorway to look around the classroom until he located who he was searching for.

"Estéban, c'mere," Baca ordered.

Ronaldo Estéban was sitting in the rear left row of tables. He pointed to himself with confusion, to confirm Baca was talking to him.

"Yes, you," Baca said.

Estéban put on his hat as he got up and pushed in his chair to head toward the door.

"Wait a minute," Baca stopped him.

Baca turned to communicate something to the agent then leaned back in to say, "Bring your stuff."

Estéban put his books and writing materials in his backpack and threw it over his shoulder and left the room, staring straight ahead with concern as everyone watched him. Baca held the door open for him then let it shut. The trainees within the classroom were quiet now, looking toward their neighbors with alarm.

When Baca came back into the classroom Estéban wasn't behind him, and everyone had the feeling that he wasn't coming back. Baca returned to the board and picked up where he left off, selecting a different colored marker from the tray. The atmosphere within the room had changed. After Baca finished writing for a minute, he put the cap back on the marker and came to the lectern. He was grinning like he had been proven right about something. He said, "If any of you left anything off your background check, or there's something that you should've told your investigator and you didn't, you better pack up."

Layne's heart dropped and a burst of adrenaline raced through his veins, causing an electric tingle to fire down his spine. He hoped the advice Matt gave him so assuredly would withstand this threatened new scrutiny. He'd been dead-level right so far.

Baca continued. "You know, the Border Patrol is gonna pay for this one day. It's gonna come back and bite them, and I'm just gonna sit back and laugh while it's happening. Because of this sudden hiring influx, DHS has a lot of pressure on them to get bodies in this place. It's obvious; you guys are the sorriest class I've ever seen. Maybe three or four of you would have graduated if you went through with my class. For you losers that lied your butts off to get here, I've got news for you."

He looked specifically at Damon. "The hiring center was in such a hurry to get people in here that some of your background investigations aren't even finished yet. So, when you got called up you probably figured you were in the clear, but you're not." Baca smiled and shook his head slowly like waving a finger.

He let out a cynical, brief laugh. "A while back, some trainees got caught smuggling dope in El Paso during their third week on the Field Training Unit. And just the other day the swimming instructor pulled a trainee out of the pool that had an MS-13 gang tattoo. Because of this stuff, DHS decided to reopen the backgrounds of anyone we suspect is a scumbag that was part of the influx. They hired a private contractor that will review your file with a fine-toothed comb. So, if you've got something to hide, I wouldn't be sleeping too good if I were you."

* * * *

LAYNE OPENED HIS EYES, MYSTIFIED BY the clouds traversing the late day sky while his mind oriented itself to where he was. As he came to, he knew instantly that he was in Damon's truck. He recognized the sound the truck made as Damon shifted gears. He sat up and stabilized himself as the truck turned. Then he rotated his torso and, through the rear window of the cab, recognized Fleming's visage in the passenger seat before vertigo forced him back into a fetal position. He could hear the drive shaft spinning beneath the cold metal truck bed. He slid from the cab to the tailgate and back when the truck slowed and accelerated. An empty pint bottle of tequila, missing its cap, was bouncing and vibrating on the truck bed while they were in motion. When the truck came to the gatehouse, the faces of the Campus Police looked down at him and laughed. The gate opened and the drive shaft spun into motion again.

It must be Sunday afternoon, Layne thought. Non-chronological clips of memory came back to him, like pictures being developed. He could remember deciding to go on a road trip two hours away to Ruidoso; the party at the Academy had lost its punch. The mountain resort had attracted him with its allure of exotic Indian superstition and mysticism. His ears still rang with casino sounds and the yelling of a horse track. He remembered cashing a $400 trifecta ticket, but there was no money in his pockets or in his wallet. His wallet was wet. He removed his cell phone from his other pocket, and it wouldn't turn on, evidently damaged by the same liquid that soaked his wallet.

Layne remembered watching a race from the rail and seeing his key horse cross the finish line first by a length, then looking for the rest of his horses behind the winner within a fury of hooves. He was too bent to be excited, even while glancing at the tote board to see that his lead horse was 26-to-1. There had been no failed attempt at self-governance like the previous weekends on base. He had told himself to have fun because he was most likely going to be fired when his background investigation was complete.

Back in camp as the sun began to set, he knew that he was in trouble. He had crossed the line; it seemed as crazy as jumping off a cliff now. He knew that he should be distraught, but he wasn't. He reasoned that he would go to bed immediately when he got to his room and he would get twelve hours of sleep and be rejuvenated to go to formation.

Layne opened his eyes the next morning after what seemed like only a few seconds. He panicked instantly upon gaining consciousness at what day it was and jumped down from the top bunk. He began to get dressed as quickly as possible. Adrenaline masked the pain of the weekend. While he hurried to catch up to his roommates to put on his uniform, he realized that he was struggling to fasten the buttons of his shirt. He had neglected to iron the uniform or polish his boots. His hands were shaking, but his roommates didn't notice anything, as he brushed past them to take shelter in the bathroom. Panic became despair when he remembered that his first class was Firearms.

In formation he didn't say a word to anyone, certain he would sound funny. He stood as still as possible, facing forward, his jaw clenched. *I can't believe I let this happen. I must be crazy*, he thought. He couldn't make it through a whole day in this condition, but he couldn't call in sick either. He felt eyes upon him, the growing focus of unwanted attention. The class had reached a comfort level over time; everyone had established an opinion of each other. Layne knew that the group of hostile Hispanics had animosity toward him because he was white and had hijacked their language, leaving them unable to talk about him out loud. His firearms ability only intensified their hatred. They were no doubt pleased to see him attempting to hide distress. So were various others. Even Melanie's eyes joined those who were watching him now. He could hear comments, tittering laughter like chirping birds, but in his agonizing condition he was helpless to retaliate and defend himself.

He tried to be invisible as he climbed on the bus and sat down in the back row of seats next to Blair, unable to greet him. The frequent glances and lip movements of the hostiles had followed him down the aisle, and he could hear Melanie's voice chime within the muttering.

Blair looked at him, concerned. "Are you okay, Layne?"

Layne could only nod in response. What good would it do to say no?

"Are you sure?"

Layne mustered his strength and said, "I'm okay. I think I'm just dehydrated." But his voice cracked before he could finish the sentence.

He felt paralyzed in the bus seat; to simply move was a chore. His motor skills were impaired, so that it would be difficult to touch his pointer finger to his nose with his eyes closed. His eyes and mouth felt as dry as the toilet paper in the stalls. He was cold, but there was a thin dew of sweat over his goose bumps. The water he guzzled from his canteen didn't aid him, traveling through him instead of into him, as if passing through galvanized pipes. The water tasted like chemicals, and it swished in his stomach when he moved. His heart stutter-stepped between beats; he was being tortured to death as punishment for a heinous crime. The smallest task seemed like a major operation that required all his strength.

It seemed impossible, even marching in formation.

The chirping birds had definitely noticed, he was certain now. He had no choice but to struggle through. He told himself to simply concentrate on each task at hand and put the time remaining in the day out of mind. Just ignore and deny, he thought. If confronted, he would think of something believable, like too much coffee. The thought crossed his mind to go to an instructor and ask to go to the Medical Building and say that he was sick. But what would he tell them when they asked more questions? The medical staff might decide to have him out-processed. No one missed a day unless there was a medical emergency, like a burst appendix.

There was nothing more embarrassing than to have a sickness that he couldn't keep from inflicting on himself. To be the cause of his own affliction was something that he forbade himself from putting into spoken words. He feared that there was a name for what was wrong with him, a term that he didn't want to know. He could've gone on pretending it was neurotic thought and hypochondria, had he not slipped up and brought it to light with nowhere to hide.

He just hoped that the hostiles wouldn't comment in front of the instructors, and he hoped the instructors wouldn't notice him at all. He made it seven of ten miles of the bus ride toward the range without incident, wincing and gritting his teeth with the pain. He knew the reticence couldn't last, and he opened his eyes to face the music when he heard Damon's voice call out to him. Damon turned around in his seat and sat up to speak publicly before his audience.

"Sheppard, you don't look so good. You alright?"

The bus broke out into laughter. Layne looked down at his hands clutching one another; he couldn't sit any lower. He could feel Blair pitying him.

Damon continued: "You should've seen the bush pig Sheppard hooked up with Saturday."

There was intense laughter; Melanie was almost out of breath from laughing so hard.

Layne vomited a little into his mouth, then swallowed the burn. *I promised myself I wouldn't do this again.* Another memory clip flashed; it was the first thing he saw when he awoke the day before—the faces of Damon and Fleming threatening to leave him if he didn't get up.

"I've never seen anyone drink that much before," Damon said.

Layne sunk even lower into the bus seat.

Blair said to Layne, "Fleming told everyone that Damon wanted to leave you there."

Layne couldn't respond to him.

The teasing had lost its momentum by the time they reached the gun range. Maybe that was the worst of it. *Just survive today somehow, minute by minute. Then you'll show them all this weekend and not drink at all, if you make it to Friday.* He counted seconds, making it past formation and the beginning of class without comment from General Lee or any of his assistants. But he had to resist the need to cry when his turn came to grab his pistol off the dowel and holster it. *I'm never gonna drink again,* he promised himself. *I mean it. If I make it to Friday, I will remember this day forever when I'm tempted.*

The sights on the pistol, which normally locked on target like a magnetic needle, were floating in every direction, and he couldn't force them into the right alignment by the time the shutter closed. It was difficult to keep the front sight itself within the boundaries of the silhouette. To aim at the bull's-eye was an impossibility, a fact he accepted after the first magazine. Struggling to force the sights to where his eye was aiming was like trying to cut the back of his hair left-handed using a vanity mirror. Right was left and left was right. The duration of the target shutter opening seemed nothing more than a flicker. He saw dirt kick up behind the target as he fired, while sensing only a fraction of a second remaining in which to pull the trigger and shoot the necessary third shot. It was like controlling the pistol remotely with a joystick he was operating with his mouth.

Agent Huston did a double take when he passed behind Layne. He stopped to take a closer look and saw that a good portion of the rounds were not even hitting paper. Layne tried to pretend he didn't notice he was being observed. But he knew Huston couldn't overlook what was happening.

"What's wrong?" Huston asked with confusion.

Layne couldn't look him in the eye. "I don't know, sir."

Agent Huston took a second to assess the situation. Then a look of discovery took over his face, and he yelled to everyone on the firing line: "Stop! Everyone, listen to me! I'm only gonna say this once!"

He walked down the firing line and didn't point out Layne while he shouted, "Sunday is for hydrating! I don't want to see anyone else show up on Monday with the shakes again, understood?"

The hostiles smiled with gratification but didn't laugh aloud. General Lee was in the speaker box, and Layne prayed that he couldn't tell what was going on.

When it came time to clean the guns, something General Lee supervised every class, Layne took the pistol apart as quickly as he could, with a quick once over. He cleaned and reassembled it before General Lee could see him in motion. But General Lee backed up when he walked by and said, "Aren't you gonna put any oil in the action, Sheppard?"

"Sorry, sir, I forgot. I will put oil on it." Layne heard the quiver in his own voice.

The hostiles laughed under their breath.

"Are you okay? You seem nervous today," General Lee observed.

"I don't know," Layne said.

General Lee realized the situation and moved on without further comment. Layne battled to stave off fatal thoughts as he struggled with the pistol's recoil spring. Firearms had been one of his classes in the plus column before this morning. Only last week he had demonstrated the skill of a pistoleer. On that occasion the pistol had stuck in his holster when the shutter opened, and by the time he freed it and drew, there had been only a split second before the shutter closed. He fired all three shots in such rapid succession that everyone on the firing line looked toward him, wondering what had happened. While the class changed targets, General Lee came out of the speaker box and strolled by to see where the shots had gone. All three of the split-second rounds were within the five-ring. Layne had his first perfect score of 360.

He snapped back to the present as he wiped the assembled pistol with a cloth. This day, Melanie had outscored him by twenty points.

When the trainees marched to formation to wait for the bus, he felt naked in the spotlight, up to his neck in the sensation that he was driving during rush hour traffic searching for an address, a string of impatient cars behind him, honking. Any sudden movement startled him.

What Baca had said to the class the week before returned to his playlist of worries. He was convinced that his background investigation wasn't finished, either. It made sense now why he had made it here. If they weren't already onto him, they definitely would be; there was no way that Baca wouldn't find out. When he did, he would alert the Hiring Center. He seemed to hate Layne more than the rest of the whites. He would be nearing a panic attack every time someone came to interrupt class from now on; he couldn't withstand such an acute concern for an extended period of time. It was hellish in addition to his basic foundation of worries about achieving satisfactory grades, Stacking, and OC.

He spent the bus ride seesawing between excruciatingly anxious feelings of impending disaster and clinical depression over regret about things he had done during the trip that were bubbling, like sewer gas, to the surface of his memory. Looking back on the contrast in his logic and judgment when he was drunk was frightening. It was as if he had been possessed by a demon. To think that he had not been in control of his actions for a period of time was horrifying.

Layne closed his eyes and leaned his head against the vibrating bus window. He tried with futility to rid his mind of horrid memories, but they arrived one after another. It came back to him what had set off such a prodigious bender in Ruidoso. The scene of Estéban being withdrawn from class by administration had been playing loops in his head. He advanced deeper into darker thoughts which normally remained locked away. The last time he had sunk into this condition, there was an I.V. in his arm and oxygen tubes tickling his nostrils. A woman without a lab coat sat in a chair next to his hospital bed with a clipboard.

He fought to redirect his thoughts. He couldn't imagine a setting worse than the Academy to endure in this condition.

He joined formation in PT class, not fully aware of how he had managed to survive the bus ride, forced to continue his part as the star of this lucid nightmare. Time continued to crawl. His organs were not functioning properly; it seemed that he would stop breathing if he didn't put forth effort to. Perhaps it would become bearable once seated in a classroom, unless someone pointed him out to an instructor. The physical pain he could handle, but he had already surpassed his threshold for humiliation.

He attempted to hide in the back of the group during a handcuffing demonstration in the mat room, Instructor Pyatt neatly cuffing Instructor Ramirez, and then announcing, "I need two volunteers."

Layne looked at his feet and scooted behind another trainee, trying to escape out of sight. But fate was unavoidable, his foul luck remarkable. The instructors rarely sought volunteers.

"Sheppard, I haven't picked you yet," Pyatt said. "Danielson, Sheppard will handcuff you. Get down on your stomach."

Layne did his best to remain steady as the pair came forward and assumed their positions like wrestlers in the center of the circle. Melanie giggled with delight and the Hispanic hostiles looked pleased enough to clap. The dexterity in his hands made it feel like he was trying to manipulate the mechanics of the cuffs wearing boxing gloves. He struggled while the hostiles watched with amusement as Instructors Pyatt and Ramirez unwittingly tarred and feathered him on stage.

Puzzled by his behavior, Agent Pyatt asked, "How much coffee did you drink this morning, Sheppard?"

The chirpers in the group were further satisfied with laughter. Then, unexpectedly, Pyatt said, "That's good. You two—Balducci, you and Rojas, you're next."

Layne considered that perhaps the instructors had been through similar experiences themselves and it wasn't a big deal; they understood. He melted back into the group, consumed by an urge to run, only movement aided the misery. The sickness brought him back in time again to the hospital within the dizzying merry-go-round of thoughts; his stamina to repulse the memory was exhausted. Only activity distracted him from the thoughts. He could still see the look of pity on the doctor's face as she filled in the blanks on her clipboard. Whether she was a psychologist or counselor he didn't know, but her attitude was devoid of sympathy or compassion. She was disgusted that it was required of her to treat such a deplorable being. He remembered her with an expression of superiority asking him what he was going to do when his parents weren't around to take care of him. He shook himself out of the trance again, his heart continuing to hopscotch. For the first time he hoped that the instructors would lead the class on a lengthy run around the perimeter fence after the drills, the farther the better.

SCHNEIDER LAY ON HIS BUNK, LEGS crossed while he turned the page to continue reading an article in *Muscle and Fitness*. He enjoyed these rare opportunities to have the room to himself after class. Just as he began to relax and truly enjoy the peace and quiet, though, he heard a weak knock on the door. He looked over his magazine and his feet to watch Damon open the door and slide in without asking permission. Damon ducked and looked to his right to see Schneider alone lying on his bunk.

"What's good?" Damon asked as he invited himself in.

"Nothing, just hanging out," Schneider said. He was finding it increasingly more difficult to pretend that he wasn't annoyed by Damon's uninvited visits. Damon had chosen Schneider to be his only friend, against Schneider's will. Schneider had begun avoiding him after the first night in Tucson; he wanted nothing to do with Damon. Yet Damon continued to seek him out, like he was pursuing a girl to court who was stubbornly playing hard to get. Schneider knew that Damon was too savvy not to be able to interpret his signals. It was an irritating mystery, but Damon wouldn't go away.

Schneider resumed his article, the magazine blocking his view of Damon looking about the room. But it was a futile hint. He would simply have to wait for Damon to grow bored enough to leave.

"What did you get on that Law test?" Damon asked.

"I got a ninety-four."

Schneider looked up from his magazine for a moment. Since the silent roommate had resigned, Layne and Schneider had taken over his locker to share. They were very respectful of each other's things. Schneider had agreed to use the bottom half of the locker while Layne used the top. Ricky, Layne and Schneider trusted each other to such an extent that they left the doors to their lockers wide open at all times.

Schneider tried to think of an excuse to leave and shake Damon off, but there was still thirty minutes until dinnertime in the cafeteria. Any abrupt attempt to leave would be awkwardly obvious, so Schneider pretended to be absorbed in his magazine. Damon began snooping around the room while he thought of more trivial questions to pester Schneider with.

"Where's Ricky and Sheppard?" Damon asked while he picked up and examined a picture of a girl from Ricky's desk.

"Ricky is studying somewhere, and I don't know where Sheppard is. He's probably in Blair's room."

"Damn, is this Ricky's chick? She's top-shelf."

"I don't know; I guess," Schneider said, although he knew that Ricky was going to propose to the girl in the picture as soon as he graduated.

Schneider kept one eye above his magazine to see what Damon was getting into next. Damon grew bored of the items on Ricky's desk and moved to stand, looking at the locker that Schneider shared with Layne.

"You guys only have three to your room—they still haven't figured out that you guys have an empty bed in here, huh?"

"Yeah, there's a lot more room in here since he left, but we don't want everybody knowing that," Schneider said.

"I'm not gonna tell anybody," Damon snapped.

Please leave, Schneider thought to himself.

"You and Layne share this locker?" Damon asked.

"Yep." Schneider rested the magazine on his lap as he looked at Damon's back, uneasy about what he was up to.

Damon reached into the top locker shelf, past deodorant, cologne and other items in front to reach for something hidden in the back. Schneider sat up. "What are you doing?"

Damon ignored the question as he stood examining a yellow pharmaceutical box. "Whose half of the locker is this?"

"It's Sheppard's. Why are you looking through his stuff?"

"Sheppard takes Paxil?" Damon said as he raised an eyebrow.

"I don't know; put that back," Schneider said as he stood up to take the box away from Damon.

Damon began putting the box back deep into the back of the locker where he had found it before Schneider could take it from him.

"What are you doing?" Schneider demanded.

"Nothing, I'm just bored. I didn't know Sheppard took anti-depressants."

"How do you know that's what they are?" Schneider asked.

"Because my ex-girlfriend took them. I don't think you can take these and work in the field. They ask you about it; it's one of the questions on the SF-86," Damon said.

"Don't be telling people that," Schneider said, irritated. "I didn't know you were gonna be going through his locker."

"Calm down; I'm not gonna tell anybody," Damon said.

Schneider was having difficulty hiding his anger. "Look, I gotta go. I'm gonna go to dinner then study for Applied Authority." He guided Damon through the door and was relieved to see him heading the other direction down the balcony walkway as Schneider locked the door.

18

ALONG WITH THOSE OTHERS WHO REMAINED, Layne had settled into a routine by week nine. Iron the uniform, polish boots, and shower at night so that he could sleep fifteen minutes longer in the morning. He made sure to have the books of the classes before lunch already in his backpack so that he could grab it and go and be in formation on time.

The gun range was the only place where he could forget about his problems. Throughout each class in the temporaries, the door was in his periphery. From the start until they rose to leave he visualized an instructor opening it, Baca becoming angry for the interruption then returning through it with an evil, satisfied grin and motioning for Layne to come to him with only his pointer finger. The instructor probably wouldn't know what he was pulling Layne from class for. Someone in Building 26 would bring him into an office and close the door. Then, whoever it was would tell him there was a problem with his background check. Layne wouldn't even ask them what it was; he would know it was the hospital visit. He would leave voluntarily without protest and would ask the administrator to please not bring up the details. The fear spun in his mind unless he was busy.

Firearms and Spanish were two classes that he would gladly attend. As they assembled themselves into formation, General Lee faced them with one less assistant on this day, but he didn't acknowledge the absence. Word had spread that the assistant had been busted by the Artesia Police for a DUI and sent back to his station, his gun taken away. Ricky had told Layne that DUIs among agents were commonplace. Matt, too, had mentioned that many Border Patrol Agents were hard drinkers, and that many of them drove drunk every night.

His interest shifted to the nineteen M4s that were waiting for the class on a rack, like guns in a gun shop. He had been looking forward to this day since Runyon had confirmed to him that the M4s were indeed the fully automatic-type A1.

The weapons looked strange without magazines in them; he couldn't keep his eyes off of them. Six trainees from Group A had quit or been forced to resign since the beginning, he realized by the gun count. He could barely remember two names and two faces of the departed. Stacking and OC were just around the corner, which were the reasons most trainees resigned voluntarily. But, Layne thought, they should've waited until after this special day in Firearms.

As Layne stared at the rifles in awe, General Lee directed the class to the bleachers with courtesy. Layne continued to stare at the rifles, looking over his shoulder at them as the class moved away toward the bleachers. General Lee was developing a fatherly affection for certain members of the class with time. He grabbed a shotgun and stood at the front of the bleachers to demonstrate, pumping the shotgun's chamber open then closed. "In the field you will run into Tonks who have an attitude because they've been caught before. But the sound of a shotgun pump will get the attention of any indigenous moron."

Layne and the other white trainees laughed hysterically. General Lee was not concerned about political correctness. He made racially questionable statements despite one of his assistants being Hispanic. No one dared correct him. His attitude conveyed that he was tolerating the Hispanics within the Border Patrol, but if he had it his way, The Service would be open only to white people.

"We'll shoot the shotgun on a different day. It's hard to miss with buckshot, and the slugs kick like a mule." General Lee put the shotgun back and picked up an M4. The sling had been removed and the swivels hung empty. He pulled back the charging handle with two fingers to retract the bolt. The M4 complimented him; the rifle looked like it belonged in his hands. He looked like a bull rider when he wasn't holding a gun.

Layne's mind wandered to whether or not he would try to refrain from drinking on Friday. He was almost sure that General Lee got drunk on the weekends. Everyone got drunk on the weekends. Perhaps he was just being neurotic about the situation. Maybe it wasn't the big deal he made it out to be at the beginning of the week. He simply needed to learn how to drink like everyone else and have the willpower to suffer through the hangovers on Sundays. The Ruidoso incident resurfaced, but he needed to give himself a break; that had happened right after Estéban had been escorted out. He had been alarmed. The incessant worry about discoveries involving his background began to taper off. No one had been pulled out of class since Estéban was fired.

Layne waited his turn in line, anxious to be issued a rifle. When his turn came, he grabbed the rifle by its pistol grip and heat shield forearm and followed the others toward the rifle range. He examined the Colt Rearing Horse emblem stamped into the receiver next to the "Property of U.S. Government" stamp. The power of the federal government's reign radiated from the gun. On the safety selector switch above his thumb on the grip were three choices: SAFE, SEMI, and when the switch was turned all the way to its forward position the arrow pointed to a notch that said AUTO. FULL-AUTO toys and video games replicated the feeling, but he knew that the real thing would be different.

From a distance of twenty-five yards, the trainees fired at the shutter targets with the switch pointing up in the semi-automatic position. The rifle felt different than he had imagined. It was light and felt hollow until the weight of a full magazine was clicked into place. With each shot he heard the exhaust escaping from a gas port. The spring within the stock could be heard absorbing nearly all of the recoil of each shot.

The class finished the first magazine and General Lee took front and center again. While everyone circled him, he smacked a banana magazine against his knee a few times to align all of the primers flush with the rear of the magazine column and shake loose any dirt. Layne and the rest of the trainees secured their ear protection and double-checked to make sure their eye protection was in place. General Lee turned the safety selector switch to AUTO with his thumb and aimed at the shutter. Instructor Huston opened the target remotely from the speaker box and General Lee let loose. The rhythmic concussion stunned the air as dozens of empty shell casings sailed end over end. Even through the earmuffs, the violent cycling of the bolt hammered Layne's eardrums.

Layne took off his hat and wiped his forehead with his sleeve and adjusted his safety glasses. General Lee pushed his earmuffs to his temples and turned the safety selector switch to SAFE with his thumb. "This carbine is too light to control with a rifle cartridge. If you try to muscle down the muzzle climb it gets even more erratic." He aimed the gun at the target to demonstrate. "If you just let the forearm rest in your front hand like you're holding a puppy and let it bounce you can keep a somewhat tight grip."

He put his ear protection back on to demonstrate, and moved forward to the fifteen-yard platform as the class moved in behind him. He checked his stance and aimed. He pulled the trigger and flinched, but the gun didn't fire because he had forgotten to take the safety off. The trainees suppressed the urge to laugh. General Lee adjusted the select-fire switch without looking at anyone. Huston reopened the target and General Lee unloaded the remainder of the magazine into the target—his cheek clamped to the stock, and his right eye focused throughout the burst. The forearm of the rifle vibrated in his palm until the chamber locked open and the action ejected the thirtieth shell. He tilted the gun like a tray to switch it to SAFE, as the ejection port and the barrel exhaled the aftermath of smoke in slow billows. "Tell Agent Huston to open the target so I can show these guys," General Lee said to an assistant.

The shutter opened, displaying the target and the trainees followed General Lee to examine it. He stood next to the target and pointed to nineteen holes all scattered within the five-ring. "This is about as good as you're gonna get on FULL-AUTO. When the target opens, you're gonna have about three seconds. You most likely won't make it all the way through your magazine. But we aren't scoring this; it's just for fun."

The time has come, Layne thought. General Lee returned to the speaker box. "Everyone ready?"

Layne eagerly rotated the safety selector switch clockwise to AUTO and pulled the collapsible stock snug into his armpit. He could feel his heart racing as he found the front sight through the aperture. He held his breath. The target snapped into the facing position and he pulled the trigger, launching an onslaught that felt like being punched in the face by a ferociously rapid combination of hooks and uppercuts. The barrage stunned his senses as he instantly lost his bead on the front sight and his eye instead focused on a stream of empty cartridges that spewed in a stampede from the ejection port. He strained to level the barrel, but the vibration destroyed his dexterity as if he were being electrocuted as two-foot flames flared in a star shape through the flash suppressor.

When Layne let off the trigger, he was disoriented, like he had just sneezed. Hundreds of spent shells echoed for seconds off the arid hills in the distance and a high-pitched ringing in his ears took over for the sound of incessant cannonade. The shutter reopened and his arms flexed to keep the sights on target to no avail until the shutter snapped closed again. He pushed the magazine release button to remove the clip, sensing there were only two or three cartridges left in the magazine.

"How many mags do you have left?" Layne asked Schneider, who was changing magazines on the platform directly to his left.

"I got two left," Schneider said.

"I'm gonna save mine," Layne said.

Huston walked by. "Don't worry. Before class we loaded three more mags apiece for you guys and we don't want to thumb them out." He handed Layne three loaded magazines and said, "Put these in the pockets of your cargo pants."

Layne smiled, the magazines weighing down his cargo pants and swaying when his legs moved. Huston was treating him like a normal person, further evidence that he was placing too much importance on the drinking issue. He was blending back in. He had decided that hard liquor was the problem. It was beer, only, from now on, and in moderation.

General Lee left the targets locked open. Layne moved his ear protection to his temples to hear what a firefight would sound like, as the guns of the other trainees blazed with stunning noise. Shells somersaulted in streams and pinged on concrete everywhere, and the air was overcome with the smell of burnt cordite. Agent Hicks, the joker among the assistants, approached Layne with an ear-to-ear smile. His hands and cargo pockets were filled with loaded magazines. He handed one to Layne. "Sheppard, shoot the whole thing without stopping."

Layne was the happiest he had been since his arrival at the Academy. All of the assistants seemed to have forgotten about the day he had been sick at the range. Maybe his suspicion that everyone was avoiding him out of scorn was just paranoia. It just wasn't a big deal—even comical, Layne reasoned. He loaded the magazine and pulled the charging handle to chamber the first round. Agent Hicks put the palm of his left hand between Layne's shoulder blades and leaned on him with a straight arm.

"Pretend it's a car coming at you, rip it!" Hicks goaded.

Layne aimed and pulled the trigger with the force of Hicks' body weight on his back to stabilize him and prevent the recoil from pushing him off balance. A relentless beating ensued. The temperature of the receiver gained heat like a stovetop burner that scalded his brow. An endless rush of burnt cordite invaded his sinuses, stinging his eye as the cartridges stampeded to evacuate the magazine. Hot gas inflated his nose and throat, like jumping into a swimming pool when he forgot to plug his nose. The pressure to carry out a dare overcame the need to let off. The action finally kicked out the last shell and his head continued to rattle as he lowered the barrel. He grimaced from the taste of sulfur in his mouth. Hicks surveyed him with satisfaction and laughed. "A couple of them hit paper," he said.

"It's like printing your name on concrete with a jackhammer to try and hit something," Layne said.

"That was awesome," Hicks laughed.

"My ears are ringing," Layne complained, disoriented.

"Don't be a pussy; here, do another one," Hicks pressed, holding out another full magazine.

The empty magazine in his rifle was almost too hot to pull out with bare hands. The heat from the muzzle warped the air surrounding it, like summer heat waves from asphalt.

"The barrel is too hot," Layne said.

Hicks relented and offered the magazine to Schneider instead, but Schneider declined.

"I thought it would be like shooting at the paper star with an automatic BB gun at the fair," Layne said to Schneider.

"So did I, but it's not. It's out of control." Schneider was using the sleeve of his shirt like an oven mitt to remove his magazine. He seemed to be in a bad mood.

"All those war movies that show guys shooting assault rifles at people aren't real. You couldn't hit a drive-in movie screen with half of the magazine," Layne observed.

"That's because they're shooting blanks; they don't have the recoil of a live round," Hicks told them from behind. He laughed and moved on.

Schneider looked around while he changed magazines. "Hey, I gotta tell you something," he said to Layne.

"What?" Layne was oblivious as to the reason as he waited for his rifle to cool off.

"Damon was in our room the other day while you were gone. He was looking at the stuff in your locker and he found a box of pills." Schneider's tone was apologetic.

Layne's joyful mood evaporated. "What was he doing going through my stuff?"

"He just comes in without asking; I can't get rid of him. He was looking at Ricky's stuff, too. I tried to stop him, but it was too late."

Layne assessed the situation in a state of distress that was swelling exponentially. Schneider looked remorseful for allowing it to happen while he prepared his rifle. Layne felt the need to explain but was considering what to say.

"What are those for?" Schneider asked respectfully while he tapped a magazine against his knee.

"They're for my asthma. I can't believe that lowlife was going through my junk. The guy is unbelievable," Layne said, growing angry.

Schneider was quiet for a moment, then said, "I kicked him out right away. If I had known he was gonna do that, I would have shut your locker."

"I know it wasn't your fault," Layne said.

Layne continued to stew and fret; they didn't even have padlocks for the lockers. It was unspoken that they stayed out of each other's things. The strain between them was growing by the second. Layne didn't blame Schneider. He knew that Damon's audacity was astounding, but regardless, he was too angry to further explain. If word got to Guillermo, it would surely be passed on to Instructor Baca, and if his background check had indeed been complete, Baca would see to it that it was reopened by the contractors.

"I told him not to tell anybody," Schneider said, regretfully.

19

"GET BACK!" LAYNE YELLED AS HE WHACKED the heavy bag with the practice baton. Schneider was straining slightly to hold the target in place. The class was paired-off around the perimeter of the mat room, taking turns practicing baton strikes on heavy bags that hung from the ceiling. Layne was hoping not to be noticed. Pyatt and Ramirez were making cursory laps around the room, observing technique and voice commands.

"Come on, Sheppard. Yell the warning commands like you mean it," Instructor Pyatt barked. Layne didn't realize Pyatt was behind him. He was hoping the instructors wouldn't notice his lack of effort. He was overwhelmed with stress and his nerves physically exhausted him; he hadn't been eating either. Schneider put his shoulder into the bag as Layne put forth more effort, only yelling a little louder to try to appease Instructor Pyatt.

Pyatt scoffed in ridicule at Layne, and Layne only glanced at the instructor as he traded places with Schneider when the whistle blew. The chirpers giggled. Layne was mad enough to fight most days because of the petty torments. But he feared he would be sent home for fighting. The thought crossed his mind to do it anyway—to punch someone and get sent home instead of waiting to be kicked out dishonorably for the background check.

"How long do we have to practice this?" Layne said impatiently to Runyon as they waited in line for a different drill. "I feel ridiculous with that baton. It's like a Nerf bat I had when I was a kid."

Runyon, the contrarian, agreed for once. "Yeah, this is stupid. Stacking and OC are pointless in my opinion."

Layne agreed, and Runyon went on. "If I'm surrounded by three aliens and they aren't doing what I tell them to, I'm not touching my baton or pepper spray. I'm going straight for my gun, and if they still aren't listening. I'm gonna start shooting."

As the monotonous drills continued, Layne proceeded to hide behind the others during the next demonstration, "the sprawl," which Pyatt was demonstrating with Instructor Ramirez. It was a basic wrestling technique to avoid a takedown.

Layne looked at the clock again and was disheartened; there was still enough time to practice it. He moped over to Schneider again to pair off for the drill. "A week's worth of drills won't help on Friday," Layne whined.

"I know. They're just filling time showing us this," Schneider responded. "Maybe they'll just have us practice against each other for a few minutes."

Layne looked at the clock as Pyatt yelled for the trainees to form another circle. He had evidently forgotten to demonstrate part of what the trainees were supposed to learn.

Pyatt held a practice baton and Instructor Ramirez put himself into a wrestling stance facing him. "The term 'Stacking' means that you strike an aggressor low with the steel baton until he falls to the ground," Pyatt began. "Once the aggressor is neutralized you lay him on the ground in front of you like this."

Ramirez collapsed to his knees on the mat as a visual aid while Pyatt explained. After the enemy had been struck several times below the waste, the agent was supposed to grab him by the shirt and pull him downward onto his stomach. Once the enemy was neutralized, the agent was to engage the next attacker and repeat the method in order to "stack" them. The drill was intended to train an agent how to handle a situation when multiple threats were not cooperating and were attempting to encircle him. Pyatt emphasized that it was critical that the agent kept the attackers in his field of vision, out of the blind areas in his periphery. Both Pyatt and Ramirez asserted on a daily basis that it was imperative never to let anyone get behind them. So much so that Layne could sense someone standing behind him, even when he couldn't see or hear his presence. But the mortal sin was to allow oneself to be backed up against a wall or into a corner.

Ramirez went for Pyatt's legs in slow motion, and Pyatt simulated hitting him in his left knee three times. Ramirez fell to one knee and Pyatt grabbed a hold of his shirt and guided him to his stomach.

Schneider moved away from Layne when he tried to whisper to him. So Layne leaned over and directed his comments to Runyon instead. "What scares me the most is being blind while someone is about to tackle me from behind."

"It's a good way to get a knee injury," Runyon whispered back.

"Did you play football?" Layne asked, when Pyatt turned to address the trainees on the other half of the circle.

"No," Runyon said.

"Two-a-days are worse than this," Layne said to comfort himself.

Runyon disagreed. "You never went through Army boot camp."

"Yeah, I heard that's rough. Anyway, at least in football there was common sense. They always teach running backs to keep their legs moving, especially when they're wrapped up. Standing flat-footed while someone blindsides you with a running start is absurd."

"I heard from guys in Class 568 that at least one person gets hurt in every class," Runyon said.

Layne wished he hadn't brought it up now. "Do you know what it sounds like when an anterior cruciate ligament tears?"

"What does it sound like, Sheppard?"

"It sounds like a tree branch breaking, then your knee swells to the size of a volleyball."

Half-serious, Runyon sighed. "I recommend that you seek help from a psychiatrist for your worrying."

Pyatt interrupted their side conversation. "Everybody, listen up! The way that the drill is gonna run is we will have a team of four PT Instructors from other classes playing the parts of the aliens."

Layne tried to listen, but stared in deep thought, recalling an incident two weeks earlier. While his group was standing in formation after a run around the perimeter, two PT instructors from another class—agents who had been detailed to FLETC by request—had approached them while they were still sweating and breathing hard. Layne had been in the second row of the formation. One of the instructors, a muscular, well-conditioned Hispanic in his late twenties, swept past the first row, brushing their chests with his shoulder to provoke a response. The instructor zeroed in on a trainee from the Valley named Navarro.

"You look like you're dragging; what's your problem?" the PT instructor fomented.

Navarro looked straight ahead, avoiding eye contact. "I'm tired, sir."

The agent bowed up. "Did you really say you're tired? I teach four classes—I've been PT'n all day, and I'm not tired."

Navarro didn't respond.

"Do you have *cohones* like a real man?" the instructor asked as spittle sprayed from his lips.

"Yes, sir."

"I doubt it." Nose-to-nose with Navarro, he said, "I can't wait until you have Stacking; I'm gonna tear you a new one. I bet you cry! Wanna bet?" Navarro looked straight ahead, and the instructor moved on looking for another inviting face.

Layne tried to clear his mind of his assorted dilemmas. He said to Runyon, "Carlos was fat when we got here, do you remember that?"

"Yeah, he's lost about forty pounds," Runyon said. When he spoke to Runyon, Layne tried to make statements that he knew Runyon would agree with.

"Unbelievable."

But talking about something else didn't allow Layne to shake the image of the PT instructors in Red Man suits in the coming week. They were now taking precedence over Damon, and grades, or an agent from administration at the door.

* * * *

RICKY WAS LEANING ON THE BALCONY railing with his legs crossed, overlooking the courtyard. He was still wearing his black boots and the green cargo pants of his uniform with a t-shirt. He was too tired to completely change clothes. The door to their dorm room was open behind him. Trainees in shorts and flip-flops were walking to the cafeteria for dinner. Layne came out of the room to join him and left the door cracked open. He had just changed into basketball shorts and sandals. He leaned on the railing to stand next to Ricky and overlook the courtyard and the red sky the setting sun created. The trainees couldn't wait to change out of their uniforms at four o'clock and wander the rest of the day about the courtyard on their way to the lounge or to one another's rooms.

"Those detailed instructors love Stacking because it's a chance for them to beat up on trainees," Layne told Ricky, as he lowered the bill of his baseball cap to shield his eyes from the setting sun.

"I know; it sucks. You gotta do it tomorrow?"

"Yeah," Layne said dispiritedly.

Ricky empathized with a nod while still watching the activity below them. He was drinking Gatorade. They were sweating, just standing outside.

Layne was silent for a moment. They had spoken about the fear of Stacking before, but without coming out and admitting they were scared. Layne envied Ricky for already having gone through it, but it still seemed to bother him. It seemed like a ritual that was like hazing in a fraternity, but with an added element of pain, like a right of passage. The detailed PT Instructors who were young agents at their stations couldn't wait to initiate the trainees. It was a tradition they took much pleasure in, a primary motivation for coming to the Academy—a chance to beat up a trainee. Instructors didn't need to be drafted to teach PT the way they did for other classes; there were enough volunteers that every PT Instructor was there voluntarily. The older instructors like Pyatt and Ramirez didn't seem to enjoy it, but they deemed it necessary and allowed the youth to have their fun.

Layne thought of something to say that he hadn't said before. "Our Law Instructor says the agents hate us even more than before because they switched the field uniform to rough gear, and the badge is sewn on the uniform when we get it. They say we are not worthy of wearing green, like we are inferior because they didn't get a badge until they graduated."

"People always say the road was harder when they went through," Ricky said.

"I know," Layne agreed.

"How has Stacking practice been going?" Ricky asked, finishing the last of his bottle in one long draw.

"It sucked. It's like Runyon said, if you're in that situation you're not gonna try to fend off three guys with a baton," Layne complained.

"Did they have you as a bull in the ring yet?" Ricky asked. He didn't seem to be enjoying the situation but was discussing it because he knew Layne was worried.

"Yeah. You can't see anything with that lacrosse helmet on. You have no peripheral vision. But at least the Red Men have to wear them, too, and they have to wear that umpire chest protector and arm and leg pads. It looks cumbersome." Layne spoke with false optimism. He shifted his position to turn around and rest his back against the railing.

"That's why they call the instructor a Red Man, because those pads are red," Ricky said. "So, what happened when you were in the middle?"

"I just grabbed a hold of my rubber gun with two hands and held on for dear life while they swarmed me," Layne said.

"Did you hold on for two minutes?" Ricky asked.

"No, they got me on the ground and two guys pulled my arms away, and Damon pulled my gun out." Layne squirmed at the memory.

"What a jerk," Ricky said.

Everyone except Damon had taken it easy on each other during practice as a sympathetic courtesy. He wanted to play the part of one of the uncooperative aliens during every round. He came from behind, running full speed to knock the trainee down.

Layne thought quietly about what else to share. He wasn't sure if Ricky had heard about Damon finding the pills. He had been acting slightly different, but Layne thought that perhaps he was reading too much into things. Layne became angry anytime the subject of Damon came up: "Even our instructors hate him."

Ricky said, "I know; everyone in the Academy knows about him. That's not good. That means his station knows he's a scumbag, too."

When it was Damon's turn to be the agent in Stacking practice, Instructor Pyatt whispered to the trainees by his sides to run full speed and knock Damon completely off his feet before he blew the whistle to start.

Layne thought of the countless reasons he hated him, and said, "We were cleaning guns in Firearms a while back. Damon was telling everybody that I hooked up with this fat chick in Ruidoso."

Ricky laughed.

Layne continued the story. "General Lee heard him and said, 'I heard you're the one that likes big girls, Balducci. Don't blame it on Sheppard.' Everyone laughed and Damon couldn't get anyone to believe him."

"General Lee is bad," Ricky said.

Layne laughed, "It was awesome. General Lee had everyone rolling, talking about how he heard that Damon had to change the springs on his truck after he dropped this chick off."

Ricky laughed. "So, you think you're ready for tomorrow?"

"As ready as I can be," Layne said. But he wasn't ready. He was dehydrated, though he didn't want to sound like he was making excuses. During PT earlier in the day, the class practiced running 200-yard sprints in preparation for the final test that included the obstacle course. The exercises were timed, and Layne couldn't hide and loaf through them.

Ironically, Ricky said, "Make sure you stay hydrated."

Layne nodded while he comprehended his doom. His urine was as orange as the Gatorade that Ricky had just finished; he felt sickly and weak. He considered a visit to the Medical Building. They would probably prescribe bed rest. But everyone would assume that he was faking it in order to avoid judgment day in Stacking. The chirpers and hostile Mexicans would be relentless with their looks and commentary. It would be less painful just to throw himself to the wolves. If a trainee missed Stacking or OC, they were required to make it up before they were allowed to graduate. The beating was only intensified by retribution from the PT instructors for trying to avoid it.

"You should just get it over with," Ricky advised.

Schneider came up the stairs and along the balcony to get into the room. He nodded but didn't say anything. Layne knew that Schneider wouldn't tell Ricky or anyone else about Damon and the pills. But Schneider's admirable integrity wouldn't prevent the information from reaching everyone at the Academy through Damon. It was hard to determine who knew and who didn't. Layne could only carry on, trying to read faces.

Ricky said, "They're gonna kick your butt no matter what you do. You can't fight three people at one time, no matter what they make it look like in the movies. You get tied up with one guy, and somebody tackles you from the side—Mike Tyson couldn't fight them all off, unless they were twelve-year-olds."

"Well, there's got to be a strategy that helps," Layne hoped.

"That's what I thought. I planned on going in there and wrapping up with one of them quick, then getting on the bottom and just riding it out for two minutes. Just holding on to one for the whole time, taking kicks from the side until they blew the whistle."

Layne listened with growing fear.

"But, as soon as I got in there my whole plan went out the window."

"What happened?" Layne didn't want to know but couldn't refrain from hearing the rest.

"I started yelling and they just closed in from all sides. I was bashing the Red Man in front of me in the knee, but he just laughed. So I just tossed the bat and started wrestling. Then they piled on me and I panicked, and the instructors stopped them." Ricky seemed pained by the memory and went back in the room to end the conversation.

Layne stayed on the balcony to ponder while he stared at the vacant swimming pool. What terrified him was exhaustion. He had nearly drowned in the ocean in California once while boogie-boarding. There was a riptide that wouldn't allow him to paddle back to shore. He had struggled for dear life to keep his head above water while the current pulled him farther out to sea. The waves pushed him under several times, and he had struggled to resurface and breathe; he thought he was going to die. After several more waves submerged him, his arms were too tired to swim and keep his head above water. Somehow, he managed to struggle back closer to shore where his toes could touch the ocean floor. He never ventured into the ocean more than knee deep after that day.

Ricky's description of Stacking resembled drowning on land, and fear never seemed to help when something was unavoidable. But there was no way to turn it off.

FELINA LAY AWAKE IN BED, STILL PUZZLING over a plan that was keeping her eyes open in the dark. Perhaps there was a way out of the confines of her past. Despite her attempt to find a way to go to college, she had never conceptualized a long-term plan of such intricacy and ambition. She turned on her side and flipped her pillow over to the cool side; she folded it in half and put her ear to it. She put herself into a fetal position to try to get comfortable enough to fall asleep. She was staring at the electronic red numbers glowing 12:18 a.m. on her alarm clock. She watched it turn to 12:19 and rolled over to reverse what she was looking at.

An idea had come to her when she left the pool party at Marianne's house. It had flickered with hope as soon as Marianne sparked it, although Felina had kept it to herself during its genesis. A plan had been developing ever since, but it contained obstacles that she had been unable to think of a way around until earlier in the day during work. Brian, the boss' son, had been trying to plan how to propose to his girlfriend for several weeks. He had several scenarios that he thought were clever, but they came off as kind of cheesy to Felina.

One of the ideas involved a puppy delivering the engagement ring by surprise; Brian just hadn't thought of the location for the proposal yet. He had asked all the women in the office their opinions of the idea. They told him it was cute, and so did Felina, although she was feigning kindness. Brian's girlfriend was pregnant, and Brian's dad suggested that they get married before the bulge became prominent. Brian's showing off the ring throughout the office caused the proverbial light bulb to turn on in Felina's mind. She had stared in deep thought as Brian proudly opened and closed the ring box for everybody. It was like a piece that made the rest of the jigsaw puzzle fall into place.

When Marianne told her that Border Patrol Agents sometimes married Mexican women who had been deported, she found it hard to believe. But Marianne always told her the truth, and Ryan had learned a great deal about the job from friends who already were agents. Felina had been thinking about it ever since.

Felina had no interest in marrying a Chicano to become a Lawfully Admitted Permitted Resident. That, she was certain, would surely lead to another life she would be desperate to escape, and anyway, the government would be suspicious of where she had resided prior to the application.

She was in her prime and her looks would last another six or seven years. She was attracted to white men, despite her dad's wish that she marry a Mexican. She wasn't going to give up and settle until she had given her luck more time. But the outlook was bleak. She couldn't date someone like the boss' son and then tell him after the courting process that she was illegal. It was dangerous; her fiancé might feel misled and used and might seek retribution. But according to Marianne, the white Border Patrol Agents often grew sympathetic toward the aliens after several years of exposure to the reality of the border wars. It was a paradox that few people knew about.

Felina thought that if Marianne could introduce her to a trainee— someone cute, someone she liked—maybe she could sweep him off his feet. And after he had fallen for her, she would tell him the truth about her past. She would tell him that she didn't see him coming and hadn't told him from the beginning because she didn't anticipate the relationship advancing. She would say that she wanted to tell him but was afraid he might turn her in. She would say that her attraction to him was a driving force that was more powerful than the fear for her safety. By the time they had reached this point, he would be smitten, and her immigration status wouldn't be the issue that it might have been when they were strangers.

She was having qualms about the moral issue of dishonesty involved with the plot. The only deceit was claiming that it was not premeditated. But she had been dealt a difficult hand and reasoned that she had no choice but to bend the truth. It would make up for the unfairness that had been placed upon her in life, and she would never have to lie again. She'd be even.

Felina came to terms with the ethics of the plan by rationalizing her rejection of other options.

She refused to use dating sites; friends had told her there was a distasteful awkwardness about the process. The manner in which potential partners met seemed to bypass the natural process of screening one another before agreeing to a date. It often left the relationship's foundation weak, which led to collapse over time. She didn't disapprove of the few that it had worked out for; it just wasn't her style.

There was nothing wrong with going to a specific type of place to meet a specific type of person either. But she didn't like bars; she wouldn't like to meet someone in a bar. She would like to date a college boy, but since she couldn't go to college it would be difficult to meet the right one. And even if she were successful in meeting an intellectual type, she would still run into the problem of how to spin why she had kept her past a secret. His opinion of immigration matters would be influenced solely by what he had learned from the media. She knew that the average Caucasian could be extremely conservative when it came to immigration matters.

She had figured out just about every aspect of how to proceed. Because she spoke English with an American accent, no one had ever asked her if she was legal; it just wasn't something that someone would ever ask. The only detail she hadn't been able to resolve until now was how to proceed after the guy agreed to marry her.

The immigration attorney had warned her that revealing herself as being in the country illegally while applying for residency was a recipe for disaster. But the puppy that Brian was planning on having deliver his engagement ring reminded her of her grandparents, specifically a picture she had seen of her family members in Magdalena. In it, she remembered, her cousin was holding a yellow Labrador retriever puppy just like the one Brian had recently acquired. If the person she met would take a risk on her behalf, she could travel to Mexico to stay with her grandparents. She was sure they would love to meet their granddaughter in person and have her stay with them. Her fiancé could apply for a fiancée visa while she was living there. Getting into Mexico would be a non-issue, and she would return to Arizona with proper documentation.

Her grandmother made corn tortillas and sold them on the streets of Magdalena for her income. When Felina was a small girl, her mother had shown her how to prepare the balls of dough, roll them flat, and bake them. She could assist her grandma for income while the paperwork was being processed, and her future husband might be able to send her the money that she needed. She thanked God that she didn't have an immigration record, although Marianne claimed it didn't matter. To the U.S. State Department, it would appear that she had always lived in Magdalena and had never been to the U.S. Her mom still had her birth certificate from Mexico; she could use it to get a Mexican passport.

It was perfect. She could claim that she had met her fiancé at Puerto Peñasco or San Carlos while they were both on vacation. Mexicans weren't fond of the beach, but most white people didn't know that. Ryan said that the agents liked to travel to the beach during their leave, posing as regular tourists. The visa would be rubber-stamped, and she would be a Lawfully Admitted Permanent Resident, on her way to citizenship within a few years. She would be able to go to U of A and get her degree. She would be accepted into Medical School, and she would have a husband who was a Federal Agent, making almost $90,000 a year. She made up her mind; she had no choice. It was worth the gamble. It was time to make her move, or live and die this way. The thought was so profound that it wouldn't let her eyes close. She was too excited to sleep.

LYING AWAKE, LAYNE WONDERED IF SCHNEIDER was asleep below him or if he, too, was tossing and turning. Layne tried to force himself to fall asleep, but he couldn't slow down the cycle of thoughts enough to drift off.

Eight hours later, he watched as his cell phone clock reached 6:00 a.m.; he had never waited so long for morning. He turned off the alarm after one chime and stepped down slowly out of the bunk. He could see the black circles under his eyes in the mirror as he washed his sweaty face.

He felt flu-like symptoms during Law class but remained in an attentive posture, kept alert by adrenaline. The entire hour he shifted constantly in his seat, trying to keep from glancing at the wall clock. For once he did not want the class to be over.

At lunch he straddled the bench seat and set his tray on the lunch table as he sat down. The normally loquacious lunch table group was relatively quiet. Stacking was less than an hour away, and the trainees in Class 590 were too nervous to converse. The lunch tables had become mixtures of trainees from different classes a few weeks after they had received their green uniforms. The trainees from other classes at the table talked quietly amongst themselves; every trainee at the Academy knew which class was going through Stacking and when.

Layne was too nervous to eat; he picked at his food and chewed small bites. Damon and Alvarez were the only trainees from Class 590 at the table with him. The rest looked to be from junior classes. Damon was sitting across from Layne, a few seats to his left. Layne usually tried to sit away from him, but the cafeteria was packed and there was no place else to sit. As Layne picked at his food, out of nowhere Damon said, "I didn't know that you take Paxil."

Layne's face became beet red as the other trainees at the table looked at Damon then looked at Layne.

"Where did you hear that?" Layne said.

"I saw them in your locker," Damon said.

"Why are you asking me?" Layne said with anger swelling.

The other trainees at the table looked at their food, trying to mind their own business.

"I was just wondering, because my son's mom used to take those for depression," Damon said.

One of the trainees got up from the table and retrieved his tray to leave.

"That's not what they're for; I take them for asthma," Layne said.

Damon sensed that his anger was growing like a pressure cooker. "Oh."

"Don't be going around telling people that," Layne said emphatically. But it was too late. Who knew how many others he already had told? Layne tried to pretend that the conversation didn't bother him because of the presence of the other trainees. He picked at his food for another minute then got up to leave without saying anything.

* * * *

LAYNE WATCHED HIS HANDS TREMBLING FROM nerves while he sat, legs spread on the mat, reaching for his toes as the class stretched. He reached for the other foot and looked around at the class stretching in formation. The tension was disturbing; no one was interested in speaking. Then, as if the Red Men couldn't wait any longer, Instructor Ramirez ordered the class to line up to leave their home mat room. "Form up alphabetically in the hallway outside Mat Room 3. The first two people in line, grab a helmet and two batons from the corner and bring them with you."

Layne was once again thankful for a name beginning with the letter S; it was fortuitous, especially in situations when observation time was beneficial.

The Red Men were already waiting for the instructors inside Mat Room 3. The trainees could hear the voices of Pyatt, Ramirez, and unidentified others. Alvarez put on a helmet and waited for word from the instructors conferencing inside. He grasped the foam baton and shuffled his feet, uncertain of which posture was appropriate for such imminent violence. He adjusted the facemask of the lacrosse helmet one last time to improve his vision. Layne stood helpless as a flop sweat began to bead on his face. Although he had barely spoken with Alvarez, he felt a bond with him for the common fate they faced: Lambs sent into slaughter. Alvarez was not one of the hostiles who whispered while looking at Layne; he minded his own business.

The voice of Instructor Ramirez intruded into the hallway. "Alvarez, you ready?"

"Yes, sir," Alvarez answered as he strengthened his grip on the baton. He entered the room and immediately could be heard yelling, "Get back, get back!"

A commotion commenced that could be felt beneath the feet of the trainees in line in the hallway. A blast from multiple bodies inside the room moved the wall several inches into the hallway. No one spoke. Those who were close to the wall moved clear. The wall-boom repeated several times, as bodies crashed into it in what sounded like a gang tackle.

Layne tried to visualize what the initial scene would be when it was his turn to enter the room. What would their positions be when he walked in? His thoughts drifted to memories of little league football. The angles he couldn't outrun and the tackles he couldn't slip or limp-leg left him tangled until they brought him down. Then the whistle blew and it was over, and there was a minute to rest in the huddle. A few times he had been knocked unconscious and didn't know his name or who he was for a few seconds. But the violence had always been in short bursts. Even fistfights lasted only seconds before they were broken up. This would be much worse, like his brush with death in the ocean.

After what seemed much longer than the goal of two minutes each trainee would be forced to endure, Alvarez came out of the room. His PT shirt was soaked with sweat. Layne expected his expression to be one of relief and accomplishment, but Alvarez was silent, stone-faced. He made his way to the back of the line and sagged quietly.

"Get back in here and grab a shield! Follow instructions!" Pyatt yelled from inside the mat room.

Alvarez hurried back in.

"Beltran, you ready?" Ramirez yelled.

"Yessir," Beltran yelled. His bravery looked authentic. He entered and more commotion ensued.

The number of trainees between Layne and the door diminished quickly. During his weeks at the Academy, his body had exhausted all adrenaline reserves. What little remained was draining away as he stood in line. He was now operating in a kind of shock, a sensation like he was piloting himself from a cockpit.

Guillermo offered a comment over his shoulder to those behind him in line. "Now I know what it must have felt like to be a gladiator going into the Colosseum."

No one responded.

Layne felt himself in the same frame of mind he had been in on the first day when they waited at the security gate to enter the base. He swallowed hard. When there was no one left between him and the door to the mat room, he heard Ramirez shout: "Sheppard, you ready?"

"Yessir," he replied. But it sounded to him like someone else answered.

"Get in here!" Ramirez yelled.

Layne entered the room, and the scene was again not what he had envisioned. The trainees who had gone before and who had already faced the Red Men formed a circle inside the perimeter of the room, holding padded shields, a human ring. Their PT shirts were soaked with sweat and there was no expression whatsoever on any of their faces. He felt like he was floating; he couldn't feel his feet or his legs.

He tried to yell, "Get down, get down!" But his cottonmouth caused the command to sound like a cry for help, a whimper. Through the tunnel vision of the helmet he saw three Red Men encircle him and begin to orbit him, like barbarians. He snapped his head from side to side, trying to look behind, constantly moving his feet like he was walking in place in mud. One Red Man left the merry-go-round and encroached, Layne struck him several times in the leg with the baton with every ounce of force he could muster. The baton striking the leg pads made a sound like chalkboard erasers being clapped together, a sound as benign as his warning commands.

"Get back!" Layne yelled after each swing.

The attacker engaged like a wrestler. The baton blows were ineffectual; they made him think of Ricky.

"Get down!" Layne yelled. The Red Man snatched Layne's left leg and hugged it while Layne tried to balance on the right. He covered his gun with his left hand in desperation. Time felt viscous; he expected to be overwhelmed instantaneously. There was absolute silence except for grunting—only his thoughts made noise, until he realized Instructor Ramirez was shouting.

"Sprawl, Sheppard! Sprawl!"

He found himself hugging the Red Man's leg and nothing more. He recognized Blair's voice shouting, "Come on, Sheppard; punch, kick, use your knees, get on top of him."

Layne punched with his left fist against the padding, spraining the ligaments in his wrist.

Pyatt yelled, "Keep them in front of you! Don't get backed into a corner! Come on, do something, Sheppard."

But his effort was pathetic, and he was relieved when he was tackled from the side and the impotent Nerf bat flew end over end into the corner.

"Keep moving, get his wrists!" Ramirez yelled.

"Ninety seconds to go," Pyatt called out.

Layne could feel burning muscle failure in his arms; he felt anemic. He was in a hopeless, non-leverage position—like he was trying to pick up a coin glued to the floor, using only his fingernails. *Just get on the bottom and ride it out like Ricky said,* he told himself. *Just like a turtle, just be in here two minutes.* But he found himself on his back with a Red Man on top of him. The fingers of the other two Red Men were weaving between his arms and torso, headed toward his gun. *Go into a jiujitsu half-guard like the UFC,* he thought.

The situation was too surreal to comprehend in real time. *I need to tell everyone that I'm dehydrated,* he thought to himself; such an ignominious performance required an explanation. Acidic sweat began to drip from the sponge forehead band of his helmet, stinging his eyes, forcing him to close them and focus on counting seconds in the dark. While he lay on his back, he squinted his eyes open to see Instructor Ramirez hovering above, his mouth was moving.

"Open your eyes," Ramirez yelled. "How can you fight with your eyes closed? Don't quit or you will die . . .

"I said open your eyes!"

Layne ignored him, unable to do more than he was doing, counting.

Ramirez yelled, "Stop!" Only then did the Red Men release him. "Go to the back of the line and do it again!"

The mat room was as quiet as a library. Nearly too exhausted to pick himself up off the ground, he slumbered back to the hallway and the end of the line. The walk to the door was long. He felt bare-naked and could feel people laughing. In the hallway he stood in a lobotomized state, wondering if this had ever happened to anyone before. Maybe this was what Ricky was ashamed to talk about. He was numb, unable to comprehend what had just occurred. Then he heard Agent Ramirez shouting, and a trainee named Sifuentes emerged from the mat room and fell in line behind him. Sifuentes was drenched in sweat as well. The remaining trainees in front of them who had not yet faced the Red Men stood dry and quiet.

"What do we have to do?" Sifuentes asked him, anguished.

"We have to go again," Layne heard himself say.

"Again?" Sifuentes almost moaned.

Layne stared in one spot for what seemed like hours. He came to his senses when two trainees came out of the room carrying another.

"What happened?" someone in line asked.

The trainee closest to the door said, "A Red Man dove at him and broke his ankle. He was standing flat-footed. I could hear it break from out here."

"Who was it?"

"Navarro."

Before he had time to process Navarro being carried out, Layne entered for the second time. He briefly wished for his own injury to avoid the next two minutes. This time he made feeble attempts to fend off the Red Man in front of him with much less baton speed than before, and he once again found himself on his back. He found himself focusing on the damp armpit odor of the Red Man on top of him, as sweat dripped off of the attacker's face and onto Layne's neck and chin. With the taste of blood in his mouth, he looked directly now into the Red Man's face and saw pity. The Red Man let up, allowing him to escape.

Like a geriatric patient, he climbed to his feet and juggled and fumbled his rubber gun. The Red Men watched it fall to the mat without reacting. Layne told himself to dive for it, but his legs wouldn't respond to the message from his brain. His leap resembled more of a collapse, the way he felt during bad dreams, always trying to run, kick, or punch with uncooperative limbs. He grabbed the gun while on all fours and pointed it at all three attackers, praying that the instructors would not make him go through this again.

"Bang! Bang! Bang!" he said.

The Red Men took off their helmets and didn't look at him as they walked away, almost ashamed of their involvement. The trainees with padded shields that surrounded him were; the chirpers among them made smug looks at one another.

"Don't be proud of that," Pyatt said.

22

UNDER DIFFERENT CIRCUMSTANCES, AWAY from the Academy, Layne would have been fascinated by the method in which the weapon was constructed. Group A sat on the wrestling mat and focused on what was being said with undivided attention.

Instructor Pyatt stood in front of them, holding a sinister-looking black canister with a nozzle and trigger mechanism. "The active ingredient in this stuff is a chemical called Capsaicin. It's extracted from cayenne peppers so that it can be weaponized. The Capsaicin is suspended in propylene glycol and pressurized with water so that it becomes aerosol. The abbreviation OC stands for Oleoresin Capsicum.

"The police-strength pepper spray that we use is a high-performance version of the kind of pepper spray women carry in their purses, but this stuff is much more potent. About five percent of the population is immune to the effects of the chemical and it only causes them to have bloodshot eyes for fifteen minutes or so. But in twelve years I've only seen one guy that was immune, so don't get your hopes up."

The trainees sat with their legs stretched out, leaning back on their hands while they listened. The scene reminded Layne of a kindergarten teacher reading a story to the class. But his amusement was muted by what he knew lay in store. The lecture was like learning about Thomas Edison and the light bulb before being walked to the electric chair.

Pyatt's voice seemed labored. "This stuff is commonly known as pepper spray. We need you to be exposed to it so that if you're ever in a situation where you have to use it, you will know what it feels like to get it on you. Worst-case scenario is that it's taken from you and used against you."

Layne visualized a woman with her hair in a ponytail jogging in the park when Pyatt called it pepper spray. Until now, he had only heard it called OC, and he had thought that they were two different things.

"Form two single-file lines facing myself and Instructor Ramirez so we can practice firing. These canisters are dummies, so don't worry about them going off accidentally." Pyatt's behavior appeared guilt-ridden and unenthusiastic, like he wanted to get the whole thing over with.

The trainees formed two lines and Pyatt resumed his demonstration. "You want to hold it just like you hold a pistol. But when you fire it, you want to have your other hand shielding your face from the spray like this, so that if any backfires or deflects you won't get it in your eyes." He held the canister in a pistol-like fashion, using his free hand as a shield, palm spread and facing forward just above the wrist of the firing hand.

"You will use the same warning commands as you did during Stacking. I know you guys are tired of yelling 'Get back!' but the warning commands are essential. You don't want to nail somebody with a baton or spray OC on their face without giving them a chance to comply first." Pyatt sounded sincere.

Layne felt silly performing the drill, as if he were on stage; he was self-conscious. To him, it felt like playing a part in a school play without ever having rehearsed. When his turn came, he pointed the canister at Pyatt and shielded it correctly, but when he tried to yell "Get back!" everyone in the class laughed at his meek voice. He wished he were invisible.

Instructor Pyatt said with a fatherly disappointment, "Do you have any balls, Sheppard?" The laughter escalated but Pyatt ignored the hostiles; he seemed to understand their malevolence. Layne damned the chirpers under his breath as he returned to the back of the line, his head still hung low because of the Stacking disaster. Ego without confidence was a difficult thing to live with.

He told himself to just get it over with. He realized that the Academy was for overcoming fear. Very little of what he retained would be of use in the field—if he could make it—the way almost nothing he had learned in college had been helpful in the real world. OC was the last physical pain obstacle in the way of graduation. But his stomach also ached over concern about an agent from administration coming to get him for the pills now, in addition to the background check. Worry about grades in academic classes occupied a different part of his gut. He was running on fumes now.

It had been a topic for conversation for over three months: Which was worse, Stacking or OC? He was next to certain that Stacking would emerge victorious. Unless he died during OC, he couldn't imagine anything more excruciating than the humiliation of Stacking. What made the experience agonizing beyond compare was that he was forced to endure it in full view of half the class—many of whom enjoyed nothing more than to see him suffer. At least OC would take place where no one could see. It was a tormenting sensation, to cherish the week of time remaining before he had to face the drill while simultaneously longing for it to be over.

Three weeks prior, his group was practicing Felony Stops while the 667 and 668 Classes were going through OC. Layne's group was at the model Port of Entry that had been constructed for Ops training, about a hundred yards down wind from the OC structure. A breeze carried the red mist all the way down to them. He could feel it tickle his nose and throat every five minutes throughout the whole class period. It tasted like what he imagined Agent Orange must have tasted like in Vietnam; it made him think of cancer.

The taste and smell of his introduction to OC were dominating his thoughts so that he could barely pay attention to where he was going as he walked through the courtyard after class. He watched his feet trade off in front of him while he returned to his room toting his backpack. He was embarrassed to even say hello to anyone. Ricky watched him approach from the railing above. When he came up the stairs to the balcony, Layne gave a two-finger salute as he passed Ricky and went into the room. He put his backpack under the bed and took off his duty belt and hung it on the bunk post. He un-tucked his uniform top and joined Ricky at the railing.

"I think it's gonna be more of a stinging pain than Stacking. Like getting a tooth drilled instead of a Charlie horse," Layne said, diving directly into the conversation.

"That's a pretty good comparison; that's about what it's like," Ricky said.

The comment caused Layne to think of another horror story from the beach. He remembered boogie-boarding in Newport Beach when he was about eight years old. It was the first time he had ever caught a wave. He surfed it all the way to the shore, and when he got there the front of the board hit a sand bar and a spray of wet sand flew into his eyes. He couldn't close them fast enough—he could actually see the sand hit the lenses of his eyeballs like mud splatting a television camera lens. The crippling sting prevented him from opening his eyes for nearly an hour. They winced closed every time he tried to wipe the sand out of them with his fingers.

"This is gonna be pushing the boundaries of what I can take," Layne said.

"I just told myself that I'm not driving a forklift for the rest of my life before I went," Ricky said.

Layne nodded with understanding, but he realized now that punching a clock at a menial job was at least painless. He wasn't sure if the pain of boredom and feeling of fruitlessness were worse than what he was putting himself through to acquire money and a respectable career. Being a peon had its appeal.

He had asked Ricky as little as possible about OC until the day before. Ricky explained that the drill was executed in a fabricated room next to the obstacle course. The structure was composed of four metal walls; the dimension roughly twenty feet by twenty feet. The walls were twelve feet high so that no one could see what it was like until their time came. There was no floor, only dirt and patches of grass beneath the trainee's feet. The trainees wore their PT uniforms, just a gym shirt and shorts with the lacrosse helmet and duty belt like Stacking. The Red Man wore the same catcher's gear and lacrosse helmet.

Layne fished for reassurance that he would be okay. "I hate that Nerf bat we have to use as a baton; it's like swinging a wet newspaper. But it's only two minutes."

"Yeah, that thing's useless," Ricky said.

"I'm worried about the part where we have to handcuff the Red Man," Layne said hesitantly.

"You just have to simulate handcuffing him; that part is easy," Ricky said in bitter remembrance.

It didn't sound easy to Layne. "And they just spray OC in your face and the Red Man comes in? Why don't you just close your eyes?" Layne asked.

"The instructor distracts you and sprays you when you're not expecting it. They're good at it," Ricky said. "Trust me, they'll get you. If they don't get you good the first time, they'll spray you again."

"And after they spray you?" Layne asked.

"The instructor leaves the room and the Red Man comes in and you have to get him down and simulate handcuffing him." Ricky waved at one of his friends from the Valley who was walking by the pool toward his room.

"How the hell can you do that when you can't see anything?" Layne asked.

"The Red Man makes it easy on you. They kind of feel sorry for you," Ricky said.

* * * *

LAYNE PUT HIS CAFETERIA TRAY in the kitchen window. He was wearing his t-shirt with Class 590 on the front and an eagle and class motto on the back, athletic shorts and flip-flops. His USB drive hung from his neck on a green lanyard that he had bought at the Student Union. He was trying to fit in. But he wished he were wearing a mask so that no one recognized him. He was only starting to look straight ahead while walking. He had returned to greeting certain people as well.

He left the dining hall and headed to the lounge. His laundry list of worries was bringing him to his breaking point, and today was one of his more insecure days. The Stacking debacle was playing loops in his head. He opened the door to the lounge and felt everyone staring at him then looking away quickly when he looked in their direction. He wished that they could have seen him in his prime, but there was only the miserable present. Blair was sitting down at a table by himself, and Layne fell into an empty chair across from him. Blair looked up briefly, then back down at his book.

"What are you studying for?" Layne asked.

"Applied Authority." Blair spoke to his book.

Even altruistic Blair was behaving awkwardly since Stacking.

"That's what I'm gonna work on, too, then," Layne said.

Blair nodded. Everyone was concerned about finals that were coming after Labor Day. Layne envied everyone else for having only the curriculum to worry about.

"Do you understand Hot Pursuit and all those terms?" Layne said to try to get Blair to talk to him.

Blair looked up, a hint of annoyance on his face. "Those are just circumstances when you don't need a warrant to enter a premises."

"I need to go over those," Layne said.

Blair flipped through pages.

"I still feel beat up from Stacking," Layne said with a deep sigh.

"Don't worry about it; it's over," Blair said.

"I was dehydrated. I was gonna go to the Medical Building, but I was afraid they would defer me." Layne felt compelled to explain himself.

Blair continued flipping through pages.

A patronizing female voice rang out from the table behind him. "You still wouldn't have been able to get out of it. They would've made you do it on a different day." Layne turned around to look. It was Lupita Gorda from Group B. She was sitting with the other Hispanic trainees from the

Valley.

"I wasn't trying to get out of it," Layne fired.

"I heard you have no *cojones*," Gorda said, and there were titters of laughter from the other Hispanics.

Layne stood up and gritted his teeth. In an uncharacteristic moment of impulsive free-fall he snared, "Screw you."

He knew it was a mistake as he was saying it, but he couldn't refrain, and the tirade continued impetuously as he pointed his finger at her. "They laid down for you and Melanie because you're girls. You think you can say whatever you want because women get special treatment?" He felt the heat rising in his face as he let the arrow fly. "You can't even run a lap around the track without stopping, you fat whore." There was a racial slur in his quiver that he narrowly held back at the last moment.

Lupita kept her smile to save face and remain defiant, but his anger caused her to return to her notebook without responding. It was obvious by the wideness of her eyes that she was doing her best to mask the alarm brought on by her overstep. The Mexicans from the Valley looked at each other cautiously, but said nothing, heeding to Layne's rage. His spring-loaded body language indicated that she had exhausted his fuse and he was ready to attack with fists at the slightest retort. He slammed his books in his backpack. He got up and left, regretting the idea to study in the lounge. He should have waited longer to integrate with the others, until the shame blew over. Nothing made him more angrily frustrated than when people didn't believe him when he was making a case.

"Sheppard, wait up!" Blair yelled from behind him as he jogged to catch up.

Layne turned to wait.

"Where are you going?" Blair asked as he matched Layne's stride.

"Back to my room."

"Are you okay?"

"No. Who is Gorda to tell me anything?"

"Forget about her," Blair said.

"It's ridiculous, man! Mexicans! What are they even doing here? And the girls know they're untouchable," Layne griped. Everyone had seen Melanie cheating on exams; she flirted with the trainees on either side of her so that they would let her look off their tests.

"I know. I'm sure Baca has seen her, too," Blair agreed. "She whispers to Greg right in front of him in the middle of a test."

Even Instructor Baca pretended that he didn't see her cheating. If he saw a male trainee cheating, he would be brought to Building 26 to be out-processed immediately. And Lupita Gorda hadn't even come close to making the mile and a half in eleven minutes. The trainees had heard Instructor Pyatt beep his stopwatch when she was only halfway around the track on her last lap. Two male trainees had been forced to resign the week before because they were over a minute too slow during their midterm PT test.

"You weren't in there when Melanie did Stacking," Blair said. He was still matching Layne, stride for stride, although in his anger Layne was picking up the pace.

Layne realized that his manic state had inspired Blair to reveal his true thoughts. "What happened?"

"When she came in, the Red Men took turns going after her in slow motion, and when she hit them, they collapsed right away. It was ridiculous. They took turns going after her like a Kung Fu movie; they Stacked themselves." Blair looked disgusted by the memory.

"That's what I figured. I don't even care, until I hear Melanie's voice chirping with all the others on the bus. She has diplomatic immunity," Layne said.

"You've been paying attention in Law," Blair said, laughing. The instructors were afraid of EEO complaints, which was why they allowed Melanie and Gorda to get away with such severe transgressions. There was a rumor that the year before, a girl was failing Law so she filed an EEO complaint against the instructor. She claimed that he commented about her buttocks and asked her out. The claim was completely frivolous, but they sent the instructor back to his station and she passed.

"There's some weird tension going on between the Mexicans and the whites," Layne said. He had seen the friction building from the first day, but nobody ever talked about it.

"I know what you mean," Blair said. "The Mexicans think that the Border Patrol belongs to them. Mexicans in general are real territorial when it comes to work—*trabajo*. It's because they're always poor with too many kids, and desperate. I've seen it before; they will go behind your back to get you fired so they can get their friends hired in your place. Also, because most of these Mexicans are from border towns like El Paso, they were brought up around Border Patrol; they think guys like us are taking what's theirs."

They both fell silent as they continued toward their dorm rooms.

THE PROVERBIAL HORIZON HAD COME within view. Three years of planning and scheming, and the last few months of physical and mental torture, all seemed to come down to this impending climax: OC. The big day fell on an unseasonably cool and overcast afternoon. The PT instructors led the quiet column out of the PT building toward the OC structure—only the sound of their shoes grinding on sand making a sound. A storm loomed in the distance to the west as the trainees waited for instructions. Lightning lit up black clouds like flashing pompons, too far away to feel the ripple of sound. PT had been rescheduled as the last class of the day because the trainees would be unable to see for a subsequent class period.

Throughout the day, Layne had been fixated on after-school fights in elementary school. The worst part of an after-school fight was waiting for three o'clock, watching the clock and the apprehension of what it would be like. The same sensation had oppressed him for the past three and a half months. It was like he had been sitting through one excruciating, drawn-out school day, knowing that there would be a fistfight before he could go home. Stacking and OC were the bullies waiting for him at the exit.

Instructor Pyatt spoke up when they reached the structure. "I need you to organize yourselves into four groups. Alvarez, you're first; everyone behind you to Fleming, follow me. The rest stay here. Instructor Ramirez will let you know when to bring your group to the other side. Group Two will be Guillermo to Lindquist; Group Three, Michaelson to Saint Claire; Group Four, Samuels to Yanez."

Alvarez and his group followed single-file behind Pyatt, around the corner to the other side of the OC structure, out of view of the remaining three-quarters of the class. Instructor Ramirez peered upon those remaining with an inadvertent expression of pity.

"I need two volunteers from Group Four to help get your classmates from Group One to the water," Ramirez said. "By the time the next group is ready to go, people from Group One should be recovered enough to help. We will need other volunteers as we go along."

The trainees looked at one another without speaking.

"So, after you recover, if you feel like you're able to function, help your classmates to water."

Most everyone responded with a timid, "Yes, sir."

Four Red Men were helping each other put on equipment near the entrance to the green structure next to a makeshift drinking trough. A garden hose was connected to the trough, which was made of PVC and constructed in the shape of a sawhorse, drilled with holes to spray water upward at low pressure like a watering can. Layne had noticed the troughs before and assumed they were for rehydrating during long distance running. They had seemed innocuous until this instant.

His fear returned to the structure; he had never been close to it. It looked like a twenty-foot by twenty-foot bathroom stall painted green. The fabricated room was only fifty yards away from the obstacle course, which ironically reminded him of a playground with its monkey bars, tubes to crawl through, and pebble sand.

Several noiseless minutes passed. Even the coal gray sky seemed to be holding its breath by the way it remained still, without a hint of a breeze. Then came shouts and sounds from inside the structure. The trainees remained stationary, all staring at nothing in particular, as if they were listening to a radio news bulletin. Then came the voice of Instructor Ramirez shouting, then the unmistakable red smell. At that moment the front arrived, and a light breeze swirled then the class inhaled a gasp of concentrated mist. They began coughing in unison.

Alvarez could be heard yelling repeatedly, "Get back!" Then a ruckus, and the trainees could feel the dirt shake beneath their feet. Then the voice of Ramirez again, and two volunteers took notice of direction from Instructor Ramirez and scurried into the structure. They emerged carrying Alvarez underneath each arm, his feet dragging. His PT uniform was soiled with dirt and blades of grass stuck to his knees and elbows. His face appeared freshly sunburned, both his eyes swollen shut, his mouth in a frown with a three-foot-long saliva string hanging from his lip, and a snot bubble in his left nostril. He looked like he had been grieving, on the verge of crying in remembrance of what had just happened to him. Instructor Ramirez trailed the three of them with suppressed compassion. "Get him to the water," he said in his everyday voice.

A Red Man came out of the structure and took his helmet off and dropped it on the dirt with fatigue. One of his comrades handed him a towel and he wiped his face and neck and then his arms. They lacked the enthusiasm for cruelty that drove them during Stacking.

The class watched speechlessly as their classmates were dragged, one by one, from the structure. Volunteers guided the blind to the trough and led their hands to water.

As the number of those who had been "sprayed" increased, they surrounded the water trough, attempting to separate their clamped eyelids and splash water in their eyes. The gathering of wounded eventually abandoned the trough when they realized the futility of water. They began pacing blindly, searching aimlessly with their hands for objects in their way. Stray bodies lay scattered, legs kicking, covering their faces with their hands. They moaned in helpless agony, unable to find relief in any form.

The Red Men yelled and cursed when they exited the room, throwing their helmets, hurrying to wash the second-hand poison off their faces. The hair on their forearms was matted with sweat, dirt, and the red pollen-like Capsicum. They walked like Robocops, as they paced and cursed, the restrictive armor they wore making their movements stiff and bowlegged.

Layne felt his slight confidence wane; he wasn't sure if he could go through with it. *I've never been this afraid before,* he thought. But it was all happening so quickly that it would be more difficult to approach the instructors and tell them that he couldn't do it than it would be to get it over with. The knight he had once thought himself to be remained bound and gagged somewhere. That person would be much more courageous, he thought, as his quarter of the group was beckoned behind the northern wall.

The horror unfolded before him before he could prepare himself mentally, like a brake failure. When his single file unit turned the corner, the secret of what had been happening behind the curtains was revealed. Agent Pyatt was preparing Samuels to go into the room, ordering him into jumping jacks. The instructors were trying to open the pores of each trainee with exertion directly before they entered the structure so that more of the chemical would penetrate their skin. Layne's heart beat out of his chest and he lost control of his breath as Samuels was sent into the room. The terror grounded itself through his toes and heels when there was no one left between him and Instructor Pyatt. He prayed for the first time, *"God, grant me strength."*

"Are you ready?" Agent Pyatt demanded.

"Yessir." He wasn't certain if his response was audible through his strangled speech and cottonmouth.

"Alright, Sheppard. Jumping jacks!"

He felt weightless.

"Faster!" Pyatt shouted.

Pyatt glanced at Agent Ramirez, who waited by the doorway to give a ready signal. A nod came from Ramirez and Pyatt ordered Layne: "Run full speed and touch the perimeter fence."

Reality was difficult to grasp as he ran, and the chain link came upon him in a flash though it was a hundred yards away. The hands that grabbed the chain link were unfamiliar to him, as if he were watching himself from above. He returned out of breath and he slowed as he approached Pyatt, who sent him directly into the room with an underhand motion.

He found himself face to face with Instructor Ramirez, who was holding two live canisters to his sides, his fingers on the triggers. Layne looked upward, only to discover there was no ceiling—as if the structure was simply a curtain to veil the sight of this. The clouds streaming over had never looked so peaceful; the dark sky had returned to blue.

As soon as the Red Man comes in, tackle him before the stuff kicks in, forget about the commands, he thought in desperation.

"Jumping jacks!" Ramirez ordered.

It was as if he were unraveling a scroll of himself as he bounced, a summary of his life up until this point flashed before his eyes.

"Okay Sheppard, this is your chance to make up for that Stacking fiasco. No head strikes," Ramirez said with purpose.

"Where were you born?" Ramirez shouted.

"Schenectady."

"What is the name of the street you grew up on?"

"Linden Street."

"When did you EOD?"

"May 19th."

"Who is your Squad Leader?"

"Guillermo."

Layne felt a bead of cold sweat drip off of his chin.

"What is your station?"

"Douglas."

"Who is the PAIC of your station?"

Kramer's name was on the tip of his tongue and he focused his memory to recall, when a blast of chemically cold gas tattooed a Zorro mask on his face out of nowhere. He witnessed particles of the mist hit the lenses of his eyeballs as it overcame him.

He cursed for not closing his eyes at the right moment. He was surprised by the force and velocity of the weapon; a solid burst extended fifteen feet and precipitated beyond his rear.

Ramirez relocated himself to stand in the doorway and Layne opened his wet eyelashes to view the crime through liquid lenses, a silver sheen cast over his vision. Sound was muffled, like listening underwater, and he sensed a sting pending as the menthol-like cold began to subside.

The Red Man entered, and Layne's attack exploded without hesitation in a cyclone of baton strikes. He felt violated and enraged by the spray. The Red Man stumbled to react in defense and the blows caught him in his left shoulder and knocked him off balance. He regained himself and a blow caught him in the side of the head and twisted his helmet sideways so that his face mask was not centered any more.

The Red Man shrieked, but the sound was drowned in the frenzy.

"I said not in the head!" Ramirez yelled as Layne pressed the attack.

The Red Man collapsed to a knee momentarily, then corrected himself and began to gallop around the room as the chemical simmered. Layne lashed out like a mongoose and snatched a grip on the collar of his chest protector before the Red Man could contemplate an evasive maneuver. He yanked the Red Man downward and the enemy's feet came out from under him. Both bodies met the ground together and the air evacuated from the Red Man's lungs upon collision with the ground. A wrestling match ensued in a cloud of dust.

Ramirez yelled, "Sprawl, Sheppard, get on top of him!"

The inexorable sting arrived, and accumulating without yield, the pain intensified almost instantly like lemon juice in a cut. His eyelids shut involuntarily, and he winced as he maneuvered in mortal combat. The chemical applied pressure to his eyeballs from every direction that caused a sensation of being crushed by an implosion. His eyelids couldn't shut any tighter and his cheeks and brow panicked and attempted to completely cover his eye sockets.

The combatants struggled for position over one another and the Red Man gained a headlock as the battle intensified in the dark. The grunts of fighting gave way to Layne moaning in pain from the sting as he heaved the Red Man on his back with a head and arm throw. Layne's shoulder crashed into his chin before he could escape, then all at once, the strength in the Red Man's arms deflated and he became limp. Layne rolled him onto his stomach like a dummy and simulated handcuffing him through the feel of pebbles and small twigs that were pressed into the palms of his hands. The chemical pressure continued to crank tighter like a vise, gripping more relentlessly with every second. He grunted and gnashed his teeth.

There was a sudden vacancy in the atmosphere; it was peaceful and quiet as he knelt and covered his face with his hands. Only the ringing of his eyes wincing made noise. He was fighting now not to give in to the pain and cry—not only the pain beneath his furrowed brow, but the merciless pain of the fifteen-month ordeal that the sting seemed to externalize.

Concern grew about the limit to his threshold for pain, and how he would continue to cope when it surpassed his capacity to endure it. The mist had gotten in his mouth, and his tongue and lips burned like he had eaten a potent jalapeño pepper. He pulled himself off his knees and crept aimlessly toward the voice of Instructor Ramirez. "You two, get him to the water. Just ride it out Sheppard. It will wear off."

Two pairs of hands grabbed him under his armpits and guided him out of the structure. One of the voices he recognized as Ryan Danielson's, the diplomat, the one who was cheerful in all weathers. Layne remembered his voice from when he had introduced his fiancée Marianne at Family Day.

"You're okay. We're gonna get you to the water. Try to open your eyelids and splash water on your eyeballs," Danielson said.

"It feels like there's something in my eye," Layne moaned.

Danielson tried to calm him. "It's just the OC. It will go away, there's nothing in your eye."

"No, I think I got something in my eye," Layne cried. He had never experienced this level of pain. Knowing that there was no medicine or remedy that could be sought for relief compounded the torture.

When he managed to pry his eyelids apart, air contact irritated the sting and they clamped back shut. The initial sting and burn had felt like he had put Tabasco sauce in his eyes with an eyedropper. But the pain was soaring now, like his eyes were being dissolved by molecular acid. The thought crossed his mind to ask someone to knock him out to escape the pain. It was still escalating, and there was no indication of a plateau.

Danielson guided his hands until he recognized the shape and contours of the PVC and felt the tiny streams of water on his palms. Danielson abandoned him as he splashed handfuls of cold water onto his face but felt no relief. Liquid only felt wet regardless of its temperature. He gave up and lay on the ground alongside the others, whom he could hear kicking and moaning. His eyes still shut, he heard Melanie crying while she yelled, "Get back," inside the walls of the structure. Then seconds later, he heard her wailing and sobbing somewhere near him. He didn't hold it against her.

THE FIRST WEEKEND IN OCTOBER had finally arrived. Layne smiled and looked out the passenger window of the rental car that Greg was driving. He was enjoying the view of the low mountains of western New Mexico through which they were passing. Prior to today, when he imagined the end of September, it had seemed like another fantasy that would require a miracle to reach. It felt dreamlike to have actually made it this far. To be traveling back the way they had come in June made him feel that someone had been looking out for him. He adjusted the passenger seat to his liking, pleased that someone else was driving again so that he could enjoy the changes in scenery. He began to relax. He reasoned that if something were going to happen regarding Damon and the pills, or the background check, it would have happened by now. There was only one week left of the Academy.

Greg was an Academy acquaintance, but Layne had little more than said hello to him in four months, primarily because Layne despised Melanie and she was usually with him outside of class. Greg had somehow remembered Layne's interest in Bisbee during the station tour and asked him if he was interested in a road trip to Arizona. He knew that Layne would probably want to go to the barbecue party at Danielson's house in Tucson to celebrate the arrival of graduation in a week, as well as look for a place to live. Greg was intent on securing a house to rent in the mysterious mining town by the end of the long weekend. He had rented a car; all Layne had to do was pay for gas. Greg didn't ask him for help driving, and Layne wasn't going to offer unless he brought it up.

Layne glanced periodically at Greg while he drove. His effeminate mannerisms and fragile build made Layne wonder how he had made it past PT. Layne had told him that he, too, was going to arrange for a place to rent during the trip. But his primary motivation was a reprieve from the Academy, and a ride to the party at Ryan Danielson's house in Tucson. He was only pretending to look for a house in order to catch a ride.

Once at Douglas Station they would need a place to stay. It was imperative that they secure boarding. Greg was certain that he was going to graduate; he had one of the best grade-point averages in the class. Layne still wasn't 100% certain that he would make it. They still had finals to overcome, and his grades were barely average in Law and Applied Authority. He would concern himself with a place to stay when he was positive that he was leaving the Academy with a badge.

"I've been counting the days until today, but now that it's here I'm already dreading going back," Layne said after thirty miles of silence. "I can feel time ticking away."

Greg nodded while he maintained concentration on the road.

"It seems like the good part of the trip is already over. The best part was when we were dismissed from class. The rest is watching it run out," Layne said, trying for conversation.

Greg nodded and glanced at his side view mirror. It was his first time at the wheel of a rental car.

Layne was excited to see what Bisbee looked like from within the town. The two of them were the only ones on the station tour in May who were interested in living in Bisbee. The others heeded the warning from Agent Ortiz and were traveling to secure apartments in Sierra Vista. Layne realized he might be in a jam if he didn't have a place lined up within the next two weeks, but to plan beyond finals in Law and Applied Authority would be a felony jinx. Out of respect for his superstition he was not going to make any commitments until after the graduation ceremony.

"I love this terrain; I don't recognize any of it from the bus ride to Artesia," Layne said, trying again to break the monotony, hoping that Greg would elaborate on his thoughts and distract him from his introspection.

"Me too," Greg said.

Now that the fear of agents from administration was subsiding, Layne's mind had searched and found a new topic for dejection. He couldn't fully suppress the guilt; that this trip would have felt like a victory lap if he had conducted himself more appropriately at the Academy.

Layne's self-absorption was redirected. He was struck by the "old mining town" feel of Bisbee as they entered the city limits. Desert sage speckled the bronze soil of the surrounding hills, and there were walls along the street painted with doves and peace/love urban art murals. Slender cypress trees towered sporadically in every direction. The unique ambiance compelled him to comment, "Remember when we first saw this place? It was from up on that hill."

"Yep, on that station tour," Greg recalled.

"I'm going to learn more about this town . . . its history. I'll bet there are a lot of wild stories in a town as old as this one."

They quickly arrived at Greg's future rental. The realtor was already parked on the street in front of the mountain-style house, waiting diligently for their arrival. The little house looked placid, tucked away just west of historic Old Bisbee. It was a two-bedroom and was nestled cozily by time among mature oak trees. Layne thought of the place they'd passed a few minutes before, on the main drag through Bisbee.

"1916 House For Sale," read the sign at the sidewalk in front of a little white frame building with a cozy front porch. "Two bedroom, 1 bath; new storage shed off back; major foundation repairs and leveling; new picket fence; new copper plumbing; total kitchen remodel (20 years ago), new roof (15 years ago), total bath remodel (10 years ago)." Layne gulped when he saw the price: $199,500.

Layne took a long look at the realtor when she got out of her car. She was middle-aged, late forties, Layne guessed, and wore glasses with her hair up. She was dressed in slacks and a white blouse—business attire, which was what he had expected. The same females at the Academy were the only women he had laid eyes on in about 130 days.

Greg met her with a timid handshake. Layne followed them silently into the house, charmed by the original creaking wood floors and living room fireplace. He approved of Greg's choice of location; it would be exotic to live in the mountains while working in a desert border setting only twenty miles away.

After the tour, they followed the realtor in her car to her leasing office on Main Street, where Greg submitted a deposit and signed the paperwork to rent the house beginning in two weeks. When they left the office, Greg looked like he had removed a great errand from his mind, causing Layne to feel envious.

"Do you want to check out any places while we're here? We've got plenty of time; we don't have to be at Danielson's right away," Greg said.

"No, I just decided that I'm gonna wait until we graduate, then worry about it."

"You sure? We aren't gonna have much time after graduation."

"Yeah, I'm sure."

They fastened their seat belts and the air conditioning resumed at full blast as Greg started the car, in search of the road that led to Highway 80 out of town, which would take them to Interstate 10 toward Tucson.

"I'm gonna have to get a car, too," Layne said. "But I want to make sure I graduate first. My grades aren't as good as yours." Layne felt the need to explain why he had not put forth any effort to look for housing like he had said he would. He wasn't sure if Greg believed him or not.

"Let's go get blasted then," Greg said.

"Okay!"

"Danielson's barbecue should be a blast," Greg said enthusiastically.

"I hope there's some chicks there; I'm starving," Layne said. "I feel like I've been in prison for four months."

The sun was descending into the strange mountains surrounding their path to Tucson as they passed near the Old West town of Tombstone, site of the famous Gunfight at the OK Corral in 1881. Layne had given up trying for conversation. They passed close to half an hour without saying anything to each other. Eventually, though, he couldn't help himself from speaking out about what was churning inside his head. "I hope Field Training isn't too rough."

Greg looked over at Layne; the statement seemed to strike him. "I don't know. I mean, I heard that they ease you into it. They're not gonna throw us to the wolves right off the bat." Greg paused then added, "I hope."

All of a sudden, Layne didn't feel like talking either. He realized that the trial had just begun, and the field in Douglas would be much more deserving of fear than the Academy was. But they were almost to Tucson; he was about to be temporarily free from worry.

The sun was almost completely gone as they entered the outskirts from Interstate 10. The conversation ran into another dead end until they arrived at Danielson's house. As they approached, Layne observed the neighborhood with intrigue. There was no grass in the front yards. The ground was composed of yellow dirt with stray desert grass and prickly pear cactus scattered about. He stared for a long moment at a lone saguaro standing next to a mesquite tree in the center of Danielson's yard. Greg pulled up along the sidewalk and turned off the engine. There already were several cars occupying the driveway space in front of the carport.

Layne itched to open the twelve-pack he carried, as they rang the doorbell. He again was overcome by the warmth of Tucson at dusk. He sensed the delight of people talking in the backyard. The awkwardness of being introduced to a multitude of people all at once would be eased if he was lubricated. But out of respect for Ryan, he had decided that it would be inappropriate to arrive partially intoxicated to this type of gathering. Once inside, he would embrace the supportive norms of social drinking. The doorknob turned and opened, and Danielson's future wife was there with a smile.

Layne remembered her face from Family Day at the Academy, and a flashback returned him to when he had met her. This evening she was wearing a sundress, which displayed her voluptuous shape. She had fair skin and curly, dyed-blonde hair; he could tell by looking at her that she was Hispanic.

"Hi!" Marianne greeted them.

"Hi," Layne and Greg said simultaneously.

"I'm Marianne, Ryan's fiancée." She waved them in through the open door.

"I'm Layne. I met you at Family Day," Layne reminded her.

"I remember. Come on in. There's people out back and in the kitchen."

They followed her past plates full of taquitos and other finger foods neatly arranged on the dining room table. The ceiling fan rocked and swooshed as it cooled the kitchen and family room. Dim lamps lit the room now that the sun had set. Among groups of strangers, Layne identified two classmates who would be stationed in Tucson. He knew their names, but he didn't know them well enough to feel comfortable striking up a conversation. He greeted them and moved on.

He found space in Danielson's refrigerator for his twelve-pack, removing a can for himself and one for Greg. The top of his beer cracked loudly, and foam rose from the opening to fill the rim. The condensation and cold from the can froze his fingers. He took a long swig and felt a tingle, like pixie dust. After four months on base, a party with friends in someone's private home felt strange in a positive way, like an airport in a foreign country.

When he turned around, Marianne had brought over two young women from the small crowd. "These are my friends Felina and Rebecca."

The two bashfully offered their hands to shake. The allure of their youthfulness was magnetic. They looked to be in their early twenties. Layne felt the smallness of their hands as he shook them respectfully. They were both attractive, but he held onto Felina's hand much longer than Rebecca's. She looked away bashfully when he met eyes with her. He liked the shininess and shoulder length of her black hair. Gold earrings dangled from her ears, and he was aroused by her shape. She had prominent hips and bust. He noticed her French manicured nails as she was fidgeting slightly with her hands after the introduction.

Layne didn't feel oiled enough to engage in conversation with new girls yet, but he felt at ease with Marianne, since they had met previously.

"Ryan told me that your family is from La Paz," Layne said to her.

"Have you been there?" Marianne asked.

"*Yo viví en La Paz por casi cuatro meses,*" Layne said, then thought about the words he had used to make sure that he had told her correctly that he had lived in La Paz for about four months.

"*¿Hablas Español?*" Marianne asked as she grinned.

"*Cómo no.*" Layne wouldn't look at the others, slightly embarrassed that they were hearing him speak Spanish. He felt in the spotlight. He considered that maybe he sounded arrogant by saying "of course" when she asked if he spoke Spanish.

"*Estoy impresionado. Hablas muy suave,*" Marianne smiled, but Layne wondered if she was truly impressed at how smooth he spoke, or if she was just being polite to stroke the ego he was letting show.

Layne felt himself blush; everyone continued to watch and listen. But within, he tingled with optimism. He would relish the moment, and worry about tomorrow, tomorrow. He resolved that he needed to learn to be more light-hearted and less critical of himself in regard to his behavior under duress at the Academy.

"So, when do you guys graduate?" Rebecca asked.

Layne let Greg answer while he concentrated on looking at Rebecca so as not to stare at Felina. Rebecca was short, with cute short blonde hair. She wore minimal makeup and her fingernails were non-feminine. She was a nurse, Layne had gathered.

"We graduate in two weeks, I hope," Greg answered.

"Are you guys excited?" Felina asked as she tried to make herself look comfortable.

"Yeah, but we have finals still," Layne said with a brief smile. He looked around the room, trying to look unimpressed by the girls. Danielson had bottles of Bacardi and Jose Cuervo on the kitchen table with the food.

Layne clung to his vow to drink beer only.

Layne turned back to Marianne, *"¿Has vivido en Mexico?"*

"Nunca, pero yo he visitado unas veses," Marianne answered. She spoke quickly, but he was fairly certain that she said she had never lived in Mexico, but had visited there a few times.

Layne grabbed a second beer from the refrigerator and drank half of it in one pull. He gritted his teeth until the sting subsided. The cold tickle and suds were polishing the hang-ups in his Spanish pronunciation, and his verb conjugation was becoming stutter-free. Beer expedited the mental word search for vocabulary while in this state. He responded with quick, intelligent answers to questions, as double R's rolled off of his tongue harmonically.

He could feel Felina watching him, and he needed more to drink in order to appear more confident. He decided to talk to her more in depth when he gathered the courage.

When the group exhausted topics for small talk, he went out back to breathe free air and examine the plant life in the yard to escape the awkwardness. Danielson met him there shortly after to relay a message of sorts.

"Some of us are going to a bar around eleven. Felina told Marianne that she wants you to go," Danielson reported.

"That would be awesome; she's hot," Layne said. But the invitation only made him more nervous.

"She just got off work; she didn't even get ready. She looks even better when she's all fixed up," Danielson said.

"Thanks for inviting me by the way," Layne said.

"You got it, buddy, Danielson said, adding in a half-whisper, "Don't say anything to the other guys about it, though. When they start leaving, we'll head out."

"I'm supposed to split a hotel with Greg tonight," Layne said.

"You can stay at my house. We have a guest bedroom," Danielson said.

"Sweet! That will save me about forty bones."

Danielson gave him a fist bump and headed back into the house. Layne felt inspired. People seemed to be approving of him, but he didn't know how to proceed with Felina. It was rare that a girl of such beauty was interested in him.

As he reentered the house, he closed the sliding glass door carefully. He felt expected to come back inside. He awkwardly avoided making eye contact with Felina; he hadn't gathered the courage to talk to her individually yet. He thought he should stay at the hotel with Greg like he agreed, but this took priority. Under normal circumstances, his failure to follow through on a commitment would have left him troubled with guilt. But considering the deprivation of the last four months, girls superseded the honor of his word. *It's alright, I don't need Greg*, he thought.

* * * *

A SUFFICIENTLY PIERCED AND TATTOOED WAITRESS brought their drinks and set the tray on their table, distributing them in a hurry. It was Danielson's favorite hole-in-the-wall, dive bar in Tucson. Nevertheless, Layne glowed with satisfaction. He could see the blue in the bulging veins of his arms and hands circulating audacity throughout his body and brain. The four of them—Danielson and Marianne, Layne and Felina—were seated on stools, around a wooden bar table. He moved in closer to Felina, brushing his skin against the soft fabric of her blouse. He was positive that he was not encroaching; she was beginning to feel comfortable with him touching her. She smiled when he put a hand on her knee for a moment, and, when she didn't protest, he moved in even closer to place his arm around her waist. The warmth of her torso made him smile at her, and she smiled back at him briefly.

Sailing on the high of new female companionship—such moments few and far between—there was no alternative but to seize them. The artificial blithe combined with the delicate smell of a new woman within his space caused eyes to sparkle and the classic rock music to manipulate his ears the way its creators had intended.

"This is awesome!" Layne shouted to the group above the music.

"You want to go get a shot with me?" Danielson yelled back.

"Does Dolly Parton sleep on her back?" Layne quipped as he got up from his stool. Danielson laughed, and the women smiled a little.

Layne's eyes wandered to the cleavage of Felina's breasts. She noticed but didn't scold him with her eyes. He pretended his glance was accidental and he wasn't embarrassed. He concluded that the way he was feeling should be the way he behaved at all times. He noticed that people were more entertained by his presence when he was confident.

Layne and Danielson headed merrily to the bar. The less than congenial female bartender waited on two regulars first, which Danielson overlooked.

"We were standing here before those two," Layne said loud enough for them to hear.

Danielson ignored the comment and took out his wallet and pulled out a twenty, paying for this round.

"Prost," Layne said, as they touched the shot glasses together before slugging them.

Layne smacked his tongue at the fragrant tequila, and the tang of salt and lime lingered in his mouth as the two of them returned to the round stool-table.

Ryan and Marianne began talking to one another over the noise, their attention diverted from Layne and Felina intentionally. Layne leaned over and kissed her quickly, emboldened by the shot of courage. She wasn't inviting him, but she didn't resist either. She grinned with surprise momentarily.

"I love this song," Layne exclaimed to Felina, while his hands were still holding her waste.

"You like Fleetwood Mac?" There was skepticism in Felina's voice.

"They are one of my favorites," Layne responded.

"You don't look like you would like that kind of music," Felina said, raising her voice so that he could hear her.

"Drowning, in the sea of love, where everyone would love to drown," Layne quoted, singing the line as best he could, although he knew that he would be embarrassed about it the next day.

"You're funny." Felina was smiling broadly now. She knew he was being sincere.

"I'm not normal. I would never admit I like that kind of music to the guys in my class," Layne exclaimed.

"Where are you from?" she asked.

"Colorado."

"Really? I have always wanted to live there. Why would you ever leave?"

"When you've lived someplace your whole life, you know, even people from Hawaii want to move after a while. I hate cold and snow, and I love the desert."

"I don't want to live in ugly Tucson for the rest of my life." Felina put her hand on Layne's knee.

"My point exactly. I think Tucson is awesome; it's intriguing to me. Probably because it's new." Layne felt the heat of her hand penetrate through the denim of his jeans to his skin.

"Will you sing a karaoke song for me?" Felina asked.

Layne felt himself recoil but made an effort not to show it. "What do you want me to sing?"

"I want you to sing Rocky Mountain High." She gave his knee a slight squeeze.

"The John Denver song?" Layne pretended to be enthusiastic about the request.

She nodded with a big smile.

He picked up his full glass of beer and drank three-quarters of it all at once. He told himself to just do it as he guzzled. Perhaps she would return his calls if he made her believe he was fearless about such things.

He knew he was drunk; his buzz had plateaued. The liquor assisted him in trying to look confident as he headed for the microphone. He could feel all eyes on him as the music started and the lyrics to the song appeared from left to right on the karaoke screen. At the sound of his own singing, his face grew hot and he felt naked. He saw people in booths and sitting at the bar smiling and turning to say things to each other, no doubt about him. He was not sure why Ryan preferred this bar; they were out of place among this type of crowd. He gripped the microphone like he was biting a stick for pain, longing for the crawling seconds to be over. Bridges and choruses seemed to be never ending.

* * * *

HE WOKE UP AND STARED AT the ceiling as his eyes adjusted. Then he gasped in an instant and reached to his right to feel that she was not lying beside him. His last memory was smelling her hair as she fell asleep with her back to him, but the broken clip was only a few seconds long. He winced at the memory. He remembered her stopping him while his fingers tussled to unsnap her bra.

It came back to him how drunk he had gotten, and the glimpse stirred alarm. The discomfort of hot pipes expanded, rising in temperature until they began throbbing with his heartbeat. His body wanted to sweat but lacked the moisture. He wondered how he had slept through such pain. He thought with panic, his ears ringing as he lay there, knowing the symptoms of another decadent night would not subside by the end of the long weekend. The good part was over, and the bill had arrived.

The regret of the night before was even more dreadful and augmented than he had anticipated it being during the beginning in the kitchen, when he had passively dismissed its inevitability. With mounting anguish, he tried to recall if he had said anything foolish, if he had offended her or somehow caused her to want to distance herself from him in the middle of the night. He imagined himself swinging a sword around in the living room in his pilotless state. Many things he could have done seemed just as appalling while grasping the anarchy of missing time.

He was afraid to peek out the door of the guest room and see Ryan or Marianne making coffee in the kitchen. If they were there, he would act normal, as if he remembered everything and he had intended every bit of whatever he had said or done. Hopefully they wouldn't bring up anything from the night that was remorseful news to him.

His next thought came unbidden from memories of seven years of loathsome mornings-after. Perhaps they were still asleep, and he could surreptitiously tiptoe into the kitchen. Crossing the line was a secret he kept guarded, because his reasons for doing so would be misconceived. His intent was not to become drunk again, but to alleviate the disquiet about the possible infractions he might have committed while he was disconnected from reason. It would in turn ease the physical pain. He guessed that they had put the Bacardi back in the cupboard above the sink if it wasn't still on the dining room table.

He pulled off the covers and walked around the bed to peep out the door, careful to make as little noise as possible. It was too late; they were already moving about, quietly cleaning up. He had no vehicle to drive to the store. Both Marianne and Ryan looked toward him in the doorway, but they didn't say good morning. They returned to their chores. He speculated that perhaps their shun was because they were just as hung over as he was. Based on their lack of greeting, he was afraid to ask if he could take a shower.

When he dressed and came into the kitchen, Marianne greeted him with a simple, "Hey." Ryan went into the living room to pick up, pretending he didn't notice that Layne had surfaced.

"Did you have fun last night?" Marianne asked, as if she had to say something.

"Yeah, I had a blast. I don't feel too hot today though," Layne admitted with regret. The night didn't seem as fun now as it had while it was occurring.

"Greg is coming to pick you up in fifteen minutes. He said to make sure you're ready," Marianne relayed. He detected a trace of indignation in her tone. She was stuffing the last of the empty beer cans from the kitchen counter into a trash bag.

"I'm ready now," Layne said.

Marianne nodded.

"Where did Felina go?" Layne forced himself to ask. Then he held his breath.

"She had someplace to be this morning." Marianne was not going to offer any more information, so Layne asked, "Can you give me her number? I forgot to get it last night."

Marianne searched the drawers and found a pen. She wrote down the number on a piece of paper and handed it to him. Layne tucked it into a special compartment within his wallet. He was torn between the urge to ask Marianne if he had done anything inappropriate, and not wanting to know. Not knowing was almost as satisfactory as her telling him that he had not, until enough time passed until it didn't matter. If he had acted improperly, he could explain, and maybe Ryan wouldn't be mad at him. But he had known Ryan for almost four months now, and Layne's next-day apologies were already losing value. Better not to know, he thought. He would worry about it either way, knowing or not knowing. The shame felt juvenile; it was years past excusable.

25

FELINA THOUGHT SHE HAD LOCATED a parking space, only to discover that a motorcycle had claimed the spot. She sighed and continued searching. The parking lot of the event center was fully occupied with seemingly nothing but pickup trucks and old minivans. Most of the pickup trucks were customized with chrome bed liners and aftermarket wheels, and proudly displayed the surname of the owner across the back window in old English lettering. Each pickup truck flaunting male machismo seemed to be forced to choose between its owner's last name or a picture of the Virgin of Guadalupe for decoration.

She was lucky to find a space in the far corner of the parking lot. She should have arrived fifteen minutes earlier, but she had taken a nap to try and recover from the night before with Marianne, Ryan, and Layne at the bar.

She turned off the engine and checked her makeup in the rearview mirror. She sighed at her appearance. Her eyes still looked tired and bloodshot despite the extra eye shadow and liner that she had used to try to conceal their fatigue. After the hour-long nap, she was delayed further when she couldn't decide which dress to wear and which heels came closest to matching. She was in need of new clothes.

At the entrance to the venue, a Hispanic man wearing a Tejano cowboy hat and western boots was courteously holding the entrance door open to allow the last of the late-arriving guests to enter ahead of him. The stragglers with last choice parking spaces were streaming through the parking lot swiftly to make up for their late arrival.

As long as she was inside and seated before 6:00 p.m., her tardiness wouldn't be considered disrespectful. She checked the clock on her cellphone; it was 5:49. She could feel the warmth of the asphalt on the soles of her feet through her nylons—it was impossible to operate the clutch and accelerator with her heels on. She grabbed her heels from the passenger seat and put them on quickly with her car door open. She used the reflection of herself in the driver's side window to check herself with a final once-over.

She had chosen to wear her aqua blue sheath dress. It was several years old, and she wasn't fond of it. But it was the only garment that seemed appropriate for this *Quinceañera*. She had worn her red dress earlier in the year for a different cousin's ceremony. She turned sideways and smoothed the dress along her torso in a rush. The only adjustment necessary was to pull the top of her dress upward to reveal an inch less of her cleavage.

She threw her purse over her shoulder and walked as fast as she could in heels. She wished she had a small purse that went better with this dress, as she zipped her keys inside. She wasn't satisfied with her only set of heels that went with it either.

The banquet room was packed full of tables with family and friends, festively settling into their seats for the celebration of her fifteen-year-old cousin becoming a woman. Felina stood holding her purse in front of her with two hands while she searched the banquet room for her parents and brother among the guests who were hugging and greeting one another. She wanted to blend in quickly; she hoped that no one noticed that she had missed the church service. She recognized the silver conchos on the hat band of her dad's Charro cowboy hat and confirmed that it was him when she spotted her aunt's feathered hair next to her younger brother Eduardo.

Her heels snapped as she crossed the dance floor to join her family at the table. After multiple hugs and cheek kisses, she became settled and placed her purse under the chair they had saved for her.

"*Estabas casi tarde otra vez,*" said her dad, Federico, who was the first to speak to her, and, as usual, greeted her critically for nearly being late again.

"It doesn't start for five minutes, Dad; I'm not late," Felina snapped as she stood up to adjust the skirt of her dress before sitting back down.

Federico chewed a bite of a roasted jalapeno pepper and washed it down with a Modelo beer then wiped his mustache with a napkin. Judging by the look on his face, tonight was an evening when he was trying to limit himself to three. He set the bottle down in front of his plate and returned his attention to his food. He was wearing his favorite western shirt with his silver bolo tie to match his hatband. His duty of reminding her that he disapproved of the life she was leading was fulfilled for the evening. He had given her a dirty look as soon as they made eye contact from across the room. He was critical of her whenever he saw her now. The chastising had begun on her eighteenth birthday. It had increased in frequency and severity every day that passed that she wasn't engaged or planning to be engaged.

Most of the guests had already fetched their plates and were enjoying the food and the occasion. The banquet room was bustling with the feast and the trumpets and accordions of Banda music. The carne asada and tempting smells coming from the adjoined food tables were calling for her; she hadn't eaten yet today. Most everyone was drinking Cerveza Sol, but just the sight of beer bottles made her queasy. She knew that grease would ease her sour stomach. She scooted her chair back out and headed for the three adjoining tables against the east wall where the line was growing long with people who had skipped lunch in anticipation of the party catering.

When her turn came, she grabbed a plate and ladled two meals worth of beans and rice onto her plate from the steam table food pans. She used the ladle to cut the blanket of cheese, separating two enchiladas for her plate. She completed the dish with a pair of tortillas and bent over to select a one-liter glass bottle of Mexican Coca-Cola from one of five ice chests full of assorted Mexican beers, Fanta and Squirt.

She was too hungry to participate in the conversation about her cousin, Arianny, yet. Felina's aunt had been planning this *Quinceañera* for the past nine months. Arianny's fifteenth birthday was Wednesday, and today was Sunday.

Felina chose to avoid participation in the standard conversation that took place when the families assembled for an event. She considered the conversations to be repetitive and shallow. Instead, she took in the room as she ate. She adored her family and the traditions of their culture, but she had decided about the time of her own *Quinceañera* that she didn't want to assimilate to the social patterns of her environment.

She was related to ninety percent of the two hundred people in the banquet room. She vowed privately to never be dependent upon government assistance, like many of the girls her age. Most of the girls in the room had illegitimate children. If they didn't have at least one child they couldn't afford by their eighteenth birthday, they were pregnant and expecting one. The pattern had become routine and was dispiriting to her. Their virginity was gone by the time the *Quinceañera* was being planned, despite their strict Catholic upbringing.

She couldn't understand why, as children, the girls didn't learn from witnessing the females in their community ruin their lives. She reasoned that it wasn't necessarily their fault and they were too young to know what they were getting themselves into. Not only did their parents condone their lifestyle choices, but some of the adults in the community even recommended that their daughters become pregnant so that they could qualify for AHCCCS (Arizona Health Care Cost Containment System) and be eligible for free health care and food stamps. Felina couldn't think of a more costly mistake that a person could make. Even a severe drug addiction had a solution; what the girls were ignorantly inviting was an unrelenting eighteen years of abject adversity.

She kept her opinion to herself, but she thought that common sense would urge them to reject the paths of the bad role models and instead use them as cautionary lessons. The mothers, older sisters, cousins and aunts exponentially compounded the difficulty of their low incomes by getting pregnant with no means of taking care of the children they bore.

To Felina, the tragedy of single motherhood had become astoundingly routine the older and more aware she became. By the time the girls were fifteen, they inevitably had chosen a bad boy to fall in love with—the alpha dog of the neighborhood, who wore his hat sideways and was constantly saving money to fill-in his sleeve tattoos or soup-up his pickup truck with a lift kit, or buy ground effects for his Honda. For some senseless reason, the boys who listened to their parents and studied for good grades were of no interest to the girls while they were childless.

Once they became sexually mature, the girls' wasted lives unfolded in three predictable stages that Felina could identify. In the first stage, they fell in love with a cocky, older boy. Despite warnings from their parents, the girls would allow the boys to talk them into sex. Birth control was taboo within their religion. Invariably, the girls would end up pregnant by the time they were sixteen, and by the time the baby was born, the alpha male father had already moved on to another ignorant young girl. In a way she felt sorry for the girls. They were sincerely in love and had no concept of the cost and responsibility that came with raising a child.

Felina took a sip of her Coke while she chewed and observed women in their late thirties who were wearing knee-length rhinestone dresses. The garments were skin-tight on bodies that shouldn't have been displayed. She continued to watch and think without participating in the conversations, partly because she didn't like speaking Spanish. She didn't blame her people for the way their culture had devolved; they weren't entirely responsible. In doctrinal areas of Mexico, girls were required to live with their parents until they were married. Once they were married, they had large families. In the old country, merely moving out of their parent's house before they were married was ignominious beyond recall. The respectable members of the community would shun such a girl. To be pregnant and not married was unspeakable. The girl would be labeled a *Puta* (whore), and her family would live in shame for the rest of their lives; it was catastrophic.

But the customs of where Felina came from had been erased during the span of what seemed like one generation. She believed that her people's way of life had been corrupted by American culture and public assistance, the way the border towns in Mexico had been corrupted by American Prohibition in the 1920s. The youth of today were helplessly influenced by the American media, and the older generations who knew better were dying off.

Her aunt told her the news that her second cousin, Lupe, had just found out that she was pregnant. It was monthly news; only one of a handful was married. Felina knew that Lupe had been trying to corral her boyfriend for several years. He was routinely philandering. Felina could predict how the situation would unfold: Lupe would remain loyal to him in hopes of winning him back, to convince him to settle down with her and raise a family. Oftentimes, a girl like Lupe would intentionally become pregnant by the same boy a second time, reasoning that the prospect of a family would be enticing and would persuade him to stay with her. She had never once seen their strategy succeed.

Her thoughts were beginning to return to Layne more frequently since she had left him sleeping that morning. She worried that his interest in her was driven by alcohol and desire for a one-night stand. She was concerned that she came off as promiscuous to him. She continued eating while she remained absorbed in her thoughts. She had never once mentioned her observations to her family.

She saw multiple girls who had graduated to the second stage of the enigma of her clan. By the time they were twenty, the girls realized that it was hopeless to try to persuade the bad boy to come back to them and help care for the children. At this stage, the mothers were desperate. They had resorted to begging family and friends to babysit for them so that they could go to work and try to earn some money. The financial assistance they received from the government took care of the medical necessities of the child but was barely enough to feed them. It didn't come close to covering the cost of rent, utilities, and clothing. Without help from the deadbeat father, the girls found themselves halfway through the second stage. The betas, the boys who the girls had not been interested in when they were fifteen, were suddenly appealing to the single mothers. The girls needed someone to help them make ends meet for their children. The boys who were desperate for female attention fell victim to the girls during this stage. The girls used the one commodity they had to barter with in order to survive.

Felina wondered if any of the others in the room noticed how prominent the boys and girls involved in this stage were. The second-stage mothers brought the fill-in boyfriends with them in public because they had to in order to make them believe that the relationship was sincere. The beta males who picked up the slack of the alpha males in the second stage appeared to be undeserving cuckolds to her. They were clueless to the fact that the child's biological father could still have sex with the single mom anytime he wished, regardless of her relationship status.

Felina laughed to herself when she imagined what the arrangement would look like if it were printed in contract form. It would say that the single mother agreed to have sex with the cuckold almost any time he wished, and she would be seen in public with him if he agreed to financially provide for and take care of another man's seed. The cuckold usually lived with the stage two mother and often married her. If necessary, the woman would tell him that she was on birth control, then have a child by him for insurance and say it was an accident.

Felina had heard nefarious stories about young mothers requesting the cuckold stay home to babysit for her while she allowed herself a "girls night out" with her friends. Once away from the house she would meet up with another guy while the unsuspecting cuckold stayed at home with the child or children of another man. The guy involved in the tryst was often referred to as a "Sancho." Felina had even heard rumors that the girls would become pregnant by the *Sancho* and allow the cuckold to believe the child was his. She had seen multiple examples of children who looked nothing like the man who was supposed to be their father.

Once the illegitimate children were old enough to begin working and the girls were no longer in danger of being destitute, their mothers moved on to stage three. They were in their thirties by stage three, usually. Now that the services of the beta male were no longer required, the girls began cheating on them with less stealth—often allowing themselves to be seen conspicuously in public with other men, men who wouldn't be suckered into the second stage, men the women had respect for. Inevitably, the beta male would become aware of the infidelity and would leave the living arrangement with the woman, which was the stage three objective. About half of the beta males would initially ignore the fact that their wives or girlfriends were cheating on him, or they would repeatedly forgive them. With no more use for them, the women would cheat until the beta male couldn't ignore the infidelity any longer. If he wouldn't leave the relationship on his own accord, the girl would break up with him, or divorce him if they were married. One of the objectives of stage three was to extract what was left of the beta male's soul through child support. The unluckiest of these poor men wound up paying child support for children that were not theirs.

Arianny's father, Hector, uncoiled the microphone cord and tested the amplifier when he found the right spot in the center of the dance floor. His voice quickly subdued the murmuring. He pulled slack in the microphone cord and tried to overcome the awkwardness of his attire in the limelight. He looked uncomfortable in his tuxedo. Felina had never seen him in anything but cowboy boots and cowboy hat until tonight. The conversations quieted as he requested the attention of all the tables, in Spanish. His speech came across somewhat planned, not quite eloquent, but fluid, his nerves suppressed by El Jimador Tequila. He fought back tears while he talked about the day that Arianny was born and how fast his *princesa* had grown up to become a woman.

Arianny was sitting at the main table near the edge of the dance floor next to her female *Chaparonas*. They wore matching pink dresses. She looked at her feet and adjusted her tiara when she felt the attention of the audience redirect to her. She acknowledged his words bashfully and began to cry tears of endearment when he wouldn't relent his focus. The chaperone boys at the male table, on the other side of the dance floor, squirmed with discomfort in their tuxedo shirts and vests. Their teenaged maturity was embarrassed by the sentimental quiet that amplified the words of a new woman's father.

Hector choked up when he switched the focus of his address from the crowd to Arianny and told her that if there was anything she ever needed that he would be there for her. Felina joined in the applause when Hector finished christening her, as she transitioned from a girl's life into womanhood.

Arianny adjusted her tiara again and wiped the tears from her eyes as her companions in matching dresses glimpsed her and clapped on her behalf. The women in the audience dabbed tears from their eyes with tissues, and the men in Charro hats smiled with pride as Hector took the first dance with his daughter. Arianny had chosen a Taylor Swift song as the theme for her ceremony. The young high school boys, who had been chosen as chaperones, sat in their seats along the edge of the dance floor and watched with awe.

Once the dance was over, the crowd offered another round of applause, and the couples within the audience took to the dance floor.

A nervous young man asked Felina to dance, and she agreed in order to be polite. The Mexican boys were persistent, but she had been successful in avoiding them thus far; she wouldn't give in.

Her partner asked for another dance after the song was over, and she agreed reluctantly. She was thinking of a rebuttal in case he asked her for something more when the music stopped. It was exhausting to continue avoiding eye contact with him. Hopefully he could tell that her cooperation was limited to the dance floor. Instead, she wondered what Layne looked like in his uniform as she looked over the young man's shoulder. In addition to her hangover, she was suffering from embarrassment. It was uncharacteristic for her to drink so much and make out with a guy the first night she met him. She feared that she had ruined the chemistry between them; he must have thought that she was a pushover.

When the second song was over, her partner could tell that she was tired of dancing and allowed her to separate from him. She thanked him for the dance and made her way back to her table. She pretended not to notice other boys watching her as she weaved. If someone else asked her, she would tell them that she was tired, or better yet, she had to wake up early tomorrow and had to leave to go to bed. She returned to her seat at the table. She could feel eyes upon her in addition to her father's. She pretended not to notice and joined in on the conversations at her table to appear occupied. She reviewed the night before. She considered that perhaps in addition to drinking too much, she had made other mistakes that would cause Layne to be disinterested in her.

She second-guessed herself about leaving in the night while Layne was sleeping; he might have interpreted it the wrong way. She thought that it would create curiosity and yearning; also she didn't want him to see her in the morning after she had been sleeping all night. She should have told him at the bar that she had to go and asked if he would be back to Tucson as a hint for him to ask for her number. She shouldn't have drunk more than six beers, but she was having so much fun in his company; he was the most interesting guy she had ever met. If he wanted her, he would find a way to contact her. She was giving him a test of sorts.

She sat staring at the half-full beers on the table. She couldn't stop thinking about him; he was so careful when she was in his arms. She could sense other boys about to approach her. Her phone dinged inside her purse to alert her that she had received a new text message. She would use it as an excuse to leave, no matter who sent it. She retrieved the cell phone from her purse; it was a message from Marianne. She opened the message and read, "Layne asked for your number. I gave it to him. I hope you don't mind." She smiled broadly. Her aunt asked her, "What are you smiling about?"

"Oh, nothing, just something funny that Marianne texted me," Felina mused as she put her phone back in her purse. She stood up to hug everyone at the table and kiss them goodbye, saying: "I have to go; I have to get up early tomorrow."

26

"I HOPE THOSE OPS TESTS I GOT FROM Ricky are good for the final tomorrow," Layne said to Blair, who was sitting at the computer next to him. "I don't know anything. I haven't studied a total of three hours for that class since I've been here." The realization of how ill-prepared he was made him feel hollow and helpless.

He had survived his binge in Tuscon, but it had set back his study schedule for final exams. He chewed his thumbnail, while his leg bounced. His USB drive was inserted in the computer port, the green lanyard hanging from it. There were only two other open computers in the Academy lab; the room was full of other trainees in t-shirts, basketball shorts and flip-flops. He plugged his current grade percentages into the fields of the grade calculator and smiled a little when he clicked compute.

"Are you gonna quit messing with that grade calculator and look at your visas?" Blair asked Layne.

"Assuming I get an eighty percent on the Law Final, I need to get at least a thirty percent on the Ops 2 Final to graduate." Layne had calculated his margin for error down to the decimal point.

"You're always obsessing," Blair said.

Layne couldn't rid his thoughts of a new loop film. In it, Instructor Baca was coming back into the temporary after running the Scan-Tron sheets through the grader. In the nightmare Baca pulled him out of the room to tell him that he was the only one who didn't pass. Everyone was celebrating while he returned to his seat in shock.

Blair by now knew better than to feed Layne's nightmares, so he changed the subject. "I can't wait to have a room to myself, and sleep

238

next to my wife again," he said. "But the downside is we won't be in a controlled environment anymore."

"It'll be cool to have that badge in our pockets, but I have a feeling that the field will make this place seem like kiddieland," Layne said.

"Hopefully, they'll ease us into it slowly," Blair said.

"I'm not gonna worry about that now," Layne said. He was beginning to form his own picture of what it would be like to move on from the Academy, and it partly included what he would be leaving. "It will be nice not to have to look at Schneider, laying on his bunk reading Men's Health with a facial mask on at night."

"He puts on a facial mask before bed?" Blair had obviously not heard the chatter.

"Yeah, it's a green mud mask for his pores. I shouldn't say anything. Schneider is a good guy. He doesn't talk bad about anybody," Layne said.

"I won't tell anyone," Blair assured him.

"Ricky used to ask Schneider where his robe and his slippers were," Layne said.

Blair laughed. "When did Ricky leave?"

"Almost a month ago. I'm gonna call him when I get back to Colorado and find out what it's like in the field—if I graduate, I mean, knock on wood."

Blair put his books into his backpack and zipped it as he stood up. "I'm going to bed early. See you tomorrow. Good luck on the finals if I don't talk to you."

"It's only nine o'clock," Layne said.

"I don't want to be tired tomorrow." Blair yawned and stretched his arms in a Y shape.

"Okay, buddy. Good luck to you. I know you don't need it though," Layne said.

"You'll do fine," Blair said over his shoulder, as he scooted sideways down the row of computer stations toward the aisle to the exit.

Layne surfed the Internet for what seemed only a few minutes. When he looked at his watch, it was 9:30. He decided he should probably try to go to bed. He gathered his things and threw one strap of his backpack over his shoulder. The other trainees glanced up at him from their monitors as he walked past them to leave. He walked tall, knowing that they could tell he was almost done.

He walked through the warm night holding the straps of his backpack, dreaming of the day that his worries would be over for good and life would be a pleasure. He took out his wallet and double-checked to make sure Felina's number was still in his special compartment. It was there, and he tucked it back in with reassurance.

Once in the courtyard, he noticed Schneider on the balcony, overlooking the empty swimming pool the way Ricky used to. Layne waved at him on his way to the stairs. Once in the room, he put his backpack under Schneider's bunk and joined him outside. He could hear the same crickets chirping from the first night, one constant throughout this whole ordeal.

"What are your plans after graduation?" Layne asked Schneider.

"We have a week before we have to report to our stations. I'm just gonna get my things to get ready to go home," Schneider said.

"I'm gonna start packing my things tonight, too, but only because I am leaving no matter what," Layne said. "Have you talked to your parents?"

"I called them earlier; you?"

"I'm gonna call them tonight while I'm ironing my uniform for the graduation ceremony. I just don't want to tell them I'm graduating. I don't want to jinx it. But I know they are leaving tomorrow morning to drive down here," Layne said.

"So, you're driving home with them after graduation on Friday?"

"Yeah, it's about a fourteen-hour drive from here to Denver." Layne didn't want to think about what the drive would be like if he didn't pass his exams.

They went back inside the room and Layne took his dress uniform out of its cellophane wrapper. He thought about his parents driving through

New Mexico as steam coughed from the iron and he continued to press the creases in the sleeves and the pant seams. He thought about Felina again. He thought of what he would say to her if she answered his call. He would apologize for his behavior and blame it on the stress of finals. He realized that if he didn't pass, he would never see her again. He considered calling her now but decided that it would be premature. She knew that he had graduation coming. If he called now, she might think he was creepy and desperate. He would need to wait until after graduation so that she would think that he had patience. Pretending to have patience was difficult. It seemed like girls could tell when he was thinking about them anyway.

* * * *

LAYNE TOOK A DEEP BREATH AS he printed his name and class number in the blanks in the heading of the answer sheet. He noticed his right uniform sleeve as he printed. He had ironed well the night before; his dress uniform was even more pristine—if he got the chance to wear it. He looked around the room. Any attempt to hawk or cheat was absolutely out of the question this late in the game.

He read the first question on the exam and froze. Although he believed he knew the answer, he reviewed the multiple-choice possibilities, and on second reading thought more than one looked correct. He made a decision and forced himself to move on. He gave himself a pep talk: Remember, if you don't know the answer, put an asterisk by it, move on, and come back. That way you don't waste more time than necessary on one you're gonna miss anyway. The voice inside his head sounded the same as his speaking voice today. He looked around to make sure that he had not spoken out loud.

Then the familiar panic set in. He expected the subsequent questions to be obvious, questions where he didn't even have to read all the choices. But instead there was one coin-toss after another. *I haven't chosen a B in a while*, he thought; then the empty circles in the *C* column that were not filled in persuaded him to choose more *Cs*. The thought occurred to him that with this low level of mastery, it was actually possible that he could score less than a thirty percent. He began to sweat, thinking of how he would tell his parents that he didn't graduate when they got here. Maybe if he failed, the instructors would disregard the score and allow him to graduate out of sheer need for bodies on the border. Maybe the higher-ups were telling them just to pass people, like they did with the driving test. Fleming didn't know what *Cómo estás* meant, and they hadn't failed him out of Spanish yet.

After the test booklets and answer sheets were handed in, the class sat for ten minutes in silence while the answer sheets were run through the grading machine. Baca came back into the classroom and said, "This is the first class I have ever heard of where someone wasn't walked out because of the Ops 2 final."

The class murmured. Baca left the room again and everyone began to talk. The atmosphere bordered on joyous.

Layne turned to Schneider and said, "That must mean that we are in the clear right?"

"I guess so," Schneider said.

"Alright, we made it buddy!" Layne said with his biggest smile in four months.

Schneider smiled and accepted Layne's high five, but with much less enthusiasm.

Layne looked around the room. "I count thirty-three. We started with fifty; almost half of the class quit or failed Immigration Law."

"Yep, everyone here will be going to Field Training at their station," Schneider said.

Layne took a deep breath as the magnitude of his accomplishment sunk in momentarily. "Everybody we know made it. Runyon, Carlos, Damon, Danielson, Blair, Fleming, Greg, and, of course, Melanie."

"Did you hear what they did to Fleming?" Schneider asked.

"No, what?"

"After he took his final in Spanish his instructor graded the tests then said he needed to speak with Fleming in private. He walked Fleming outside of the temp in front of the whole class," Schneider said.

"Oh man."

"Then his instructor said, like, 'I hate to be the one to tell you this, but you passed by one percentage point,'" Schneider said. "Two other Spanish instructors were hiding behind some bushes, because they wanted to see the look on Fleming's face."

"That sucks," Layne said.

"Fleming would agree. Even after they told him it was a joke, he was still ticked," Schneider said.

Layne considered Fleming's situation for a moment. Ricky had told him that the instructors weren't doing the trainees any favors by allowing them to pass Spanish out of charity. Supposedly, the Spanish Oral Boards they had to take once at their stations were hell to get past. He said that it was better to fail out at the Academy than to become situated in another state, then get fired at one of the two Oral Boards.

"Where's Baca?" Layne suddenly became aware that the Instructor had been gone for quite a while.

"He went to go get our badges so that we can verify the information is right on the credentials. They'll present them to us tomorrow at the ceremony," Schneider said.

Layne had forgotten that they had their pictures taken a month prior for the IDs. His head was spinning; back then he thought that there was no way he was going to make it. If he could have traveled back in time to tell himself not to worry, he wouldn't have believed himself.

Baca finally came back into the room carrying a box. He looked like he wanted to punch Damon as he walked past him. Judging by the look on his face, Baca was disappointed that none of the trainees had failed any of their finals. He dropped the box containing the wallets on his desk. "When I call your name, raise your hand."

"Alvarez," Baca said.

Alvarez raised his hand and Baca threw the wallet like a Frisbee to him. Alvarez caught it in his chest.

"Beltran," Baca said.

Beltran raised his hand, and the trainees sitting at the table in front of him ducked as the badge sailed over their heads.

* * * *

"DON'T SCREW THIS UP. THE PAIC in charge of the Academy is gonna be here. Don't embarrass me on my last day," Baca said as he stood before the soon-to-be graduates on the graduation stage.

Class 590 was in line alphabetically, awaiting further instructions. The ceremony started in thirty minutes. Parents and families were not allowed into the auditorium yet. Layne's parents were on campus. He flipped open his cell phone and read a message from his mom. He closed the phone and put it back in his pocket in the nick of time. Baca almost caught him looking at it.

Baca instructed, "After the trainee in front of you gets his badge, wait until he's off the stage. Wait until he steps off the last stair before you approach the PAIC. If the timing isn't right, it's gonna look like a fire drill up here."

Layne looked around at the green Border Patrol flag and American flag near the podium. He looked at everyone in their dress uniforms. It was peculiar, but it was satisfying to see everybody wearing the outfit—even people he couldn't stand, like Melanie. She had her blonde hair pulled back into a neat French braid beneath the strap of her Smokey. Layne readjusted his Smokey to the right tilt before all the parents entered the auditorium.

Baca continued with instructions: "Now, when you approach the PAIC, you extend your right hand to shake hands with him, then reach for the badge and accept it from him with your left hand. Turn and smile for the camera. Once you see the flash, head for the stairs and get off the stage. Then form up over by that table."

Families began to stream in. Layne saw his Christy and Dutch Sheppard talking to some of the Hispanic parents as they all filed into the auditorium. His mom covered her mouth when she saw Layne on stage, and his dad smiled and gave a thumbs-up. He had heard from some of his classmates that nearly three hundred people would be in the amphitheater. Everyone graduating would have family there, except Damon. Layne smiled; he deserved it.

He bore down to concentrate. He went over what Baca had told the class: Accept the badge with your left hand and shake with your right. Make sure you watch Schneider and wait until his foot reaches the floor from the stairs. His mind was complicating the maneuver into a dance routine. He made himself focus; he was more nervous than he was for the exams. *Get out of here as fast as possible after you get your badge. Just don't mess up the handshake. Wait for the picture and get off the stage.*

The camera flashed at the moment his handshake connected with the PAIC. The PAIC's hands were heavy and thick. Layne stepped down the stairs to join the rest of the group in formation, waiting for those behind them to receive their badges. When the ceremony ended, the class went individually to claim the lock boxes that contained their pistols.

With his lock box under his arm, Layne searched the crowd for his mom and dad. They were waiting for him to make eye contact, and when they saw him, his mom extended her arms, waiting for him to arrive for a hug. She was fighting back tears, and his dad was wearing the biggest, proudest smile Layne had ever seen on him. His parents took turns hugging him, and Layne wondered if he would ever grow out of being embarrassed by such moments.

He rushed his parents through the mingling. As was their tendency, Christy and Dutch had made fast friends with the parents of several other trainees. Some of them were parents of his enemies, who, he noticed, were making the connection between Layne and his convivial parents and were keeping their distance. He would rather have gone to the dentist to have his teeth drilled than to pretend to be friendly with them.

The urge to leave came quickly upon him. His bags were packed, so he told his parents he would meet them in the courtyard. He raced across the grounds and sped up the stairs, two at a time, to retrieve his bags from his room. No goodbyes. They just made him uncomfortable, and what more was there to say? He would see Fleming and Schneider at headquarters pretty soon anyway.

When his parents arrived, they walked to the car and Layne threw his bags in the trunk without looking back. He stared at the Academy in the side view mirror as they passed by the Campus Police in the gatehouse. He wished he hadn't ruined the moment on stage with worry.

27

LAYNE'S EYES THROBBED AND BURNED with fatigue. He rubbed them and they glassily resumed focus on another pair of semi-truck tail lights a quarter mile ahead in the dark. He put on his blinker and moved into the left lane to pass as the truck's engine roared. The noise tailed off and the truck fell behind in the rearview mirror as he turned off his blinker to return to the right lane. It felt strange steering and operating the controls of his mom's car. He hadn't driven on a public road in four months and was accustomed to driving around a track through orange cones in the old Border Patrol Crown Victorias that were used in driving class.

After graduation he and his parents had had dinner at The Wildcat, but Layne had been in a hurry to leave Artesia forever. They were attempting to drive non-stop to Denver through the ghostly New Mexico night. Christy and Dutch were both sound asleep now, his mother resting her head on a coat against the passenger side window and his dad lying across the back seat.

Reunited with his parents, it seemed that he had been away for only a few weeks. At the Academy he had counted the endless days like tally marks on a prison wall. Now, looking back on his time there was like waking up in the morning and reflecting on the duration of time spent asleep. Further distorting his perception, his headlights on the highway through deserted land created the illusion of time travel. He hoped that this was the beginning of a new era. There was nothing he cared to reflect on during the past four months. He attempted to cram the memories into an overflowing closet along with the memories from the past seven years, then close the door quickly before they all spilled out onto him.

Around midnight he woke up his dad and told him that he was too tired to continue and suggested maybe a motel in Sante Fe. But his dad told him he was confident they could make it home driving straight through, if Layne could stay awake. He was too exhausted to argue with Dutch. His dad was proud of his son again, and Layne wanted to sustain the impression. So, he pressed on, the way he had within the concertina wire fences of the compound.

The glowing lights of Sante Fe were growing dim behind him as the car hummed deeper into the night. To divert his mind from sleep, he attempted to create a sense of celebration over what he had attained, but his mind rejected the Academy as an accomplishment, assigning no value to it. Four months prior, he had been certain that he would gain a new sense of self-respect on this special day. Still, no perceived crowning achievement to date had ever earned him a lasting sense of fulfillment. He disapproved of himself more than ever. He considered that perhaps it was because his achievements hadn't involved a significant and sustained monetary gain. He convinced himself that the salary and panache of a GL-11 Federal Agent would be the answer. But he wasn't quite ready to ponder and face what would be required of him. He bowed his neck and looked upward through the windshield to distract his thoughts. He felt his arm hair stand up with goosebumps as he gazed upon the billions of stars in the spectacular night sky.

He began to nod while creeping north across the Colorado border; still, interval thoughts of Felina came to him. A fantasy about a storybook romance with her flashed in ten-second clips among the oncoming yellow stripes and high beams. The fairytale ended with him taking a knee before her as she covered her mouth, then looped back to him courting her again.

The starry darkness and hypnotic drone of NPR radio lulled him into waking dreams, and Felina blew a kiss goodbye to him. In the dream, he was back in class at the Academy in one of the rows of tables to the rear, and he had forgotten to put on his duty belt before leaving his dorm room. He was trying to hide as instructors passed by that he didn't recognize.

He was cowering and hoping they wouldn't notice. Thoughts inside the dream involved irrationally strange decisions. He had enough time to run back to his room and put on the belt, but he decided to try and make it through classes without it. Along came another dream without sequence. He looked down at his wristwatch only to realize that it must have stopped. He was at least fifteen minutes late and running after the bus, headed for the temporary buildings, and his legs weighed hundreds of pounds apiece. The bus continued to pull away from him into a cloud of road dust. When he made it all the way to class on foot, there were only a few minutes left in the period. No one noticed him sit quietly.

* * * *

LAYNE WOKE UP IN HIS BEDROOM. As he came to, it didn't seem possible that less than twenty-four hours earlier he had been so far away, standing next to Instructor Baca. All of that was in the past, he told himself. He spent the afternoon worrying about the future.

He forced himself to wait until three to call Ricky. His heart pounded as the phone dialed. On the third ring he remembered Ricky saying that they had weekends off during Field Training. The connection opened and he heard his old roommate's voice.

"Hey, it's your boy Layne."

They both laughed.

"So, tell me what it's like and don't jack with me," Layne prodded.

"I learned more in the first few hours in the field than I did the entire time at the Academy," Ricky explained.

His voice sounded different. He took his time speaking and he sounded more sure of himself.

"What's it like?" Layne asked him.

"The first day I thought that we were gonna do classroom-type stuff. But our FTO's took us out into the field. I was riding with a guy who took me out on the highway outside of Rio Grande City, pretty far from the station. The traffic in Texas is different than it is in Arizona."

Layne listened intently, grateful that he was safe over a thousand miles away in Denver. What Ricky explained seemed to be taking place in a different world.

Ricky felt obligated to elaborate. "It's all highway vehicle stops down here; every station is different. We laid-in on the side of the road in an area where this FTO said that every passing truck or van that's heavy on the back springs is good."

"How did you hide?" Layne asked.

"We parked beside a tractor, so oncoming cars couldn't see us until the last second," Ricky said. "We weren't out there an hour and my FTO got behind a load vehicle and turned on the emergency lights. The truck was still rolling on the shoulder and five people bailed out the bed and started scrambling into a field. The FTO got out so fast—we skidded and he was running before our truck even stopped." Ricky's story scared Layne, producing a metal taste on his tongue as he licked his lips. "Did you catch one of them?"

"I yelled at this one to stop and he kept running full speed. I tackled him and handcuffed him and brought him back to the vehicle," Ricky said.

"Did you handcuff him like they showed us in PT?" Layne inquired.

"No way; the chain was all tangled. I didn't even lock the cuffs. They were probably choking the blood flow in his wrists. The FTO just said to get them on him as fast as you can. Those guys laugh at the Academy. They say, 'Just forget everything they tried to teach you.'"

Layne laughed. "So what do you think, so far?"

"I don't know. I mean, I like it so far. It's actually kind of fun. I think I'll do it a couple of years then try for something else, like DEA or ATF. I don't wanna live in Rio Grande City the rest of my life. But it's a longshot; it would be like winning the lottery. They wanna keep us where we are," Ricky said.

Layne knew what Ricky meant about the desire to transfer. He said, "Me, too. I wanna transfer to a different agency after two years, like the State Department or something. I don't want to live in Douglas for twenty years. Once I got into the Academy my whole plan was to use the hiring influx as a way to get my foot in the door with the Feds."

"Everybody says the same thing," Ricky said, "but it's hard to get in with another agency, and they won't let you transfer stations in BP unless you wanna go to the Canadian border and freeze your balls off. If they let people transfer, they wouldn't have any guys left at the stations in crummy locations. The only way to transfer stations is to pick up a supervisor position somewhere, and it takes a long time. You gotta know somebody to hook you up if you wanna be a Supe because of the politics. Even if you kiss up for eight years and pull it off, there ain't gonna be any openings at good stations, like San Ysidro. Guys in those places aren't letting go of those plush jobs. You gotta get really lucky to land a gig like that."

"Can you imagine the tail you could pick up in San Diego?" Layne fantasized.

"Yeah, I'm sure the chicks are nails. Even if you would've put in for San Ysidro when you applied, the waiting list is so long you never would've got it. And it's not as good as it sounds. The cost of living in San Diego is off the charts. You gotta make bank to survive there. A hundred grand there ain't nearly enough. The guys in my class that are stationed there have to live, like, four guys to an apartment until they make GL-11. They waited about three years for an opening."

Layne was silent, digesting the futility of his plans.

"Did you hear about Damon?" Ricky said, regaining Layne's attention. "He lost his gun. A guy who was in my class is at his station."

Layne smiled broadly with satisfaction, astounded by the karma. "How did he manage to lose it?"

"He drove all the way back to New York and went straight to some party on the way home. Some high school punks broke his truck window and took his backpack, and some of his uniforms, too."

They both laughed.

Layne said, "He's screwed! Lose your gun before you even show up at the station?"

"He's done. The FBI has to investigate when an issued weapon is stolen, because of the serial numbers," Ricky explained.

"How long do you think it will take to fire him?"

"It takes a few months to complete the investigation. He'll be in plain clothes for a while, doing janitor work until they can get all of the paperwork done. But he's gone, for sure."

Layne never let the pistol out of his sight. He didn't even feel comfortable locking it in the trunk of his car like they were supposed to. He had ordered a concealed carry holster online that Runyon recommended. He brought the $800 pistol with him under his waistband everywhere he went.

"I can't wait to fly on a commercial flight with it concealed. I heard you show your creds at the ticket counter and they take you completely around the security strip search.

"Have you ever considered being an Air Marshal?" Layne asked enthusiastically.

"No, you don't want to do that," said Ricky. "Back when 9/11 happened, I heard a ton of agents transferred to be Air Marshals. But they found out quick, it sucks. You're like a flight attendant. I heard it's so boring."

"It sounds cool, though, James Bond-style," Layne said.

"It's not; you waste your life away sitting in airports and on planes. You're always worried your neighbor is tapping your wife because you're gone all the time, like a truck driver. Like when guys in the military get deployed to Iraq," Ricky said. "I guess after a year all those guys who became Air Marshals were begging to come back to BP."

"I'm nervous already about FTU," Layne admitted.

"I wouldn't be," Ricky said. "You should be relaxing, not thinking about training. You've got a week off."

They talked for a while longer, but Layne already had confirmed what he feared all along—that the field would be something altogether different, and that he would be ill-prepared for it.

He wondered, too, what the future had in store for him with Felina.

ABOUT THE AUTHOR

Sherryl and Christopher LaGrone

Sherryl LaGrone, who is producing The Delta Tango Trilogy, is the mother of the trilogy's author, the late Christopher LaGrone and his sister, Aimee Hestera. She is a retired high school teacher who now enjoys being a "snowbird" in Mesa, Arizona, which is a couple hundred miles to the north of the setting of *The Delta Tango Trilogy*. Sherryl and her life partner spend their summers in the mountain town of Grand Lake, CO.

For more information about *The Delta Tango Trilogy*, please go to www. thedeltatangotrilogy.com, email us at Deltatangotrilogy@gmail.com, or follow us on Instagram or Facebook, searching for Delta Tango Trilogy.

CPSIA information can be obtained
at www.ICGtesting.com
Printed in the USA
JSHW032115181220
10382JS00003B/44